THE HOUSEWIFE ASSASSIN'S KILLER APP

JOSIE BROWN

A BOOK BY

SIGNAL PRESS

ONE OF MANY GREAT SIGNAL PRESS BOOKS

San Francisco, CA

Library of Congress Cataloging-in-Publication Data is available upon request

Cover Design by Andrew Brown, ClickTwiceDesign.com

Digital Formatting by Austin Brown, CheapEbookFormatting.com

Trade Paperback ISBN: 978-1-942052-18-0

Hardcover ISBN: 978-1-942052-32-6

V022319

"This was an addictive read–gritty but funny at the same time. I ended up reading it in just one evening and couldn't go to sleep until I knew what the outcome would be! It was action-packed and humorous from the start, and that continued throughout, I was pleased to discover that this is the first of a series and look forward to getting my hands on Book Two so I can see where life takes Donna and her family next!"

—Me, My Books, and I

"The two halves of Donna's life make sense. As you follow her story, there's no point where you think of her as "Assassin Donna" vs. "Mummy Donna', her attitude to life is even throughout. I really like how well this is done. And as for Jack. I'll have one of those, please?"

—The Northern Witch's Book Blog

Novels in The Housewife Assassin Series

The Housewife Assassin's Handbook (Book 1)

The Housewife Assassin's Guide to Gracious Killing (Book 2)

The Housewife Assassin's Killer Christmas Tips (Book 3)

The Housewife Assassin's Relationship Survival Guide (Book 4)

The Housewife Assassin's Vacation to Die For (Book 5)

The Housewife Assassin's Recipes for Disaster (Book 6)

The Housewife Assassin's Hollywood Scream Play (Book 7)

The Housewife Assassin's Killer App (Book 8)

The Housewife Assassin's Hostage Hosting Tips (Book 9)

The Housewife Assassin's Garden of Deadly Delights (Book 10)

The Housewife Assassin's Tips for Weddings, Weapons, and Warfare (Book 11)

The Housewife Assassin's Husband Hunting Hints (Book 12)

The Housewife Assassin's Ghost Protocol (Book 13)

The Housewife Assassin's Terrorist TV Guide (Book 14)

The Housewife Assassin's Deadly Dossier (Book 15: The Series Prequel)

The Housewife Assassin's Greatest Hits (Book 16)

The Housewife Assassin's Fourth Estate Sale (Book 17)

The Housewife Assassin's Horrorscope (Book 18)

Principle of Least Astonishment

Despite our claim to be great at multitasking, the fact of the matter is that, unlike computers and their offshoots of smart phones and electronic tablets, human beings can only pay attention to one thing at a time.

This is where a well-designed app (short for "application") comes in!

The "principle of least astonishment," or POLA, is the app designer's mandate to ensure that these little software goodies think through the logistics of getting from Point A (for example, "I wonder if I can download a book…") to Point B ("Wow! Yes, I can. In fact I can search for all sorts of books, and within different online bookstores…") to Point C ("Gee, I can purchase and download the book into my account, and read it on any of my ever-growing number of devices!")—

So that all you have to do is push a button to get what you want!

In fact, a well-designed app is like a great lover because it:

- *A: Anticipates your every need, want, and desire.*
- *B: Listens to your instructions, and performs accordingly.*

- *C: Meets your greatest expectations.*

For some reason, no one has perfected a Husband app. Go figure.

"DO YOU WORK FOR UPS? I COULD HAVE SWORN I SAW YOU checking out my package." The portly goombah whispering this pick-up line into my ear is Walt "the Wolf" Squarcialupi, a capo with the Carducci crime syndicate.

Believe it or not, I've heard worse pick-up lines. Tonight, in fact. In other words, the wise guys who frequent Mama Giacomini's Ristorante in New York's Little Italy aren't the silver-tongued devils they imagine.

No wonder this infamous mob hangout has trouble holding onto its waitresses.

If all goes well, I'll be the next to turn in my uniform. Not that there's much to it—just a too-tight, barely-there vest worn over short-shorts that would make a Hooters girl blush. To add to my image as a woman willing to do anything for a tip (hopefully a cash one, as opposed to best odds during the fifth race at Belmont), I'm also squeezed into fishnets and totter through the lounge on six-inch heels.

Seriously, Walt the Wolf's timing couldn't be worse. Tonight, I'll be serving Lawrence Raley, an NSA intelligence analyst who made too many losing college basketball bets and couldn't pay the vig. When Phil "the Fixer" Rugassi, an underboss in the Moretti organization, showed up with a metal bat to collect what was owed, Lawrence convinced him that there's a much better use for his brains than smearing them all over the sidewalk—

Like assessing the telephone text and voice metadata files of Empire State Technologies, Limited—a phone company that just so happens to be one of the most successful (and supposedly legitimate) assets of the Moretti crime syndicate.

Here's a newsflash for you: when it comes to organized crime cash cows, the old standbys like drugs, prostitution, and gambling are so last century. A more lucrative new side business is cybercrime. For the Morettis, that means Empire State—which just may be your discount phone company. You see, once you've signed up, you've given the Morettis your charge card.

Then the real shakedown begins. Let's say you download a gaming app or two or three. Or you subscribe to a sports gambling website or a porn site, let alone any other of the millions of promotional services pitched to you on your cell phone. Soon, strange charges start appearing on your credit card bills.

But you don't notice, because you're having too much fun.

Forget breaking a leg with a lead pipe. Now when the Cosa Nostra reaches out and touches someone, it does it via an auto-debit, to the collective tune of tens of millions of dollars a year.

Lawrence has taken it to the next step. Over the past six months, his data mining on the Morettis' behalf has pulled up the dirty little secrets on rival mobsters like the Carduccis, who enjoy generous "family plan" discounts with Empire State. He's also given the Moretti Syndicate enough dirt to blackmail a few celebrities, not to mention a politician or two.

It's one of these politicians who asked my employer, Acme Industries, to pull the plug on the Morettis' new venture.

As you can imagine, this is an important operation for Acme. Not only will a successful racketeering sting endear us to the FBI, it should help us avoid losing our own very lucrative contract with the NSA.

So, no, I can't let Walt the Wolf get in my way. I pop my gum in his face, but he takes it as a sign that I'm being coy.

His follow-up line is pretty blunt: "You know how I know we're gonna have sex later? Because I'm stronger than you."

Wrong.

"Promises, promises," I coo. I let my gaze fall to his crotch. Seriously, if there's a bulge there, I can't see it. Maybe I need glasses. Still, I open my eyes wide to feign awe and wonder.

I deserve an Academy Award for this performance.

With a come-hither smile, I beckon him into the ladies' room, then lock the door behind us. A moment later, my punch to his throat, followed by a knee to the gonads and a sharp elbow to the back of his head, leaves him face down in a toilet.

So that he gets the point that I don't take threats lightly, I flush it a few times.

Everyone can use a facial now and then.

"Mrs. Stone, try your best to stay on track," my boss, Ryan Clancy, mutters into the wireless ear bud too tiny to be seen, even if my right ear wasn't hidden beneath a long, blond feather-cut wig. To hold its pouf in place, I have a banana clip secured at the crown. It's teased up so high that I have to duck to clear the doorsill.

"With all due respect, Ryan"—I'm feeling like a Jersey girl, what can I say?—"I had to shake the guy somehow. Can I help it that I'm the only woman in this joint who isn't making goo-goo eyes at the piano player?"

I can't see it, but I can imagine the smirk on Ryan's face. "That's only because he'll be going home with you tonight."

He's got that right. The man with his finger on the pulse of his audience's rapidly beating hearts is none other than my main squeeze and mission partner, Jack Craig.

He wears a custom Armani tuxedo that fits his man-candy physique like a glove. The way he's crooning *In the Wee Small Hours of the Morning*, you'd swear Ol' Blue Eyes himself coached him on which beats to hold the longest in order to tug at a woman's heartstrings.

In their minds, he's fabulicious.

"Donna, you've got a customer." That's Ryan's way of telling me Phil the Fixer has arrived.

And off to work we go.

But, by the looks of things, it isn't going to be easy to get Phil's attention. He's brought a woman—some teased-out tart, barely twenty if that, with a *Penthouse*-worthy set of knockers and a 'do that's high enough to stop radio transmissions in a six-block radius.

"My God, is that his wife? She's got to be thirty years younger than him," I murmur to Ryan.

"Hardly. Like Phil, Angelina Rugassi is in her fifties. She also happens to be the daughter of a capo with the Carducci family."

Noting my gaze, Phil gives me the once-over. I murmur, "Talk about playing with fire."

The mobster and his cupcake take the booth reserved for them—the one farthest from the piano. Even at that distance, it only takes Cupcake a minute to fall under Jack's spell. Phil realizes this too and raises a brow at me, as if to say, *Don't be shy.*

He's got nothing to worry about in that regard. My mission is to get close enough to him so that, when the time is right, I can switch Lawrence's thumb drive with mine, which will release a worm into the Moretti syndicate's database.

"What can I get you?" My question is innocent enough, but the way I say it, so slow and husky, leaves nothing to the imagination—Phil's, anyway.

He nods in Cupcake's direction. "Get the little lady anything her heart desires."

"Martini," Cupcake purrs without turning her head. "Dry as toast."

"I'll have one too. And two orders of the calamad, and two of the linguini and clams, and a side of mozzarel." Even as Phil slides closer to her, he sticks a fifty-dollar bill between my breasts. "Keep me happy, and there's more where this came from."

I have half a mind to tell him that he'll need it to buy cigs in prison, but then I remember Ryan told me I could hold onto my tips, so hell yeah, I'm keeping it.

Besides, the others in the crowd are lousy drinkers, and even worse tippers. You'd think that, with all the salivating they're doing over Jack, they'd be thirstier.

Noting Phil's generosity, Cupcake snaps her fingers at her sugar daddy. "Gimme sumthin' for the *pee*-an-is." Because she said it with a silent T, it sounds as if she's said, "penis."

Over her dead body.

The bill he hands her is a Benjamin.

Jack's tip will be bigger than mine?

She smirks over at me as she shimmies out of the booth and toward Jack.

Phil murmurs, "I like my women like my meatballs—soft, round, and extra spicy." He leers as he runs his eyes over my posterior.

Oh boy. Another lousy pick-up line. These guys need new material. The next time the lounge manager wants to do his patrons a favor, he should hire a dating coach for the floorshow.

Frankly, Phil deserves the same treatment as the last guy. But, ironically, I'm not here to put a hit on him, but to hit *on* him. I bat my lashes and murmur, "Sure. Look me up if she runs off with the pee-an-is."

He's still roaring with laughter when Lawrence stumbles into the lounge. Seeing Phil, Lawrence straightens his collar and heads over to the table.

I wait until he plops down beside Phil before asking, "And what can I get for you, sir?"

"A…a Manhattan, please." The kid's voice is shaking.

The men don't shake hands. In fact, Phil's smile has totally disappeared.

I can tell there won't be a lot of small talk between these two guys, so I've got to move fast. I give their orders to the bartender and tell him there's a twenty if he can turn the drinks around as fast as possible, along with their pasta.

The bartender is on it, like lightning. The night is slow, what with most of the ladies ordering the lounge's ready-made mix of Snooki Snacks.

Cupcake has lingered as long as she can by the piano without looking like a crazed stalker. So that Jack notices her, she practically drapes herself over the top of the baby grand. He gives her a smile and a nod, and sings the next stanza of the song staring into her eyes.

To show her appreciation, she tucks the Benjamin into his shirt between the buttons that are nipple high.

As far as his bill collecting goes, I don't think Jack could have done better if he were the headliner in the Las Vegas Chippendale's review. His tip jar is overflowing.

I wonder how much he would have taken in if he were wearing just a banana hammock. If times get tough for us again, maybe I'll suggest it to him.

As I drop off Phil's drinks, I pretend I'm not listening to the interchange between the men. Not that I have to strain too hard. There's an audio bug in the lamp on their table, allowing Ryan and me to hear them loud and clear.

That's how I know Cupcake is pissed that Phil can't keep his eyes off me.

When the food arrives, I slide the plates on my stainless steel tray and time my return to Phil's table so that I'm front and center when Lawrence slides the thumb drive toward the wise guy.

At that point, I pull an oopsy that pushes Cupcake's linguini onto her lap.

She screams, "Oh, my GAWD!" Her faux leopard whore couture now looks like a cat crawling out of a muddy sewer. "It's leather—and you've ruined it!"

With one hand, I grab a napkin and wipe her down. The other hand is palming the duplicate thumb drive.

I'm just about to exchange them when I see Phil reach for the real one.

To stop him, I flip the second bowl of linguini into his lap.

Cursing, he leaps up so fast that he upturns the table. The drinks land on the floor, as does the silverware, the table lamp, the breadbasket—

And both thumb drives.

Lawrence looks from one thumb drive to the other, confused. "What the hell…"

Phil's eyes follow his gaze. The next thing I know, he's staring at me.

I scoop them up and start for the door—

Only to be tripped by one of Lawrence's size-fourteen flat feet.

I land face down. The breath is knocked out of me.

Through my earpiece, I hear Ryan murmur to Jack, *May Day*. Even after stopping abruptly in the middle of *Come Fly with Me*, the women in the lounge crowd around him adoringly. Seriously, he could have been humming the phone book off-key and they wouldn't have known the difference. The mob is so thick that he can't wade through in time to stop Phil from lifting me up and shoving me toward the lounge's entrance.

I have just enough time to grab one of the fallen forks off the floor before he hauls me up by my waist. I stab him hard, in the thigh.

His roar fills the bar. Angrily, he pulls out the fork and tosses it away, then slams me up against the wall. He's got one hand around my throat. The other is mauling my shorts and vest for my pockets. Angered that he can't find the hidden thumb drives, he hisses, "Where did you hide them?"

It's not that I won't answer the idiot. It's that I can't even croak, let alone breathe, what with his fingers on my throat. Now that I'm running on fumes, my eyes roll downward.

For some stupid reason, Phil takes this as a broad hint and puts his hand in my vest and rummages between my breasts.

Suddenly, a woman screams, "Why, you two-timing son of a bitch! So, this is the scrawny whore who's keeping you company these days?"

All eyes turn toward the doorway. I've never seen her before, but apparently Phil knows her, and from the loss of color in his face, he wishes he didn't.

"That's Angelina Carducci Rugassi," Ryan mutters into my ear.

No wonder Cupcake is trembling—and sliding under the table.

Then again, it could have something to do with Angelina's gun, which seems to be aimed at Phil one moment, and me the next.

"H-Hand to God, Angelina, th-this isn't what you th-think!" Phil stutters.

"The two-timing son-of-a-bitch is right," I assure her. "In fact, he's roughing me up because I wouldn't sit in his lap, and I had the nerve to question his taste in bimbos."

I point to Cupcake, who's peeking out over the top of the upturned table.

"Her? You're two-timing me with our babysitter?" Her first

shot hits him in the groin, putting him on the floor. As he bleeds like a stuck pig, he groans in pain.

Angelina stalks her next victim, Cupcake. "That ring on your finger better be a fugazi," she shouts as she shoots. A bullet singes her rival's bouffant, who barely ducks in time.

Just at that moment, Walt the Wolf stumbles out of the ladies' room. Apparently the women who came in after our little altercation weren't kind to him either. I presume that they, too, were victims of his threatening pick-up attempts, which is why such commentary as LIMP PRICK and JERK and LOSER is now scrawled all over his white button-down shirt in a rainbow of lipstick shades.

Walt is out for blood—mine. Finally spotting me, Little Italy's Raging Bore charges my way. Suddenly, Walt is aware of the melee around Angelina.

By now, Jack's fans are screaming at the top of their lungs and hightailing it out the back door. This gives him just enough time to jerk Angelina's arm straight up before she gets off another shot. The bullet slams into the ceiling instead of Cupcake, who crawls away on her hands and knees.

Like the rest of us, Walt watches as Jack wrenches her arm straight up, assuring that Angelina's jilted-wife defense doesn't turn into an indefensible homicide rap.

Angelina stares at the tall, handsome stranger who has just knocked the gun from her hand with his fist. Burying her head into his broad chest, she sobs, "He promised to love me forever!"

Lawrence sees this as the perfect time to leave the scene. He's making a run for the door—

But he doesn't get far, because I trip him.

He falls face down. One good turn deserves another.

I turn to find Phil staring at us. He reaches for his gun.

I grab the closest thing I can find for cover—my stainless

steel serving tray. Holding it like a shield, I leap in front of Jack. Phil's bullet bounces off the tray and ricochets into his own shoulder.

He's howling like a banshee, but he'll survive. The ambulance and police cars can already be heard coming from all directions.

Lawrence too will live to see another day. But, beyond that, I'm sure that the wise guy who takes Phil's place will be gunning for him, unless he's willing to play double agent for the Feds, and pray that he makes it into the Witness Protection Program before the Moretti syndicate finds out it's been double-crossed.

Despite his questionable eau de toilette, it must have dawned on Walt that saving Angelina is one way to come out smelling like a rose to the Carducci family. "The family owes you one," he promises Jack as he scoops her gun off the floor and ferries her toward the door.

"Hey, where did you hide the thumb drives?" Jack asks.

I reach into my pouf, where they've been held in place by the banana clip.

He laughs. "I would have never guessed."

Partial payment comes with what's in Jack's tip jar, which I shove into my vest until I'm pushing a DD width at the very least. When Jack raises a brow, I shrug. "Pay day," I say, as I push the rest of the bills into his jacket pocket.

In fact, there are so many dollars that they don't all fit there, either, so I tuck some under his waistband.

He laughs. "You can't buy me."

"I think I just did."

He smiles. "I guess it's time to pay up."

Before I can answer him, he grabs my arm and pulls me toward the kitchen door, and we disappear into the night.

2

Emoticons

In case you didn't know it, those cute little smiley faces you use in your emails are called "emoticons." They're supposed to give the recipient some idea of how you're feeling, be it happy — — or sad — — or dismayed — :/

As emoticons go, not all are faces made out of keyboard strokes. In fact, some are actually complete messages. For example, this one says, "I love you":

I <3 U

Others are symbolic of something easily visualized. Case in point: this one is a rose:

@-→-→---

Oh, and this is a bucktoothed vampire with a missing fang:

:-F

Frankly, in the time in which it would take you to learn every emoticon out there (including and especially the bucktoothed vampire) you could have picked up your cell phone and called to say, "Hi, hope you're having a great day." Or you could have plucked a rose and handed it to your friend, and seen a real smile on her face.

Best of all, you could have called your beloved to say, "I love you."

As for the bucktoothed defanged vampire, all I can say is that if you've found a use for it, you have too much time on your hands.

No, I'm not suggesting you create a costume depicting said vampire in order to scare the bejesus out of some pal. Actually, a better use of your time would be writing a note on beautiful stationery, then walking it out to the mailbox.

Etiquette beats netiquette every time.

Real emotions are more effective than emoticons. Trust me on this one.

JACK AND I HAVE A PRETTY GOOD REASON TO BE SMOOCHING ON the N Train. Keeping face-to-face and wrapped in each other's arms is the easiest way to avoid being caught by the subway's security cameras.

Hey, I'm not complaining at all. My only regret is that our stop—Union Square—is a mere five minutes away.

One of my hands cups the nape of Jack's neck. The other is pressed against his chest. Whereas the adrenaline rush of being roughed up by bad guys and dodging bullets has my heart pounding against my ribcage like a metronome, Jack's is several beats slower. Ha! Maybe next time I should take on the role of lounge singer.

The thought of my off-key crooning and one-handed *Chopsticks* wowing the crowds and launching my diva career is forgotten in the heady sweetness of Jack's kisses.

Be still, my heart.

All around us, the sights, sounds, and smells are raw and unyielding. A homeless guy plays a tarnished saxophone with the chops of someone who once was a somebody. The wild-eyed man sitting across from us is picking fleas out of his hair. The dude on the far side of Jack is high as a kite. He lays into a box of greasy fried chicken, devouring it, bones and all. The college student standing in front of us bops her head to a techno-pop ditty, which is so loud that it drones beyond the confines of her Beats. The standing mob around her nudges each other for more space. No one else notices the kid pick-pocketing his way through the undulating throng.

Despite all of it, I wish I could stay here for the rest of the night, entwined with the man I love with all my heart.

"So listen," he murmurs into my ear, "I noticed this great little French restaurant just a few blocks from our hotel. What do you say to a little foie gras and some coq au vin, with a nice Bordeaux to set it off?"

"Sure, okay," I purr, "if that's what you want."

His right brow rises. "Do you have a better idea?"

Tenderly, I touch his cheek with my hand. "Here's my scenario: you join me in our hotel room's large double tub. Lots of candles, lots of bubbles, lots of sex. Afterward, we pay the bellboy to run down the block and pick up our food order. *C'est bon?*"

Before Jack can answer, my cell phone buzzes. It's a text that reads, simply: *You're needed.*

Oh…no. Not now. Please…

"You were saying?" Jack stares down at my phone, then back up at me.

"I…have to go." I try not to look down at the cell as I text back: *ONE HOUR.*

Jack's smile fades. He shrugs. "Leave after dinner."

I shake my head. "I can't. We need him."

"I think you're wrong. Lee is using you." Jack's frigid declaration sends a shiver up my spine. "He thinks of you as his pet—a komodo dragon. Anytime he wants to rattle Carl's cage, he pulls you out so that you can snarl and wreak havoc."

"Your metaphor is less than flattering. I'd like to think of myself as something more beauteous than a two-hundred-pound scaly lizard with a forked-tongue."

Jack isn't laughing.

Hmmm. Okay, move on to Plan B: remind him why we agreed that I have to stay close to Lee Chiffray, the President of the United States. "The lives—and livelihoods—of our co-workers are also at stake, not to mention my children's wellbeing."

"You mean 'our children,' remember?"

I nod. He's right, of course. For the past two years, he's proven it, time and time again.

Right now, I'm doing everything I can to stop their biological father, Carl Stone, from coming back into their lives. So far, so good, but it hasn't been easy. I've been dodging summonses that are delivered now almost on a weekly basis. To that extent, it helps to have friends in low places. The gate guards for our private community, Hilldale, appreciate my homemade pies enough to warn me when yet another server is coming my way.

"Maybe it's time for you to play hard to get," Jack continues. "My God, Donna, it's been almost seven months since you made your deal with Lee to backchannel Acme intel before it goes directly to the intelligence agencies controlled by Carl! Since then, Acme—and more to the point, you—have jumped through every hoop Lee has tossed in front of us. And yet, Chiffray still hasn't made any changes where it counts most—Carl's removal from power. In fact, things have only gotten worse."

He's talking about the fact that my ex, Carl, is still Director of Intelligence for our country.

This is quite a feat for someone who was once considered a known terrorist.

His name was cleared, thanks to Lee.

At the time, Lee felt he had no choice. He's regretted it ever since.

Time for Plan C: appeal to Jack's sense of duty. "Jack, in all seriousness, you know the protocol."

"Is that what you call it, 'protocol'?"

I grit my teeth. "What would you call it?"

He shrugs. "You don't want to know."

"Yes, actually, I do. Because I care about your feelings." This is my way of saying, *What you say next may hurt mine and forever ruin what we've built together these past two years—so think before you speak.*

Any notion I may have had that Jack can read minds is put to rest when he declares, "I call it a liaison. A rendezvous."

I glare at him. "Next, you'll be calling it a booty call."

He's silent, but his shrug says it all.

The fact that he's put me in this position angers me to no end. "Jack…really? You doubt my love for you, after all we've been through together?"

"No, never." He hunches down in his seat. "If our profession has taught us one thing, it's to separate love from sex. But, Donna, I know you well enough to realize you'll do anything— use any skill at your disposal—to take down the Quorum, once and for all."

He's not coming out and saying it, but he means sex.

For us, it's an occupational hazard.

"You sound like a jealous schoolboy," I chide him. "Lee is not 'my boyfriend.' You are, or have your forgotten?"

"Prove it." He looks me in the eye. "Don't go."

I sigh. Then I reach for his hand and hold it tight. "For the record, Jack, he and I don't have sex."

"I'll take you at your word," he smirks. "Of course, that doesn't mean Lee doesn't want to have sex with you."

In my heart, I know Jack is right. All it would take is one signal from me.

Jack and I are too close, physically, for him to miss my blush.

And we are too close, emotionally, for him to ignore this unspoken truth.

"Ah, I see." His eyes are angry, but he keeps his voice deadly nonchalant.

"Jack, I swear he's been a perfect gentleman! You have to trust me when I say that I'll never betray the love we share… with my body, or my soul."

His way of showing that he believes me is to pull me in close.

His lips are warm. They part naturally at the touch of my own. Their taste leaves me tingling. I lose all sense of time and place.

I ache, mind and heart, when he pulls away.

"This is my stop," Jack mutters. "Last call."

I sigh and shake my head. I have four more stops to my exit —Grand Central Station—where I'll flag down a taxi, then exit it a few blocks from my real destination.

Without another word, Jack rises and heads toward the door. But before strolling out, he tosses the homeless guy playing the sax one of the dollars crammed in his coat pocket.

With a grateful smile, the man tips his hat at Jack.

The rest of the trip, he serenades me with *Blues in the Night*.

How appropriate.

When it's my turn to hop off, I also bend down and put a buck in his hat.

He grins at me. "Your man—he's a good one. Now, don't you go two-timing him."

I nod stoically.

Then I run off, so that he can't see my tears.

Jack is right about one thing. When Lee and I meet, it's always off the books—that is to say, never in the Oval Office or the West Wing, and certainly never in the presence of his staff.

And certainly his wife, Babette, knows nothing about it. Her suspicions of me are worse than Jack's.

That's okay. The feeling is mutual.

Today's meeting is to take place in the private penthouse apartment on Riverside Boulevard, overlooking the west side's Hudson River. I don't know if it is owned by Lee, or one of his many companies that are now held in a blind trust until he leaves office, or if it's a second or third home of a loyal constituent who honors POTUS's ask-no-questions criteria.

I honor it too.

According to the protocol that Lee and I have set up, I'm to arrive before him and his entourage. Despite any protestations of his advance team, he insists on entering the residence alone. That way, his security detail never sees me.

Thank goodness, too, because the way I'm dressed now, they'd worry they have another Slick Willy on their hands.

Not to mention, Lee would jump to the wrong conclusion too—

And try to prove Jack right.

I've got to find some different duds, and fast.

By the time I emerge onto Forty-Second Street, I've only got half an hour to do something about it, which means I don't have time to run over to Saks. Besides, it's already closed, as are most of the decent clothing stores between here and my destination.

Out of the corner of my eye, I spot a couple of streetwalkers giving me the high sign. One lets loose with a lowdown whistle before exclaiming, "Whoooeeee! You are *swanky*, girl! Where'd you get them hot pants?"

I hold up a twenty. "Hey, doll, I'll give you this for your coat."

She strips it off in a flash.

When you're meeting the leader of the free world, you've got to have some coverage, even if it's hooded, hot pink, fake and furry—and barely grazes your thighs.

Desperate times call for a desperate wardrobe. If her micro-mini wasn't so short, and lime green to boot, I'd have her throw that in as well.

By the time a taxi gets me to my destination—forty blocks north and on the west side of Manhattan—I've got less than five minutes to spare.

It's not my first time here. I've long memorized the security code that gets me inside the building. As in past rendezvous, I lift the coat's hood over my head so that the security camera can't pick up my face, or the color and cut of my hair. Yet another code gets me inside the express elevator to the penthouse, and another opens the front door to one of Manhattan's most exclusive residences.

The floors are marble. The walls, gold in tone, are at least fifteen feet high. The top eight inches are adorned with intricate moulding designed with a baroque flair of deep swirls.

Completing the fantasy of being transported to a wing in St. Petersburg's Hermitage Museum are the sumptuous rooms' high-backed, deep-seated furnishings in white silk brocade.

So that none of Lee's security detail spots me when he opens the door, I head for the penthouse's terrace. When I open the large glass sliding door, a tuft of hot-pink faux fur floats back inside, alighting on one of the settees.

I'm tempted to leave it there, but I know better. The last thing Lee or I need is to leave behind even a trace of evidence that can be analyzed by the best forensic labs in the world—a most likely scenario if Carl should ever find out about this place.

The building is tall enough that the penthouse's four-sided terrace has a three-hundred-degree view. I look east and south, so that I can gaze upon the most iconic landmarks in New York's midtown skyline: the Empire State Building, the Chrysler Building, the GE Building; and further to the south, the spire of the new Freedom Tower.

I don't hear Lee walk up behind me, but I feel his presence, which is usually the case.

He likes watching me without my knowledge.

Like all guilty pleasures, his fleeting voyeurism has a price. Time to pay up.

I turn to him. Every time I see him, his hair is a little grayer around the edges, the circles around his eyes are a shade darker, and his worries are etched even deeper on his brow.

Dealing with the world's most challenging issues is already taking its toll.

Despite this, he's smiling, and I'm sure he hoped I'd be too. But no, this time I must disappoint him. "Mr. President, to what do I owe the honor of your summons?"

Noting my curtness, his smile wavers ever so slightly. "Ryan mentioned you were in town. Since your trip coincided with my own—one of the party's many fundraisers—I thought you might catch me up on how it went."

I nod. "Mission accomplished. Jack and I were able to intercept a thumb drive containing cell phone metadata stolen by one of New York's mob syndicates, something both the NSA and the FBI will appreciate."

"I appreciate it too." He holds out his hand.

I hesitate, but yes, I take it.

His palm is large and warm, but dry. My eyes lock onto his as I grasp it firmly. I've been out here long enough that my own hands are cold. There is a chill in my voice, too, as I counter, "Duly noted. Perhaps you can show it with a little quid pro quo—specifically, catching me up on Carl's status within your administration."

"I thought you'd never ask." His sarcastic tone indicates otherwise. "Since we last met, Carl has been busy doing end-runs on my handpicked IC directors."

This is serious. If my allegiance with Lee is to pay off, he needs the intelligence community directors who must report to Carl to be POTUS's eyes and ears on our mutual enemy. They'll be in charge of agencies within the DOD, like the heads of the NSA, Military Intelligence, and Defense Intelligence; or those under the auspices of the DOJ, such as the FBI and DEA; not to mention stand-alone agencies such as Homeland Security.

"He can't get away with that, can he?" I ask.

"Thus far, he's been successful in two out of four attempts. In one, the vetting caught something that later turned out to be a false accusation. Still, the Congressional subcommittee approving the appointment—not to mention the press—had a field day with it." Lee frowns. "The second didn't even get that far. While waiting for his acceptance, my appointee candidate arranged a private meeting to let me know he was passing on the honor. He was scared off by what he called a blunt threat to, quote-unquote, look so far up his rectum with a microscope that something was sure to be found."

"Did he name Carl, specifically?"

"He did better than that. When I asked him who said it to him, he wrote Carl's name on a sheet of paper and handed it to me."

"Did you confront Carl?"

Lee smirks. "His response was that he had the obligation to conduct his own due diligence on the candidates, to assure that my choices aren't an embarrassment to my presidency, a legacy he cherishes as if it were his own."

"I guess that's his way of saying you're his bitch."

"How kind of you to point it out, Mrs. Stone."

I wince at the name.

He shrugs. "Yes, well, neither he nor I was happy with how the conversation ended."

"What exactly does that mean?"

"I told Carl that a new mandate is in effect. First of all, he's to leave the vetting of my candidates for any and all agencies to the DOJ, under the supervision of my chief of staff, Lavinia Stanhope. And second, the acting heads of the agencies under his auspices now copy me on all correspondence to him."

"Let me guess. He didn't take it well."

"That's putting it mildly. But it doesn't matter, not after a recent cyber threat on his watch."

Finally, there's something to make me smile. "Don't leave me in suspense, Mr. President."

"It's one of the reasons I wanted to meet with you. The U.S. Intelligence Community's data servers have been hacked. Files throughout the IC were compromised. I presume it's only a matter of time before the hacker releases them to the press. Worse yet, it could have been a successful cyberoperation from an unfriendly nation."

Well, that certainly wipes the grin off my face. "Wow! Was it an inside job?" Even today, the fallout from the Snowden affair is the first thing that comes to mind.

"Carl claims it wasn't, based on the fact that the perpetrator left a calling card. He calls himself 'The Mad Hacker,' and went so far as to leave the icon of Lewis Carroll's Mad Hatter from *Alice in Wonderland* with three clues. FBI cryptographers don't know what it means yet, but they're leaning toward the theory that the message refers to a Doomsday Clock of some sort. You'll soon be getting a dossier on the incident." Lee smiles despite the gravity of this news. "Acme will be conducting the IC's database audit. As you can imagine, Carl hit the roof when I told him."

Lee may have just redeemed himself in my eyes.

"Is there any reason to think that Carl is the real culprit, leaving a red herring to take everyone off the scent?"

"Frankly, I'm hoping you prove exactly that. That way, we'd get rid of him once and for all. By the way, until the mission is announced by Ryan, my one request is that you'll not say anything to anyone about it."

He means Jack, of course.

"You know, Lee, you can trust Jack."

Lee shrugs. "Why would I, when he doesn't trust me?"

He's got a point there.

"By the way, you'll be the mission leader," Lee continues. "This will give you free access to all of the IC's computers—including Carl's." He pauses to take a deep breath. "Donna, about that thing we discussed back in Hilldale, around seven months ago—I have a feeling that Carl is keeping it on his laptop."

Without coming out and saying it, Lee is asking me to do the one thing that will free him from Carl:

Erase the evidence that Carl is using to blackmail him.

That way, Carl can be brought to justice without any repercussions to Lee.

I can't help laughing. "If I do, he'll finally know where he stands with you."

"I could not care less." Lee shrugs. "A bigger question is where I stand with you."

I'm taken aback by his declaration. When I finally answer, it comes out in a stutter. "Lee...I...I hope that I never let you down...or our country."

"The country and I aren't one and the same." He frowns as he takes my hand. "Donna, are you saying that you don't feel anything for me?"

"I...of course." Yes, I feel something for him, but it's not what he thinks, or what he'd want to hear.

I feel pity.

I'm sorry—almost as sorry as him, no doubt—that his company's acquisition of the conglomerate previously owned by one of the thirteen leaders of the Quorum, the now-deceased Jonah Breck, put him squarely in Carl's sights—and in due time, also under Carl's thumb.

When Lee married Jonah's widow, Babette, I guess he never figured the relationship was really a *ménage à trois*—one that includes Carl.

At Babette's behest, Lee put money behind a presidential candidate—Congresswoman Catherine Martin. In due time, Catherine realized that his wide-open pocketbook and international business connections made him an ideal running mate, a heady proposition for a self-made billionaire from the Kansas corn belt. But when Catherine's husband Robert learned that another source of her funding was the Quorum and threatened to divorce her right in the middle of the campaign, Carl convinced Catherine that it was Robert who was her biggest liability.

A telltale video caught her sanctioning Robert's assassination. Unfortunately, Carl hid his features well from the camera, but I could tell he was her co-conspirator. A wife recognizes little things—the slope of her husband's shoulder, the way he arches his fingers to make a point, even the pauses in a voice that has been electronically altered.

I was once his wife. Now I'm his enemy.

Even with Catherine in jail for life, Carl had his ace in the hole: Lee. His hold over our new president is information explosive enough to put him behind bars for murder.

Lee searches my face as he waits for the answer to his question: what does he mean to me?

I put my hand over his heart. It's beating much faster than it should in the presence of someone whom I desire as no more than a caring friend.

I know my answer isn't what he is looking for, but it's the best I can do:

"I'll always have your back, Lee."

I keep my hand there, even as his eyes grow dark with the understanding that this is as good as it gets.

Impulsively, I lift myself up to give him a peck on the cheek.

He stares down at me. For a moment, it looks as if he's going to draw me in close to him, but something in my face stops him. He, too, knows:

If it were to happen, it wouldn't—it shouldn't—in this way.

His shoulders straighten with his resolve as he nods his goodbye, then heads out the front door.

I wait fifteen minutes before I follow him out. But I don't take the elevator. Instead, I walk down the fire exit. It lets me out in the back of the building.

It pisses me off that, no matter how loudly I whistle or how broadly I wave, for some reason, three empty cabs refuse to pick me up.

Finally, a fourth one pulls over to the curb. When I open the door, I don't like the way the cab driver's eyes sweep over me, as if I'm a piece of meat. Still, I jump in. "Union Square. Step on it."

"Are you sure? You know, on the square, they patrol for you girls pretty heavily. And with all due respect, lady, you ain't exactly the type that the Hyatt lets stroll through its lounge." Through the rearview mirror, I watch as he eyes my cleavage, which is in full view, since there are no buttons on my furry pink coat.

I bat my eyes at him. "Oh, they'll let me in alright. Come on back here and I'll show you why."

That's got his attention. I might have whiplash, what with the speed in which he pulls over into a deserted alley.

He jumps in the back seat with me and yanks me onto his lap, but I slap his hands away. "First things first," I promise, as I unbuckle his belt and pull it off. The next to go are his pants, which I jerk down to his knees. "Wow! Look at that," I gaze at the tent in his shorts. He's so proud of it that he doesn't react at first when I yank off his socks. When finally he opens his big mouth to squawk, I cram one of them into it, then I pull his sweatshirt up over his head.

He's gagging, so I can't exactly make out what he's trying to say, but it sounds like, "What the hell are you doing?"

"Hold still, big boy. I'm just helping you get comfortable," I purr, as I jerk his arms up over his head and lasso them together.

He gets the hint that something isn't right when I pull it tight and loop it over the handle above the side door. To make sure he stays that way, I roll down the window just enough that the belt can slip out, then I roll it up again.

He squeals through his stinking sock when he hears me say, "You may think I'm no lady, but I know you're no gentleman."

As I jump out, I lock the door behind me, slipping the key over the driver-side wheel.

I'd rather take the subway, where no one judges you. If

they're going to talk smack, at least you don't have to pay more than two bucks for the privilege.

Maybe Creepy Taxi Driver is right—how I look now would make me stand out at the Hyatt. But that doesn't matter because our room is at the W Hotel, and by its standards, I could be a boho artist, or a slumming starlet, a rocker's groupie —or yes, one of the many call girls casually lounging in the bar.

Jack is already asleep when I enter our room, but he stirs when he feels me slipping into bed with him.

"Sorry I came off like a jealous fool." By his drowsy drawl, I can't tell if he's awake, or if he's saying this in his sleep.

To prove to him there is nothing to forgive, I spoon him tightly. My arm snakes slowly through the smooth valley that falls between the hill of his hip and his mountainous rib cage. As we lie together like this—with my fingers nesting in the curly chest hairs over his heart—I realize just how large he really is.

He will keep me safe—from others, and from myself.

Slowly, he rolls over so that he's facing me. There's enough light slipping in through the shuttered windows for me to see that his eyes are open. One of his hands finds one of mine, and holds it tight. The other hand's index finger strokes my face gently. His deep kiss sends a pulse through my body.

Still, I wait for the inevitable: a question about Lee.

But, no, he stays silent.

Yes, I am grateful. To know he loves me.

To know he trusts me.

Granted, he sucks in his breath when I take him in hand. And there is a sigh of anticipation as he hardens.

When I ease onto him, he groans with joy.

In no time, he matches my pace. I plunge. He thrusts. I squeeze. He surges.

Together, we explode.

Spent, he lets loose with an ecstatic groan.

Afterward, I lay in his arms. Silently, he circles my nipples with his fingertips until he falls asleep.

As his chest rises and falls beside me, I finally realize that he's taking me at my word—

That I know what I'm doing.

I wish I were as confident.

3

Trojan Horse

Hi, ho, Silver! Away—

With your files, your pictures, and all the work projects you had to put on your boss's desk in the next twenty-four hours.

That's what happens when you download a "Trojan horse"—a.k.a., malware (a malicious code) program designed to corrupt your files—onto your computer.

The email or text that put it there seemed innocent enough. Apparently, you clicked on it because it promised, YOU CAN BE A HOTTIE! ALL YOU HAVE TO DO IS—

Of course you clicked the link.

Ouch, wrong move! You've just allowed some baddie to slip into your computer through the back door, and now he knows more about you than, say, your mother.

She may have warned you about wearing dirty underwear, but he knows where you hide it.

THE TEXT ON MY CELL SAYS:

LET'S HAVE DOUBLE DARK CHOCOLATE DEVIL'S FOOD CAKE FOR DESSERT TONIGHT. OKAY? XO J

I guess this is Jack's way of saying that he doesn't want to share my diet misery. How thoughtless of the man!

But, hey, I can think of a few ways he can make it up to me when he gets home from coaching my son Jeff's baseball game.

My youngest daughter, Trisha, is tagging along with the boys. My oldest daughter, Mary, will be returning from a sleepover later this afternoon.

In other words, I have the whole morning to myself—a rare treat indeed.

But, alas, the cake will have to wait. Yard work is long overdue. Besides some unsightly weeds, I'm ashamed to say that my sweetly pink Heritage roses now flow so far beyond the front picket fence that they are nudging passers-by practically onto the roadway.

Time to get clipping. I don my broadest sun hat and I grab my sharpest shears from the garage, along with a pair of gardening gloves and a bucket.

Many of my neighbors are of like mind regarding the best way to spend this beautiful Saturday morning. I wave at those who live closest to us—the Shumways, who own the hacienda-style mansion to our left. The husband, Will, salutes me with his hedge clippers, but the wife, Mitzi, frowns. I guess she hasn't forgotten the FBI SWAT team's middle-of-the-night visit to my house last year.

Talk about holding a grudge.

And since I also stopped the annihilation of several major cities all over the world, frankly, I think it's time that Mitzi cut me some slack.

The arrest was a mistake. A Department of Justice wonk thought I was aiding and abetting my terrorist soon-to-be ex-husband, Carl. Ha, as if! Despite Carl's attempts to sully my reputation, I handled the situation in a most honorable and lady-like manner. Granted, it meant executing the island jailbreak of a Mexican drug lord, only to lose most of him to a hungry shark. But, all's well that ends well, since I was able to hold onto his head, which was tattooed with the bank vault combination containing the floor plan to the Quorum's secret hideout.

It's still early enough that the sun isn't so hot as to make a lady glisten, as my mother used to say.

Until recently, we've been houseguests of an Acme colleague—Dominic Fleming, whose pseudo-chateau is right around the corner. Our own house was rebuilt after a tremendous fireball scorcher, which left nothing but ash and cinder.

Did I forget to turn off the iron, or leave the stove unattended? If only! In truth, Jack and I were escaping from another raid—this time, by an NSA SWAT team.

And you thought your neighbors were pains in the ass.

The move back was a bear. For the first three months, the contractor dragged his heels—that is, until I took him to the shooting range. Watching me drill fifty rounds into the genital area of a paper target man convinced him to take me at my word when I said I wanted to be in our house no later than Mother's Day.

Besides buying all new furniture, the kids needed new clothes. It was like Christmas all over again.

I'm sure I won't feel that way when I see my next home insurance rate increase.

The wind picks up as I snip the most egregious rose branches. The fragrant scents of the flowers drift over me in the now-cool breeze.

A half-hour later, though, the sun has ducked behind a dark bulging cloud. I'm not very far along in my work, but already a few fat sprinkles have dampened the sidewalk. I've been placing the fallen flowers stem-side down in a bucket. It's now time to separate those holding fresh roses from those with petals long past their peak. The former will be placed in vases throughout the house. As for the latter, I'll ask my daughters—fourteen-year-old Mary, and seven-year-old Trisha—if they'd like to help me make sachets from the roses' petals and an old lace curtain I've held onto, for just this very reason.

Only then do I notice that I've got an audience. An elderly woman, wheelchair-bound, sits just a few feet from me. Is she visiting the MacMillans, the neighbors on our right? I don't remember them saying they expected company.

As our eyes meet, she smiles shyly. "You're Donna Stone, aren't you?"

"Yes," I say, as I push back the brim of my hat to get a better look at her.

"My, my! I heard your roses were beautiful," she gushes. "I can see why you're celebrated for your green thumb."

"Really? Well…thank you for saying so." Better that, than night raids by local agency SWAT teams.

I pick up a dozen of the fresh ones and walk over to her with them. "Would you care for these?"

"How generous!" Pleased, she holds out a hand and takes them. "One good turn deserves another. I've got something for you too." With the other hand, she gives me an envelope.

"Oh! Why…thank you." Of course, I take it. Graciousness was drilled into me from the time I was a toddler. "Should I open this now?"

"That's entirely up to you. Don't take it personally, but you've been served," the woman says over her shoulder, as she wheels away from me. "Thanks for these!"

I stare after her. A moment later, I've ripped open the envelope to discover that Carl is asking for full custody of our children, based on his claim that I'm an "unfit mother."

The nerve of the man! Why, he made the Interpol Most Wanted List a full year before I was placed on it. Talk about selective memory.

I don't have to accept his reality. For that matter, I don't have to accept this subpoena, either.

I shout, "Wait!" But the woman has already rounded the corner. I have to hurdle over the Shumways' red-tip hedge to catch up. Even Mitzi's glare can't stop me from cutting across her front yard.

Doing so puts me neck and neck with Miss Wheelchair 1964. I grab her chair by its handles and pull her to a halt. "How dare you!"

The woman shrugs. "Lady—I'm just doing my job."

I move to the front of her chair and lean on the arms with both hands. I don't care that a couple of neighbors across the street have stopped their gossiping in order to stare at us. "Nope, sorry. This is unacceptable," I insist. "You came up to me under false pretenses."

She rolls her wheels over my feet.

"Ouch, that hurt!" I hop on my right so that I can grab the left one and rub the soreness out of it.

She smiles up at me and murmurs sweetly, "Well, dearie, I asked your name, and confirmed you were the party being served. By law, it's the only thing I have to do—that, and hand you the papers."

"It wasn't right! I was on my own property, which means you were trespassing."

She shakes her head. "Technically, you were on the public sidewalk."

Okay, yeah, she has a point.

Still, that doesn't stop me from snatching the flowers out of her lap.

"You gave those to me!" She grabs them back.

"Buy yourself a dozen with whatever money you've made by making my life miserable." I yank back as hard as I can—

The buds come off in my hands. Worse yet, the thorns have shredded my palms to bits.

I'll survive. Besides, she's left holding nothing but the stems.

Her involuntary reflex—to roll away from me—deposits her left wheel in a rain grate. Every attempt to maneuver out of it only secures her right wheel even deeper into a crack.

Hopefully, she'll be stuck there until the next Great Flood.

For a moment, her rage reddens her face. But then her lip quivers. "You can't just leave me here! I'm a defenseless old lady!"

"Oh, no? Watch me."

I turn to leave—

Only to bump into the small crowd that has gathered around us. I guess I should be concerned that everyone thinks I'm some sort of bully, but quite honestly, I'm so angry right now, I can't see straight.

As I rush by my neighbors, I hear Tiffy Swift, one of my carpool partners, mutter to Mitzi, "How could anyone be so cruel to that poor thing?"

If only she knew.

I guess she will, and soon. She and the rest of her coven— Hayley Coxhead and the all-time queen of mean, Penelope Bing —will have yet one more reason to snicker when I'm in view.

By now, sheets of rain are falling. Soaked, I toss the crushed buds into the bucket with the rest of the cut flowers and make a run for the house. Now, besides making Jack's cake, I've got another task:

Telling my children that the man I love is not their father.

First things first: I've got to see my divorce attorney.

I AM NOTHING LIKE THE THREE OTHER WOMEN IN ALAN SHORE'S waiting room.

I don't accessorize cropped razorback running tees and ass-lifting yoga pants with precious diamond tennis bracelets worth more than my home mortgage.

I'm not on my third, fourth, or fifth husband—and trying to get away from him.

And I don't bring my maid to my appointment with my divorce attorney so that she can take notes for me.

In fact, I don't have a maid.

Admittedly, it's the one thing I covet from these ladies.

Okay, that and the tennis bracelet.

I may have walked in last, but my name gets called next. The twenty-dollar bill I palmed to Alan's receptionist buys me VIP status.

At the same time, it earns me laser-sharp glares from the other women. Well, too bad. My children's wellbeing is at stake, so, hell yeah, baby, I'm jumping the line.

Besides, it's cocktail hour in Paris. At least, that will be Alan's excuse for tippling even this early in the day. And let's face it: he may be a conniving bastard genius, but he's less lucid when he's too far into his cups.

So, yes, I'm next in line for some of his sage, if cockeyed, advice.

I wouldn't trade that for a million tennis bracelets.

ALAN DOESN'T RISE WHEN I ENTER. FOR THAT MATTER, HE DOESN'T even look up.

Maybe that's a good thing, since his personal barber has a straight razor at his throat.

"Joanie, long time no see! January, two years ago, right? Wasn't that the big shakedown for Husband Number Three? Gee, how time flies when you're having fun."

By the way I open a spare straight razor with a flick of my wrist and trim Alan's cowlick into a Mohawk without him feeling it, the barber knows I'm serious about getting Alan's undivided attention and does the smart thing: He grabs his gear and scurries out the door.

"Alan, it's not Joanie." Of course, he knows my voice.

Slowly, he peeks out from under the warm towel wrapped around his face. Seeing me, he practically falls out of his chair. "Donna! I—I wasn't expecting you—"

"That's quite alright. Your receptionist understood the severity of my emergency and slipped me in." My voice oozes peaches and cream, but by the way I hold the razor—next to his neck—he knows I'm not a happy camper.

He frowns. "Yeah, okay, what can I do for you?"

I snort. "According to your billable hours—over a hundred, to date, and counting—you should have done it already! Don't you remember? You're supposed to be my first line of defense in my divorce from Carl Stone, lately of the District of Columbia! Or have you forgotten it's why I pay you such a princely sum?"

"If I remember correctly, I've got you on the 'practically pro bono plan,' which, frankly, makes me a gentleman, considering nothing about this divorce is easy."

"Pro bono? Is that what you call it?" Oops, my bad, I've pricked his neck.

He yelps, but only after I lift the razor so that he can see the droplet of blood on its blade.

He leaps out of the chair and backs away. "On top of driving a hard bargain with me, and considering that you refuse to take a dime from him, yes, that's exactly the right word for it."

"Of course I won't take money from him! If I do, it validates his role in my children's lives, even after he deserted them—and me." I'm trying hard to keep my eyes from clouding up with tears. "Not to mention the lies he'll tell them—about himself, about Jack…and about me."

"Believe what you want, but if this goes his way, you've only yourself to blame," he mutters.

"Oh? How so?"

"Since you won't take alimony or child support, Carl doesn't believe you're willing to play hardball." He dabs the towel to his neck. When he sees a spot of blood, he gulps hard and backs away from me. I can tell by the worried look in his eyes that he's wondering if he should say what he really thinks.

To encourage him to do so, I toss the blade to one side.

Relieved, he sighs. "Look, Donna, I'm doing the best I can. But to tell you the truth—I know, rare in my profession—my people have had a hell of a time getting anywhere near Carl to subpoena him for a deposition, because he's surrounded by his personal storm trooper battalion…twenty-four seven. Not only that, he's got everyone but the justices of the Supreme Court offering themselves up as character witnesses as to why he should share custody with you. Let me put it this way, my dear Mrs. Stone: you can't fight city hall, let alone Capitol Hill. He won. You lost. Suck it up."

I brush away a tear. "I can't do it, Alan! I can't allow him near them!"

"If that's the way you feel, keep doing what you do best—

dodging the summons server. Maybe Carl will get tired of all these shenanigans and blow it off."

"I...well..." I hand him the subpoena. "Unfortunately, a process server got to me."

Alan's eyes narrow. "Part of your 'pro bono' fees went to buying off—I mean, retaining—every process server in the LA metro area, so that they could pass on the honor of serving you. So, what did this guy look like?"

"It wasn't a guy. It was a little old lady—in a wheelchair, no less! And it wasn't a prop either, because she couldn't get out of it when she accidentally fell into a ditch."

Alan snorts. "Yeah, those kinds of accidents happen—around you, anyway." He walks over to his desk, opens a drawer, and pulls out a stack of cards.

Glancing over his shoulder, I see that someone's picture is pasted on each one. "What are those, sports trading cards?"

"Something like that—and even more valuable if you've got a reason to stay just out of reach of the long arm of the law. I should have had you look at these when this case heated up." He flips through the stack until he finds the one he seeks: a front-on shot of the woman who served my summons. He holds it up. "Let me guess. It was this woman—Greta Larkin."

I grab it out of his hand for a better look. "Yes! How did you know?"

"Your Carl is a sly dog! He hired the best process server in the San Francisco Bay area. Let me put it this way: if she were a trading card, she'd be the Babe Ruth of the deck. Her record is nine-eighty-nine and oh." Alan shakes his head in awe. "Don't feel bad. One way or another, she would have gotten you."

"Oh, really? Well, thanks for the vote of confidence." I'm tempted to pick up the razor again and do a little manscaping —around his heart—only I'm afraid it'll be a waste of time, since he doesn't seem to have one. "Okay, genius, what's our next step?"

He shrugs. "If you don't give in, you'll be in contempt of court—and he may be able to convince the judge to take your kids away from you."

Adamantly, I shake my head. "Nope. That will never happen."

Seeing me pick up the blade again and fiddle with it, he backs up as far as he can go without falling out his third story window. "You've always had excellent powers of persuasion. Maybe you can use them to come to some sort of agreement that you both can live with," he says with a leer.

If he's suggesting I sleep with Carl, I'll make his third-story fall look like a successful suicide attempt.

However, if he's suggesting that I kill Carl, well, duh. That niggling little task has been on my to-do list for quite some time now.

Not that he needs to know this. Despite attorney-client privilege, a lady must always keep an air of mystery about her—not to mention any and all incriminating evidence.

I shrug nonchalantly. "Maybe you're right. I should at least attempt a meeting of the minds—for old time's sake."

"That's my girl!" He nudges me toward the door with one hand. With the other, he towels off the rest of the shaving cream. "In the meantime, I'll stall on the actual meet-and-greet. But the judge has already warned us that it should happen in a timely fashion, so whatever you have in mind, make it happen —quick."

That's the plan—quick.

Although not necessarily painlessly.

For Carl, anyway.

4

Hardware

Your brand spanking new laptop computer comes out of its box so pretty and so shiny—and loaded with tons of bells and whistles that will have you moving at warp speed through the Etherworld!

Which bring us to the three things that should never be allowed near it:

- *Forbidden Item Number 1: A can of soda.*

Nothing mucks up a keyboard faster than heavily sugared seltzer water. For that matter, when it seeps into your hard drive, you can forget your computer's memory too. (But, hopefully, you remembered to buy a warranty plan.)

- *Forbidden Item Number 2: Your child.*

He may like the fact that your computer doesn't freeze while he plays his favorite video games, but the last thing you need is for him to erase any emails from your boss (by mistake), or the latest email from his teacher (on purpose).

More than likely, he will also be the one who spills the soda on your keyboard.

- *Forbidden Item Number 3: Your significant other.*

Porn may look better on your large, hi-def screen with 200x zoom, but since you're less interested in counting the moles on some naked nympho's breasts than he is, tell him to stay away from it.

Or to get his own computer.

Should his porn obsession get out of hand, spill a little soda on the problem.

I'M ICING ALL THREE COOLED LAYERS OF CAKE WHEN JACK, JEFF and Trisha get home from the game.

Despite the fact the he's soaked to the bone, Jeff gives me a peck on the cheek. "We would have won by three if the game hadn't been rained out."

I give him a hug. "Did you pitch?"

"Give me a break! What do you think?" He flexes a muscle.

Like his father, he's not exactly the modest type.

By that, I mean Carl.

The thought that he'll soon know the truth makes me want to throw up.

Jack takes my left hand and holds it up, so that he can examine my bandaged palm. "Don't tell me you cut yourself with the shears."

I flinch—not because my wounds are still tender, but because I don't want to tell him the truth. That is, not yet, anyway. "No, I…had a run-in with some…rose thorns."

He sticks a finger in the icing bowl and licks it. "So, now, you're drowning your sorrows in chocolate cake?"

I slide the bowl away from him. "How dare you!"

He frowns. "What's wrong? You told me to remind you whenever you're tempted to go off your diet."

I shove the whole cake in his direction. "I'm not making it for me. It's for you! Remember?"

"Since when?"

"Since ten-thirty this morning, when you texted me." I grab my cell phone off the counter and thrust it in his direction. "See?"

He takes it and reads the message. Then he stares at me, shaking his head. "Donna, I swear I didn't send this." He takes his phone from his pocket and hands it to me, so that I can see his list of recent texts for myself.

"But then…who?"

He shrugs. "I guess your phone has been hacked."

"That's impossible! At least, if you're to believe Arnie."

"Even Arnie isn't infallible. In any event, he needs to know as soon as possible." He's about to punch Arnie's number into his phone when it rings. Caller ID shows that it's Ryan. I can't hear what our boss is saying, but Jack's face has a curious look on it. "Will do, boss. We'll leave immediately," he mutters.

"What did Ryan want?" My heart is pounding. My guess is that the call is about what I heard from Lee last night. Still, I have to pretend that I don't know what it's about.

Jack shrugs. "He wouldn't say, but he wants us in the office, pronto. Do you think Aunt Phyllis can cover for us?"

I nod nonchalantly. "I'll see if I can rustle her up."

I text Aunt Phyllis:

Calling in a chit. Can you watch the kids for the rest of the afternoon?

A minute later, she texts back:

Hola! I'll head over as soon as my samba class is over. Besos!

Jack is reading my cell screen over my shoulder. He winces. "Couldn't she throw out a hip?"

"After thirty-some years of yoga, I'd say the odds are good that she'll outlive us both."

He opens his mouth to say something, but then realizes it's something I already know: In our line of work, longevity is questionable anyway.

I look over at Jeff. "I'll need you to watch your sister until Aunt Phyllis gets here. It should be an hour, tops."

"No problem." He licks his lips. "Can we have cake?"

"Yes, but after dinner. I'll text Mary now, so that she knows to make spaghetti if we're not home by seven."

He wrinkles his nose. "Her noodles are too soft. She never hears the timer, because she's always on her cell phone."

"With *Trevor*," Trisha says with a knowing grin.

The last thing I need to worry about is Mary and Trevor's raging hormones. "Her noodles will be just fine for tonight," I assure him.

To guarantee it, I text Mary: *Need you at home.*

She texts back: *Still with BFFs, studying.*

The library closed a half hour ago. My next text tells her I know it: *WITH TREVOR????*

A moment later, she texts back: *B home in 5*

Relieved, I smile. "Jeff, afterward, you'll help Mary with the dishes. Trisha will set the table. For lunch, there's chicken salad in the fridge, with organic greens." I grab my purse. "Until Aunt Phyllis gets here, don't let anyone in the house except for Mary."

"Not even Trevor?" Jeff asks slyly.

"Especially not Trevor," I say, as I follow Jack out the door. "And please stay inside."

Not that they'd want to go out, anyway.

There's a storm brewing.

BY THE TIME WE GET TO THE OFFICE, THE REST OF THE MISSION TEAM is already assembled in the conference room with Ryan. There are at least twenty tech-ops personnel, as well as their fearless leader—Arnie Locklear, who personally provides tech-ops for Mission Quorum, which is headed up by Jack.

Emma Honeycutt, my mission team's communications intelligence specialist, is also here. She's engaged to Arnie, and is now well into her seventh month of pregnancy. I wish I could say that things have been smooth sailing for those two, but after the initial proposal euphoria, reality has set in.

They must be in the midst of some new battle, because they're sitting on opposite sides of the room. They haven't even tied the knot, but already they fight like an old married couple.

Other members of the Quorum mission team have also been summoned. Abu Nagashahi, a field operative who is our mission's cut-out and cleaner, is sitting behind Emma. And, finally, there is Dominic, who, like Jack and me, is an F3—he finds, fixes, and finishes—on black-ops missions.

For the majority of these operations, we're naked—and by that, I don't mean we aren't wearing clothes (albeit in some cases, we aren't), but that we go solo.

When it's Jack's turn to go naked, I hold my breath until he walks back through the door.

He does the same for me. Too much can go wrong. We know this from experience.

Frankly, when it comes to my dealings with Lee, I'm totally naked—figuratively, that is.

No doubt he wouldn't mind if I were in the literal sense either.

But that ain't happening. I think I've given him that message loud and clear. At the same time, I'll be honest: I don't mind being the pawn—make that the queen—in some deadly chess game of wits and power with Carl.

I have a vested interest to keep Carl in check.

Now that everyone is here, Ryan gets right to the point. "Acme has been called in to do an audit of the U.S. Intelligence Community's main database. Apparently, the IC's intrusion software is less than stellar. Security vulnerabilities have been found in our most highly classified files concerning terrorism, both foreign and domestic."

Jack gives me a sidelong glance. I know he's now wondering if this was the reason for Lee's call to me. I look straight ahead, as if I'm not aware of his stare.

He's about to say something to me when Ryan holds up his hands to counter the shocked murmurs and questions from the crowd. "We don't know much, but from what we can tell, the hacker is a pro, not just some kid looking to prove something. It is cyberespionage of the highest order. And yet, he chose to leave a calling card. Three, in fact."

From his iPad, he flashes an image onto the wall-sized video screen: a wild-eyed man in a top hat—the classic illustration of the Mad Hatter in *Alice in Wonderland*. Only this hatter is sitting with a laptop. Alphabet letters swarm the screen like flies. When they align, they read:

It is better to be feared than loved.

Spooky.

Dominic taps his lips with a forefinger. "From what I

remember of *Alice in Wonderland*, that line was spoken by the Red Queen."

Ryan nods. "Thanks for that, Dominic."

The next clue says: *What a funny watch! It tells the day of the month, and doesn't tell what o'clock it is!*

"Alice, of course," Dominic says, matter-of-factly. This knowledge earns him a few grudging nods.

"Here's the final clue," Ryan says, as it appears on the wall: *Everything's got a moral, if only you can find it.*

"This quote is directly from the Duchess," Dominic declares.

I notice that a couple of fivers are handed around. Those who get them must have bet correctly that Dominic could go three for three.

Emma pats him on the shoulder. "How did you do that?"

Dominic shrugs. "It's nothing, really. Every student at Ludgrove has memorized the entire text of *Alice in Wonderland* by his second year."

"Ludgrove? What?…And all this time, I thought you'd gone to Hogwarts," Arnie mutters. He turns to Emma. "Isn't that what you told me?"

She sighs. "I didn't have the heart to tell you Hogwarts isn't a real place."

"Yes, well, I'm sure Princes William and Harry were also disappointed," Dominic sniffs. "But they got over it soon enough. As is the case with the rest of Ludgrove's alumni, eventually they learned to appreciate its academic excellence sans wands and motorized broomsticks. What one must tolerate if the swish of ermine and the rattle of sabers is in one's blood."

"Back to the matter at hand, please." Ryan scowls, warning them that he's got a lot more to say. "We are now also aware that government contractors with access to these files were hacked as well."

Dominic raises his hand. "Does that include Acme?"

A ghost of a smile rises on Ryan's lips. "As a matter of fact, we are the only contractor who wasn't infiltrated. I attribute that to two things. I'm sure we're on the hacker's radar, but Arnie Locklear's crackerjack intrusion software, doubled with his other tech security initiatives, have kept us safe. The second is that Acme had nothing to do with the IC projects with access to the breached data files."

For once, Carl's hatred of his old employer has done us a favor.

"That being said, POTUS feels that Acme is the logical choice to conduct the security audit. It'll be all hands on deck. Finding the perpetrator assures Acme's status in the intelligence community will once again be second to none."

"Yet one more thing that puts Carl on POTUS's shit list," I murmur to Jack.

"Don't kid yourself," he mutters back. "They've got some sort of bromance going on."

I hold up a finger to my lips, to shush him.

He must have noticed that it's my middle finger, because he snorts.

Abu raises his hand. "Ryan, is there any reason to believe it may be an inside job—say, a disillusioned government employee, or a government contractor with security clearance?"

Or more to the point, the IC director himself, since his own ties to the Quorum are still very much in question.

Ryan shakes his head. "Good question. In answer to the first scenario, our illustrious intelligence director insists not, but we won't presume anything. Anyone could be the Mad Hacker. Of course, Director Stone would prefer the second scenario. In fact, if the culprit was found here at Acme, it would make his day."

An uneasy chuckle can be heard through the room, but no one is really laughing. Ryan's answer has bound us to a singular mission: to prove our former colleague and current nemesis wrong.

Ryan nods toward Arnie and Emma. Both begin to make their way through the room, distributing the stacks of file folders in their hands.

"Each and every one of us in this room is to play an important role in assessing the damage, and identifying the hacker. The majority of you—those working in tech-ops and systems analysis—will report to Arnie Locklear. You'll be placed on a team with specific audit duties, such as looking for security exploits—bugs, viruses and Trojans—packet sniffing, or doing rootkit detection. Your team's mandates are spelled out to you in your individual mission folders." Ryan scans the faces in front of him. "The rest of you will be conducting personnel interviews, suspect interrogations and persons-of-interest investigations—all of which will be coordinated by Jack Craig. Here at Acme headquarters, Emma Honeycutt will be heading up the cyphering team, which will work here at Acme headquarters on the three original riddles left by the Mad Hacker in the IC database."

Ryan passes out mission folders. Everyone gets one but me.

Noticing this, Jack murmurs, "Whatever we find is going to rattle Carl's cage, so Ryan is smart to keep you out of this."

I'm just about to come clean to him about my role in all this when Ryan adds, "This mission's leader is Donna Stone. Any and all questions should be addressed to her. Take the next half-hour to look at your files. Afterward, we'll meet back here. At that point, you can address your questions to Donna and your team leaders."

Jack's eyes open wide. His head turns my way, and his stare says it all: *You knew about this?*

"I can explain," I start.

Jack shakes his head. He doesn't wait for me, but heads toward the front door.

I start to run after him so that I can pull him aside and remind him what he told me—that he trusts me—but I can't get to him because suddenly I'm surrounded by other Acme operatives. They pat me on the back and congratulate me for this plum assignment. Even those who haven't worked with me before know me by reputation, or my personal history. It's why they're pledging their all—body and soul—to make our mission a success.

They will never forget Carl's disloyalty—not just to Acme but to our country as well.

They want to take Carl down too. And I'm their fearless leader.

Hmmm…well…

In any regard, I'm their leader.

BY THE TIME I MAKE IT TO THE LOBBY, JACK'S LAMBORGHINI IS already pulling out of the parking lot. Damn it, what does he expect me to do, walk home?

Seeing Dominic, I wave him down. "After the audit debriefing, do you think you can give me a lift?"

He shakes his head. "Sorry, old girl. Afterward, I'm heading to my new private club."

I raise a brow. "Oh? Which one? Déjà Vu? The Spearmint Rhino? Plan B?" These are all strip clubs, and there's nothing private about them—unless you're willing to hand over a Benjamin in order to get a private room and a dancer who'll warm your lap for you.

"I've been accepted into the Grand Havana," he sniffs.

That's about his speed. Cigars, an overpriced menu, and a

mediocre wine list—not to mention some of the most gorgeous women in LA, whose job is to make its power ranger members forget that they're upping their odds for throat cancer every time they walk into the joint.

Maybe Arnie and Emma won't mind taking me home. I find them standing in a cubicle by the window. Their backs are turned to me. When I get closer, I hear why—they're in the middle of a very heated discussion.

I'm about to walk away when Arnie turns and sees me. "Donna, do you need me?" He sounds so desperate. I guess, at this point, he'd do anything to avoid Emma's bad mood. Emma's hormones have her swinging like a pendulum—not a good thing for a woman who is naturally acerbic anyway. To top it off, she isn't taking well to the physical changes that come with pregnancy. Not only are her cravings crazy (pickles? Forget about it! Try chicken apple sausages, beets, and mango sherbet), she's frustrated that she can no longer squeeze into her tight low-slung jeans.

Been there, felt that.

"I hate to ask, but Jack took off already, and I was wondering if you'd be kind enough to give me a ride home after the briefing."

"Oh, Donna, sorry, but we can't because we came on my bike." Emma's wheels are a Brutale 800 Dragster.

Suddenly, Arnie is all smiles. "As a matter of fact, we can." He turns to Emma. "I was going to save it as a surprise. But hey, now's as good a time as any." He reaches into his pocket, takes out a car key, and dangles it in front of her. "Sweetie, this is for you."

Emma stares down at it. "What is it, exactly?"

"The key to your new car! I bought you a Yukon Denali XL hybrid." He points out to the parking lot. The SUV is in the front row: black and gorgeous. "It's fully loaded," he says proudly. "Four-wheel drive with a V8 engine, coil-over shocks, multilink rear suspension—I even got it with bullet-proof glass."

Emma's eyes narrow. "You got me *a mommy mobile?*"

His smile fades. "Em, sweetie, it's not as if you can slap a baby seat on the back of your motorcycle. I don't think California law allows for that."

Emma lets that sink in. Then she starts to hyperventilate. As she bursts into tears, she slaps the keys out of his hands and storms off.

Arnie turns to me. "What did I do now?"

I don't want to tell him that I think the Yukon was a bad idea, especially when it's my dream car, and especially since it's my ride home.

It's ten o'clock at night by the time I get back to the house. Thank goodness Arnie is too morose about Emma's reaction to be much of a conversationalist. However, when I jump out of the car, he asks, "It gets better, right?"

I pat his hand. "Yes. But, Arnie, take my advice—let Emma grow into the role of mother."

He gulps. "What if she doesn't?"

"Trust me, she will—starting with the very first time she holds her child in her arms."

"That's a relief. Still, I don't think it will change how she feels about me." His head is weighted by this thought.

Arnie loves Emma. And yes, at first, he was hurt that he wasn't the father of her child. That honor goes to Reed Horwitch, an actor who seduced her while she and the rest of our Acme team was undercover with a film crew while trying to clear our names from Interpol's Most Wanted List.

At the time, we all needed some diversions to get our minds off our situation. Unfortunately for Emma, she now has a constant reminder of that very anxious time in our lives.

Despite Arnie's heartbreak over her affair, he's embraced the idea of parenthood with open arms.

When he pulls a tiny velvet ring box out of the Denali's glove compartment, I realize just how badly he wants Emma to accept him—not only as the father of her child, but as her husband.

I open it slowly. What's inside makes me gasp. "Arnie! This is…beautiful!" The diamond, at least a carat, is placed on an angle in its platinum setting. The companion ring, a man's, is angled in the opposite direction. So that when the wearers' palms touch, the rings' surfaces fit like two pieces of a puzzle.

He blushes. "I designed it myself. I was going to give it to her tonight, after she took the car for its first spin around town. But now…" He stares down at it. When I hand it to him, he tosses it back in the glove compartment.

I pat his arm. "She's got a lot on her mind. Bide your time. Let her tell you when it's right."

He nods, but his eyes are clouded with doubt.

I know what he's wondering: *how long will I have to wait until she accepts me?*

I watch as he pulls away from the curb. For his sake, I hope Emma has calmed down by the time he gets home.

For my sake, I hope Jack has forgiven me too.

I ENTER THROUGH THE KITCHEN DOOR. THE FIRST THING I NOTICE IS that all but a quarter of the cake is already eaten.

It's no wonder the kids have gone to bed early—with belly-aches, I imagine.

The guest room door is cracked open. The television is on, but Aunt Phyllis is on the bed, snoring.

It's for the best. If Jack and I are to have a civil conversation about why I'm on this mission—and why I've been chosen as its leader—better that no one else is in the line of fire.

But he's not in our bedroom. So, where is he?

I glance out the window. The inky darkness is cut only by the pale glow of a half moon. Once my eyes get used to it, I see Jack: on the back terrace, sitting on a chaise lounge.

I practically run downstairs to the kitchen.

I grab a tray. On it, I put my peace offering: what's left of Jack's double chocolate cake, along with a knife to cut it, two plates, two forks, some napkins, and a couple of tall glasses filled with milk.

In this case, I don't kid myself that chocolate cures all ills, but it's a start.

IF JACK HEARS ME COMING, HE DOESN'T SHOW IT.

Perhaps the half-empty Scotch bottle beside him has something to do with that.

I ignore it. Instead, I make it a point to walk in front of him before placing the tray on the picnic table. I cut him a generous slice of the cake, and take it to him with a glass of milk. "Peace offering."

He takes the cake, but waves away the milk, pointing to the tumbler of Scotch beside him. "My thirst is quenched, thank you very much."

I drop down onto the wrought-iron settee beside him. "So I see."

He scowls as he stares back at me.

Aw, heck. Why didn't I keep my mouth shut?

He jabs the cake with his fork. After taking a bite, he mutters, "Not bad. Why don't you join me?"

"I'm…not hungry." By the time we were done with our meeting, I'd devoured three hefty wedges of pizza—not that Jack needs to know that.

"Oh, yes, I forget. Must keep your girlish figure if you're to entice the real Mr. Stone into divulging his deepest, darkest secrets."

Silently, I count to three. "Jack, I know you're hurt that I didn't tell you about Lee's plan before Ryan divulged it to the team as a whole—"

He stabs his fork at me. "Ha! I knew it!"

Firmly, I nudge his fork away from my face. "Knew what, may I ask?"

"That it was Lee's idea."

"What of it?"

"Don't you see, Donna? You're Lee's pawn! He moves you around the board, knowing full well that Carl will chase after you. Carl corners you, and he corners Carl." As Jack spits out his concern, he spews a couple of crumbs in my direction.

Because I know how much he cares for me, I resist the urge to take the milk and throw it in his face. Instead, in a soft but determined tone, I counter, "Isn't that what we want as well—to corner Carl?"

"Not at the cost of your safety, or your children's wellbeing." He takes a swig of his Scotch. "Have you forgotten that this mission puts you in close proximity to Carl—something which, up until this afternoon, I thought you were opposed to, considering you've been dodging his subpoenas for the past few months?"

I pull the subpoena out of my back pocket. "Too late. Happened this morning."

"I see." The cynical glint in Jack's eyes softens just a bit.

"Maybe it's time to call that deadbeat lawyer of yours and put him to work for real."

"I did better than that. I paid him a visit. A lot of good it did me. He says I'll be in contempt of court if I don't acquiesce to the judge's ruling for joint custody—that is, if I can't convince Carl otherwise."

Jack shrugs. "So that's what this is really about."

"What's that supposed to mean?"

"Don't be coy, Donna. All Carl has to do is be within sniffing distance of you and he goes wild with the desire to do one of two things: kill you"—he stabs another bite of cake with his fork, but just stares down at it—"or fuck you. Granted, the first desire makes sense. If he gets away with it, you're out of his way once and for all, and legally, nothing can stand in his way of getting full custody of Mary, Jeff and Trisha—not even me." He frowns. "But something tells me he loves keeping you around just so that he can taunt you—or better yet, bend you to his will. And thanks to Lee, now more than ever, he's in a position to do so. Which brings us to the sixty-trillion-dollar question: just how far will you go to make sure he stays out of the children's lives?"

Jack is just about to dig into the cake again when I snatch his plate away. "Are you insinuating that I'd…I'd…" I'm so angry that I can't even say it.

He grabs it back. "In a word, yes."

I rise to my feet. "Thanks for your vote of confidence. I'll keep it in mind. By the way, I don't appreciate the fact that you've walked off this mission. You told me you'd always have my back."

"You don't need me. Lee has your back, remember? If you're right—and in my book, that's a big if—I presume he admires the view." As he cranes his head, his gaze goes downward, to my ass. "I don't think he'll mind sharing it with Carl, since it gives him the leverage he needs. For once, I look forward to telling you 'I told you so.'" He crams another forkful of cake into his mouth.

When I reach for the plate again, he jerks his hand away—

And the cake goes flying.

Devil's food icing on a white silk blouse is not a good fashion statement.

I grab the plate in order to fling it at him, like a Frisbee.

He ducks and it soars right over his head. When this precious piece of my Lenox Vintage Jewel collection hits the branch holding Mary's old tree house—now Trisha's domain— it shatters into a dozen jagged pieces.

I storm back into the house before I'm tempted to shave his jugular with one of them.

I fall asleep while doing my homework: reading a digital copy of *Alice in Wonderland*.

5

Backside Bus

A "bus" is a collection of wires that distribute data within your computer. The size of the bus dictates how much data can be transmitted (for example, 16- or 32-bits).

Your computer has two buses. The "frontside bus" carries data between the CPU (central processing unit; in other words, the computer's "brain") and its main memory.

The "backside bus" runs data between the CPU and a Level 2 cache. Typically, it runs at a faster clock speed than the frontside bus.

This being said, no need to punch out someone who compliments you on the speed of your backside bus, since in no way are they implying that your ass-kissing is second to none.

CARL STONE, THE DIRECTOR OF NATIONAL INTELLIGENCE, KEEPS me cooling my heels outside his office for over two hours.

Still, I keep a sweet smile on my face. In fact, I brought along a dozen homemade double butterscotch brownies, which

I've placed in a white box with a large blue ribbon. When Carl was the love of my life, it was his favorite dessert.

Perhaps all things taste bitter to him now. I wouldn't doubt it in the least.

Time to test that old adage, *the way to a man's heart is through his stomach.*

No, I'm not kissing ass. It's a peace offering. As the Acme team leader, I have to meet with him as a courtesy anyway, to go over the specifics of the audit. While I'm here, we might as well have a civil conversation about the children too.

Besides, if Jack is right and Carl is still smitten with me, who knows? As my mother used to say, "You'll catch more flies with honey than vinegar."

And edible panties.

Not that I'm wearing any.

I don't need them. Today, I'm not playing the whore, but a madonna—specifically the mother of Carl's children. As such, I look demure as well as fabulous in my navy pencil-skirted suit, which I'm wearing over a sheer white blouse.

Not the one Jack ruined for me.

Now that Jack has gone AWOL, Dominic is taking over as the interview team's leader. To that end, he's combed through the IC employee photo database in order to ID his own interview candidates. Whereas Jack would have chosen the most obvious suspects, Dominic's are all female and under thirty— no surprise there.

For the duration of the audit, the Acme team has booked two floors of the Tyson's Corners' Hilton, diagonally across the Three-O-Nine from the ODNI headquarters, known as Liberty Crossing. I would have been bunking with Jack, but since he's opted to take an unpaid leave—something that has Ryan furious—I'll have a room by myself.

Maybe absence does make the heart grow fonder.

But I won't bet another white blouse on it.

Except for the layers of security surrounding it, the ODNI campus looks like any of the other nondescript multi-story buildings located in the many faceless office parks that ring DC's Central Beltway's northeast side.

And inside the facility, the offices and cubicles are just as vanilla.

This way of life is the antithesis of everything I know about Carl. He hates offices, and loves the danger of being out in the field, totally naked.

Yes, literally and figuratively.

Finally, Carl's comely administrative assistant (what did he do, raid her from a *Playboy* photo shoot?) simpers, "Carl—I mean, the director will see you now."

Just as I rise, the door opens and two men in military uniforms exit. From their abundance of chest candy, I gather that they're generals, but I don't recognize them as any of the heads of the agencies within the Intelligence Community.

Carl comes out after them, smiling broadly. I haven't seen him since the U.S. Senate subcommittee hearing in which his appointment was cleared. I can only imagine the dirt he had on the committee's members. "Donna, my dear wife! Well, aren't you a sight for sore eyes!"

His pleasant demeanor leaves me speechless, not to mention this false term of endearment. In shock, I hold out my hand, but he does more than shake it. Instead he uses it as leverage to pull me into his arms.

Before I know it, his lips lock onto mine. What...the *hell?*

He steps into the kiss until we're chest to breast. I'd push him away, but that would mean dropping the brownies.

No need. By the time I recover from his kiss, he's whisking me into his office.

Are the generals snickering because they notice the way in which he pats my bum before closing the door?

From the angry pout on his assistant's face, I know she certainly saw it.

This is not going according to plan.

Mine, anyway.

ONCE THE DOOR CLOSES, I STOMP DOWN HARD ON HIS SHOE WITH my stiletto-heeled pump.

He grunts as he raises his bruised foot. Now that he's off-guard, I could elbow him in the stomach, which would buy me enough time to snatch the letter opener off his desk and pierce him through his heart.

Nah, too messy. Don't need a gusher of blood to ruin this blouse too.

Or I could slam him up against the wall and twist his nutsack so hard and for so long that he could spend the rest of his life touring as the lead in *Jersey Boys*.

But then I remember that neither of these acts will help me achieve my long-term goals. (Goal Number 1, Carl back in Gitmo; Fallback position, full custody of our kids.)

Through gritted teeth, I hiss, "Despite your untoward manhandling, for the good of the country I'm willing to set our personal issues aside during my stay here in DC. This national emergency deserves our mutual attempts at professional respect, not to mention a modicum of graciousness"—I extend my olive branch: the brownies—"so, here."

I hope you choke on them, asshole.

He eyes the box suspiciously. "What's that, an unpinned grenade?"

I shove it hard, into his gut. "Just—open it!"

He's weighing the odds that he may be right. Since I'm not inching toward the door, I guess he figures I'm not a suicide bomber. Slowly, he pulls the ribbon and opens the lid.

"Hmmm." He nods, but by the way his eyes narrow, I can tell he's still not sure I'm on the up and up. "Let me guess—they're poisoned."

I take one and cram it into my mouth. Through chewy chocolate and dense butterscotch, I mutter, "Convwoinced nowww?"

He shrugs. "How do I know the poisoned ones aren't buried in the middle somewhere?"

Okay, he's got me there. I would have asked him the same question. I gulp down the rest of the brownie. "Go ahead, pick one—any one."

He looks down into the box. Finally, he plucks one out of the center, in the bottom row, and hands it to me.

I cram it into my mouth. "Thewrre!" I'm choking, but I've got a point to prove:

My baking never killed anyone—

By that I mean, no one I hadn't meant to eliminate, and proudly without a trace of evidence.

"Point taken. Just the same, I'll pass. No offense, doll, but… well, some of us are better than others at resisting unwanted calories." As his eyes sweep over my backside, he brushes one of my spewed crumbs off the front of his suit jacket.

How dare he!

"It's all part of the new me," he continues. "I exercise, I eat right—I revel in clean, healthy living."

"Right. Does this mean you're no longer looking to rule the world through terror, blackmail, and mayhem?"

He laughs heartily. "Quit being so melodramatic."

"I beg your pardon?" I lift a hand, so that I can count on my fingers. "You almost blew up a stadium full of children. You tried to shoot down Air Force One. You targeted thirteen international cities for missile launches. You slaughtered a baker's dozen of your Quorum homies, as well as the Federal agents interrogating them—Oh! And let's not forget that you assassinated the spouse of a presidential candidate—"

"Yada, yada, yada. That's so last year." With a whisk of his hand, Carl swats away my contentions as if they were wayward flies attempting three-point landings on the sticky ointment of his fantasy life. "Now that I've gone legit, what say we let bygones be bygones?"

"Ha! If, by that, you mean playing husband and wife, you can forget it."

"Don't be so full of yourself." He snorts raucously. "I'm having too much fun as a single man."

"From what I hear, marriage never dampened your sexual appetites, either."

He shrugs. "You know the game we play for God and country—"

"And libido." I shake my head in mock wonder. "Cut the bullshit. As for joint custody, forget it. I'd prefer you'd stay out of our children's lives, if only for the fact that you're a terrorist—"

"Despite your never-ending attempts to sully my reputation, I was cleared on all counts. It's why I hold down this nifty little government gig, or have you forgotten that?"

"As I remember, the reason you're even in this office is because you're blackmailing the president."

His eyes narrow. "Is that what he's told you?"

"Yes. And, Earth to Carl: I have no reason to question it."

He smirks. "You've always been a lousy judge of character."

"Duh! Our marriage was proof of that," I mutter under my breath.

"Truth be told, Lee begged me to take the position. File it

under the heading, 'Keep your friends close, and your enemies closer.'" A smirk rises on his lips. "My God, Donna, who do you think headed the Quorum in the first place?"

I rummage in my purse for my miniature travel mirror. When I find it, I point it at him.

"Well, you're wrong. Lee Chiffray was the last of the men who underwrote the organization's initial financing. Granted, his vision was more altruistic than the rest of them. He thought that buying off terrorists might be a smarter move than financing them. You know, sort of like paying farmers to not plant surplus crops. But, the fact of the matter is, he had no qualms at all in hiring me to initiate a very final, and very fatal, exit strategy for his twelve partners. To start with a clean slate, as it were."

"I don't believe you."

"No? Don't take my word for it. Catherine Martin will back me up."

"As if I'd believe her! After what she did to Robert—"

"You're still holding a torch for your old crush, aren't you?"

"Don't be silly, Carl. Robert was a childhood friend."

"And I was your husband. Remember?" His eyes sweep over me, as if in search of something—anything still alive from the past we shared.

"Yes, you were—that is, until you left us by pretending to be a corpse. Carl, if you really care about the kids, you'll honor the fact that they already have a father who's totally devoted to them."

Hearing this, his smile wavers. Still, he holds his game face. "Ah, yes, your rebound mistake—the unwavering Mr. Craig. Awesome. Should I find myself in need of a manny, I'll know whom to call." Carl feigns a glance over my shoulder. "Speaking of your guard dog, don't tell me he agreed to letting you come into this lion's den alone!"

"Jack…isn't part of the audit team." I meant to say this as nonchalantly as possible, but I have a feeling he noticed that Jack's name got stuck in my throat.

"I see. Well, that's certainly a step in the right direction." An eyebrow arches in anticipation.

"Don't read too much into it, Carl. It was Jack's decision, not mine."

"Even better! Now I can have you all to myself—"

Seeing the anger flare in my eyes, he quickly adds, "—If only to convince you that I mean you and the children no harm." He leans against the wall, as if the wind has been knocked out of him. "I don't want to torture you anymore, Donna. All I want is your approval to share custody of Mary, Jeff, and Trisha. As we both know, I've already got the court's approval."

I wince at this reality. "And we both know that my children have every right to resent the man who deserted them and their mother. You think that if I've forgiven you, they'll do the same, which is why you want my approval so badly." I cross my arms at my chest. "What makes you think you'll ever get it?"

"Because, deep down in your heart, you know I love them too." His smile disappears. "Look, I know you find this hard to believe, but every event leading up to and since my disappearance was done with the intention of saving you and the kids from danger and…eventual heartache." His hand reaches out to me. He touches my arm, gently stroking it, as if he doesn't believe I'm really here, beside him. "I realize you don't love me anymore. I've accepted that, and I've moved on."

"Good to hear." Seeing the shadow of pain in his eyes, I add gently, "What I meant to say is, we've both made our peace with our personal consequences from your actions. Perhaps it's time we look forward instead of backward."

"My point exactly! It's your choice. Do I force the issue in court, or do we come to some sort of amicable agreement, just the two of us?"

"Carl, I really don't think there's anything else you can say or do to convince me to change my mind about you staying out of our children's lives."

He chucks me under the chin. "That's exactly my point, hon. I'm not the one who has to do the convincing."

He's right. We both know it, unless the Acme audit team finds a hacker's trail that leads right to this office.

"Damn it, I'm running late to a meeting with the joint chiefs and your most ardent admirer, POTUS. I'll be sure to give him your best." He looks down at his watch. "Tell you what, I'll give you a final chance to convince me—tonight, over dinner in fact, in Georgetown. My assistant, Susan, will give you the address."

Perfect. A nice meal, in public, just two mature exes working out the final details of their children's custody.

And if he still insists on following through and ruining their lives, I'll lace his food with an untraceable poison and blame it on the chef.

I grit my teeth into a smile. "Sure. Say, eight o'clock?"

"Perfect! I'll be sure to ask Lee if his ears were burning this morning, what with all our dishing. Not to worry, though. I'll leave him with the right impression—that your devotion to him knows no bounds."

Once again, Carl is hustling me out the door.

And, once again, he pats my ass.

I turn angrily, only to find the door shut firmly behind me.

Even before I ask for it, Susan writes down an address. In fact, she bears down so hard with her pen that she practically shreds the paper.

When she rips it from the pad and hands it to me, there are tears in her eyes.

I can't get out of there fast enough.

On the way out the door, I text both Arnie and Dominic to meet me in exactly an hour, in Hamlet Park, a short distance from the IC campus. I want to make sure that what I say to them won't be overheard. Here, the walls have ears.

Oh, who am I kidding? No matter where we go, we'll be seen and heard. It's the new reality of life in the good old U.S. of A.

And so, amidst a playground filled with squealing toddlers, barking dogs, and gossiping moms who seem to not have a care in the world, we'll have a chance to figure out our next move.

"OKAY, SO WHAT HAVE YOU GOT FOR ME?" I SNAP MY FINGERS TO get both Arnie and Dominic's attention.

When I got to Hamlet Park, Dominic was eyeing the toddlers suspiciously. Having just watched one child projectile vomit after a five-minute ride on the swing set, he is spooked by the thought that one of them might run into his arms and do the same all over his new six-thousand-dollar Hardy Amies bespoke suit.

In contrast, Arnie practically glows as he watches the children at play. He misses Emma terribly and eagerly awaits the birth of her child.

I wish I could say she feels the same, but in truth, she needs some time alone, to process all the changes taking place in her life in such a short period of time.

I'm in the opposite frame of mind. I could do with a large dose of Jack.

Arnie sweeps his hand broadly in Dominic's direction. "Age before beauty."

Dominic looks up from what he's doing—entering in the

telephone numbers of those women he feels would be, as he puts it, "receptive to a more thorough interrogation on my next visit to DC"—and scowls. "Why, I can't be more than a month or two older than you!"

Hearing this, the root beer that Arnie is guzzling spews up through his nose.

In my sweetest voice, I murmur, "I'm sure all Arnie meant by that is that he doesn't mind at all if you go first."

Grudgingly, Dominic nods. "As Arnie will soon detail for you, the vulnerability affected two relatively new programs that are part of the RTTI, or Rapid Technology Transition Initiative."

"What do they do, exactly?" I ask.

"One of the programs provides continuous diagnostic and mitigation capabilities, protecting the IC's IT network from all the cyber threats it receives daily," Arnie explains. "The other program controls the LNI—the Library of National Intelligence. It's a virtual card catalogue offering access to at least 10 million analytic products. For example, the FBI's Biometric QuickCapture Platform program is on it."

"What form did the vulnerability take?"

Arnie frowns. "In this case, it was malware that released a virus. Happens quite often, in fact. Over the past six years, the number of incidents reported by federal agencies has increased by nearly seven hundred percent. In fact, if the Mad Hacker's calling cards hadn't been found, the virus would have never been revealed. Interestingly enough, the virus had been planted at least a month prior to the Hacker's clues revealing themselves."

"That's odd," I murmur. "Why re-enter, just to leave footprints when you're already well clear of the crime scene?"

Arnie nods. "My point exactly. As for this specific incident, whereas many of the files were accessed, only one file in the LNI was completely erased."

"Which one?" I ask.

Arnie's brows furrow into two fuzzy caterpillars. "Something called Operation Clark Kent."

"You mean, as in Superman?"

He nods.

I shake my head, confused. "It doesn't make sense. Why take a file when you're already hiding in plain sight?"

Arnie shrugs. "Excellent question. Once we track down the malware's port of entry, the answer to that may be revealed."

I shake my head. "We're talking about what is supposedly the most secure IT network in the whole world. Isn't it logical to think it was an inside job?"

"It's a strong possibility, yes. But considering that both it and the LNI are part of the IIO—that is, an interagency intelligence operations technology—and can be accessed by contracted analysts in addition to any one of one-hundred-thousand IC employees, it could have come from any access point," Dominic declares. "Today alone, each of my fifteen team members is spending the day on the ODNI campus, interviewing twelve people a day—predominantly IC analysts who monitor RTTI. At the same time, Arnie and his team are running security diagnostics on their computers." He sighs. "In other words, we could spend the rest of our lives interviewing personnel with access."

But we know where it came from: Carl. We've just got to prove it.

It's times like these that I miss Jack. But he's not here. So, instead, I have to ask myself: *What would Jack do?*

He would rally the troops by instilling a sense of urgency.

He'd let them know that he never doubts their abilities to finish the job—

Before it's too late.

I turn to Arnie and Dominic. "Tomorrow, start with the DI's office and work your way out from there. I want you to handle it personally."

Arnie turns white. "You mean interview Darth Vader himself?"

"Yes. In fact, treat it as a hostile interrogation. Run every diagnostic you can think of on Carl's computer, smart phone, and any other device he owns. Run a proctoscope up his ass, if you have to." The thought of watching them do so makes me smile. "In fact, I'd like to join you, if you don't mind."

"Sure, no problem." Arnie is practically relieved. "Thanks, boss lady."

I blush. "That's not necessary. I'm just plain old Donna."

Of course, if it turns out that Carl had nothing to do with it, my name is mud.

It's a chance I'm willing to take.

I have no other choice.

6

User-Friendly

The term "user-friendly" describes either a hardware device, or software interface, that is easy to use, learn, and understand. Most aren't overly complex, have well-organized interfaces, and provide quick access to their features and commands.

Wouldn't it be nice if the man in your life were as user-friendly as your computer? Is it too much to ask that he stay organized, obey your commands, and understand your every need?

How wonderful would it be if, when he screws up, you could reboot him!

Or, better yet, replace him while he's still under warranty—

Say, a decade later.

Ha! As if.

GRANTED, THE ADDRESS SUSAN WROTE DOWN IS IN GEORGETOWN—

But it isn't a restaurant at all. It's a three-story Federal-era mansion on one of the neighborhood's most elegant streets, just a couple of blocks off the M Street-Wisconsin retail hub.

Is this a private residence?

Damn it! He invited me to his home—*where we'll be alone.*

I stand outside for so long that, inevitably, his security camera zooms in on me. Realizing this, I scurry down the massive marble steps—

Only to freeze as I hear Carl's voice. "Great, you found my humble little hovel! Come on in!"

Slowly, I turn around. He's changed into khakis, but he's still got on the white button-down shirt he wore in his office. However, the sleeves are rolled up.

He looks relaxed. And normal.

Just like the Carl who left me.

I point toward M Street. "I…I thought we were meeting at a restaurant."

His chuckle is deep. "I figured I should convince you that I'm still parenting material. That being said, I've made dinner for us, here."

Still, I hesitate. If I go in there, no telling if I'll be drugged and sold into slavery—or worse yet, murdered.

It must be easy to read the concern on my face, because he adds, "Trust me, I don't plan on poisoning you. Granted, I'm not the consummate cook you are, but I have been taking private lessons, from the chef at 1789." He ducks his head, as if he's embarrassed.

Carl cooked dinner, for me?

Okay, this I've got to see.

Slowly, I make my way up the steps. "'*Entrez vous,* mam'selle," he says, as he steps aside, sweeping his arm into a bow.

Hovel? The damn thing is the West Wing in miniature! The green-and-white marble checkerboard floor is in a foyer that is two stories tall, and the size of my living room. It boasts a circular staircase. On both sides of the door are Empire settees, upholstered in yellow-and-white stripe brocade. Beneath the staircase is a large room, with French doors that lead out onto a private terrace.

"Nice pad," I murmur.

He shrugs. "Got it at auction. Ill-gotten goods of some high-flying perp. One of the perks of my gig."

Oh, yeah? Well, when you're whisked to the clink, someone will be saying the same about you.

"After dinner, I'll take you on the grand tour. But, if you don't mind following me into the kitchen, I'd like to pull dessert from the oven—a chocolate soufflé. You know how delicate they can be."

"Of course." I try hard not to stare as I walk with him through the room on the right—a large, formal dining room. Its walls are painted a deep burgundy, whereas the Dentil moulding around the ceiling is painted a stiff glossy white. All of the room's furnishings are antiques. The eighteen chairs surrounding the table have shield backs. Their seats are upholstered in thick brocade. The oval mahogany dining table has a broad rosewood crossbraiding within an ebony and boxwood line inlay.

The table is already set, for two: one end chair, and the chair next to it. Cozy. In front of them are five-piece place settings of Wedgewood's Renaissance Gold pattern, as well as Waterford cut crystal wine glasses, and the Wallace silver pattern, Grand Baroque.

Ah, so he remembered.

During our engagement, I coveted these styles. He knew it because whenever we passed one of Los Angeles' fine china shops, I'd sigh longingly. I'd inherited my mother's china and silver, so we skipped the expense of buying them. In time, I've grown to love what she left me. How could I not? Each piece holds a bit of her soul.

Carl pretends not to notice the impact the table setting has on me. Instead, he goes through the double doors at the end of the room, into a spacious gourmet eat-in kitchen. It boasts an eight-burner Viking range and three built-in convection ovens, all surrounded by an orgasmic amount of cabinet space and marble countertops.

"I promise you, the rest of the meal is healthier. I want you to know I'll take the care and feeding of our children seriously," Carl explains, as he ties a full-length apron around his waist. He then grabs a mitt for each hand, in order to lift the soufflé from one of the built-in ovens. "With that in mind, I hope you'll enjoy the feast I've prepared for you: poached salmon, Yukon Gold potatoes, and braised Brussels sprouts—just like you'd prepare for the kids."

Ouch. My kids are the pizza and burger types. I can't imagine what their reaction will be to some stranger forcing them to eat Brussels sprouts.

Before I know it, he spears one of the sprouts from the small round Le Creuset casserole dish with a fork, and holds it up to my mouth.

I remember his fear over my butterscotch brownies, but I shake it off. It helps that I've slipped a knife off the counter and behind my back. If I feel myself getting woozy, I'll stab first and ask questions later—

Yum! Wow! Talk about an explosion of flavors!

"Ah! So, you like it?" The cloud of worry in Carl's eyes dissipates in the warmth of my pleased smile. As hungry as I am, he's lucky I don't grab the pan out of his hand and gobble up all of these tasty morsels.

I guess he's testing my resistance, because he hands me the pan, then picks up a large covered tray. "Great, we're all set. Follow me."

Back into the dining room we go.

But if he thinks the way back into my heart is through my stomach, he'll be sorely disappointed. Of course, I'll wait until after a second helping of his chocolate soufflé to break the news to him.

~

So far, so good.

By that, I mean I haven't been shot, stabbed, bludgeoned, or poisoned by my ex.

Truly, I'm surprised by this turn of events. By now, he should be fuming angrily. All of his points for why we should share joint custody have been countered with my own calm, common sense rationale as to why it just won't work out.

For example:

Carl: "You know, I can take the kids off your hands during the summer, so that you can take a breather."

Me: "How sweet of you to offer! But I don't think the children will take too kindly to me leaving them for three months with a known terrorist, former or otherwise. Both Mary and Jeff have done sleep-away camps, but nothing as extreme as the militant jihadist ones you and your Quorum homies fund. By the way, what kind of badges do your campers earn for suicide missions?"

Or this, halfway through the meal:

Carl: "So, what do you think of Mary's high school? It's public, isn't it? Even in a community like Hilldale, it can't compete with the curriculum and staff—not to mention the connections—of Sidwell Friends School, which of course she'd attend if she and Jeff and Trisha were here with me in DC. And just think how much further you could climb up the career ladder if you were full-time in your job. Of course, you'd have them every other weekend, and for summers."

Me: "Just so you know, professional honeypot isn't a 'career path.' The work is dangerous, the hours are lousy, and you associate with lowlifes. But, thanks for always thinking of us! Oh no, wait—you're *never* thinking about us. Otherwise *you would have never left us in the first place.*"

And, finally, noting that my wine glass is empty—yet again—Carl pours what's left of the three-hundred-dollar bottle of 1991 Dominus Bordeaux into it and muses, "At first, the thought of sharing my children with Jack bugged me. You know, I was worried about how I'd measure up. But now that I've accepted it, I look forward to the challenge of making up for lost time, and showing them what it's like to have a real man around the house."

Trying hard not to rise to the bait, let alone toss my cookies all over this sparkling white tablecloth (note to self: must get his laundry service to give me her secret as to how she gets real linen so snowy white and so wrinkle-free), I respond, "A real man? Ha! Carl Stone, here's a newsflash: real men don't desert their families."

Game, set, and match to me.

I can tell by the way Carl stabs his chocolate soufflé with his spoon.

I presume he's wishing it were my heart he was piercing instead.

Well, too bad.

We finish our soufflés in silence. Finally, he pats his mouth with his napkin and rises. "Perhaps we should call it an evening. I've had a long day. I'm sure you have too."

"So, you agree with me, to leave the children alone?"

"Not at all." His tone is ominous. "The judge has ruled. There's nothing more you can do about it."

He's claiming the joint custody. Period.

My children will learn that we've been living a lie.

They'll learn who their father really is—that he isn't Jack, and never was.

They'll be hurt. Crushed. Angry. At me of course.

"Unless you want to strike a bargain of some sort." Carl bares his teeth into a smile.

"A…bargain?"

"Yes." He leans in. "All you have to do is spend the night here, with me."

"Never." I toss my napkin on the table and stand up.

"Donna, you once loved me. You lived to make love to me. You can't tell me now that you've forgotten how we were… back then, before…before I made the biggest mistake of my life."

He searches my face for something that validates his beliefs. But, no, he doesn't find it. "Okay, I get it," he mutters. "You don't want me anywhere near them, or you. But one way or another, you're going to pay for that dubious honor. If you want me out of their lives, you have to give me just one night."

The look in his eyes is one I remember from so long ago. Love. Longing. Lust.

It's the same look he had whenever he came home to me.

Home, from those trips in which he killed and double-crossed, and sold state secrets to save his own skin.

To save us.

Or so he said.

He broke my heart once. For what we once had, I won't hurt him the same way. All the more reason I have to tell him the truth:

"Carl, even if I said yes, I'll never love you again."

The hope in his eyes dissolves into the cold reality. He laughs. "Donna my sweet, I'm not doing it in the hope of changing your mind. I just don't want the evening to be a complete waste of time for either of us."

The icy realization washes over me: *Carl will hold it over me, forever.*

He'll tell Jack. Or I'd have to tell him.

Jack would be devastated. I'd die of shame.

Either way, I lose: my children's respect, and Jack's love.

I loathe the knowledge that, to make Carl back down, I'll have either have to let him inside me—inside my body—

Or kill him.

Not such a bad idea.

I slip the knife I used on my salmon up the sleeve of my blouse. Slowly, I stand up. As if in a trance, I walk through the door to the foyer.

SLOWLY, I CLIMB THE GRAND STAIRCASE, EACH STEP LEADEN WITH the dread of what awaits me, should I miss my mark. I don't have to look back at him to know he smiles triumphantly. I feel his eyes scrutinizing me, hungering for me. I can't stand the thought of his hands on me. Or his mouth.

By the time I reach the top of the stairs, Carl is right beside me. He leans in close in order to whisper into my ear, "The master bedroom is through the double doors at the end of the hall."

Instinctively, my head turns in that direction. The doors are dark stained oak, ornately carved, with large brass knobs. One knob has a keyhole, which holds a skeleton key.

My torture chamber.

Where he will hurt and humiliate me.

Or do his best to pleasure me, to make me desire him.

If I don't stop him, once and for all.

I start down the long, softly lit corridor. I hold my head high, but I feel my lip trembling.

I reach the doors. I turn the key in the lock. The hinges creak as I slowly open the door—

And I'm staring at Jack.

What the hell…

He stands on the far side of the room, in a small alcove holding a large ornate desk. He holds a laptop in his hands. A thumb drive is blinking in one of its USB ports.

He glances up. When he sees me, he does a double-take. He holds up a hand with three fingers.

Aw, heck. He wants me to stall for three more minutes.

Quickly, I flip around, closing the door behind me. Turning my face up to Carl's head, I seek out his eyes so that he can read in mine what I want from him—

A kiss.

He is so surprised that he freezes.

Not me. I lean into him. My lips part as I curl my arm around his neck, drawing his face closer to mine.

At first, my kiss grazes his lips shyly—

Before parting them with my own.

His mouth is hungry, filled with desire.

Mine responds in kind, as if I've missed him. As if I've always loved him.

As if he never left me.

We stay in this state of suspended reality for an eternity—

Until Carl reaches around me and pushes open the door.

Quickly, I turn around. No one is in sight. Jack is nowhere to be seen, thank God.

Carl shoves me into the room. Before I know it, he's thrown me down onto the bed and is straddling me; his mouth bruises mine with insatiable kisses. I slip the knife beneath the pillow at my head while he rips the buttons off the front of my silk blouse.

Damn it, I should buy a dozen of these things and just be done with it.

With lightning speed, he unbuckles his belt. With one quick motion, he strips it through the loops of his pants and stares at it for a second before dropping it on the bed, beside me. "Later," he promises me. "What's pleasure without a little pain? But don't worry. Afterward, I'll kiss it and make it better."

Two minutes and twenty-four seconds left, and counting…until I kill you.

Ever the tease, he pulls his shirt out from his pants.

I reach up and tear off his buttons, exposing rock-solid abs and bulging pecs under broad shoulders.

He roars with laughter. Then again, his buttons weren't expensive seed pearls. And besides, he's got someone to chase them down and sew them back on.

He wags a finger at me. "Eager, are we?"

You betcha. There's now less than a minute before I will stab you and be rid of you, once and for all.

As he yanks my skirt up to my waist, I slip my hand back under the pillow. It grasps the handle of the knife, blade down. *Thirty-three seconds left…thirty-two…thirty-one…*

Carl takes time to admire the view of my pink lace cheekini. After giving a low whistle, he hooks the right side with his index finger. Slowly he pulls it down—

Twenty…nineteen…eighteen…Isn't Jack finished yet??

Out of the corner of my eye, I see him, inching his way to the door—

Until a floorboard under his foot creaks softly.

Carl freezes, but before he turns his head, I stroke his taut abdomen with a nail on my free hand, raising it slowly, toward his left nipple. When I reach it, I tweak it between my thumb and forefinger.

Yes, this has his full attention. He leans down. His mouth hungers for my breast—

Exposing his neck to me.

Perfect.

In one quick motion, I swing my arm out from beyond the pillow and up, deep into his jugular—

My hand is just a mere inch from his jugular when I feel someone grab my wrist—

Jack.

Before I can wrest it away from him, his raises his other hand, and with one swift motion, he jabs Carl's thick, muscled back, close to the base of his spine—

With a knife?

No, it's a needle.

The result is almost instantaneous: Carl grunts. His eyes cross—

And he passes out, flopping down on top of me so hard that he knocks the breath out of me.

As I struggle beneath him, I hiss to Jack, "Why didn't you let me kill him?"

"Because I'm tired of breaking you out of prisons. And, besides, if you're right, the files on his laptop will put him away for life."

"'If I'm right?' About what? Seriously, Jack, I don't know what you're talking about."

"Oh no?" He whips out his cell phone and presses his email app. "I got this email from you last night, begging me to forgive you, and asking me to come to DC as soon as possible to help you prove he's the source. So, I lined up Aunt Phyllis to stay with the kids, and—"

"Did you say…to forgive *me*?" I try to shove Carl off, but it's no use. He's too heavy. I'm feeling claustrophobic. Not to mention pissed.

"That's not all. When I got to the hotel this afternoon, I received a text from you, telling me that Carl had invited you out to dinner, and that I should break into this mausoleum and run a diagnostic on his personal laptop. You even sent me the code to disarm his home security alarm and webcam feed."

"I swear to you, Jack, I didn't send anything to you!" *Who keeps hacking my email and texts?*

"Yes, it's now obvious to me, because, A, the thought that he'd have a second computer wouldn't have occurred to you. And, B, you would not have appreciated me walking in on you, with Sleeping Beauty"—Jack lifts Carl's head up by his hair, only to let it drop again, onto my chest—"here in his bedroom."

"He…I…we…" The truth sticks in my throat, like a lump of shame.

Just then, the thumb drive flashes green. Jack removes it from Carl's computer.

Instead of shoving Carl off me, he heads for the door.

"Whoa, whoa…wait a minute! You're not just going to leave me here—like this!…Are you?"

He stops short and turns around. He raises a brow. "Say it."

Carl must be having a bad dream because his hand goes around my waist, holding me tight.

"What the hell are you talking about?" My voice cracks with panic. The last thing I need is for Carl to wake up and find me under him, holding a knife no less. I'll never leave this Munster Mansion alive.

Jack crosses his arms at his chest. "You know what to say."

Ah, I get it. "Yes, Jack Craig, you were right! About Carl pulling a stunt like this, and about me falling for it. There, is that better?"

He shrugs. "It still doesn't explain why you were walking into his bedroom with him."

"If you must know, he gave me an ultimatum. He said he'd

leave me and the children alone, for good if I…if I spent tonight with him." Because I can't move my head, I'm choking on my tears. "Just…one night."

Instead, I would have killed him—if it hadn't been for Jack stopping me.

Jack flops down beside me on the bed. He stares down at the knife, then takes the knife out of my hand.

Best of all, he shoves Carl off me. "The old boy's put on weight," he says with a grunt.

A second later, Jack pulls me up, off the bed—

And into his arms.

He's kissing me, as if he never wants to let me go.

No, it's more like he never *should have* let me go.

He's right about that.

To play it safe, he goes to the window, opens it and tosses the knife into the large privet hedge below.

"That knife is an antique. He's going to have a hell of a time finding a replacement."

Jack holds up the thumb drive. "If the hacker who brought me here is right, Carl will be eating with plastic utensils for the rest of his life."

A frigid breeze wafts in through the window. I shiver. "Aren't you going to close it?"

Jack thinks about it for a moment, then shakes his head. "Nah. If we're lucky, Carl will get pneumonia, and all our problems are solved."

I nod. "Good point. Natural causes."

Not as dramatic as a knife to the jugular, but it'll do.

7

Cold Boot

Starting a computer that has been turned off simply by pushing the "power" button is called a "cold boot," as opposed to a "warm boot," which is to restart your computer after it's already been on for a while.

There are other ways in which one might experience a cold boot. Literally, by standing in a foot of snow for two hours. Or, metaphorically speaking, should you offend an associate, you experience a cold boot as he shoves you out the door—a gesture that means you are no longer welcome.

Cold-booting a computer gets you what you need: access to information.

Standing too long in the snow will result in sneezing, frostbitten toes, and the need for a nice warm bath.

Receiving the cold boot from a new frenemy is a call to arms, so don't be afraid to push back—

But before you slam the door behind you, toss a grenade.

"Nothing," Arnie hisses as he passes Dominic and me in the DI's reception room.

That is to say, there is nothing on Carl's office computer to tie him to the security vulnerability.

Not good.

Hearing his news, Dominic and I wince in unison. While all the other audits and interviews have taken place concurrently with the IC employees and their computers, Arnie's audit was a solo operation, because Carl's never-ending series of meetings has left Dominic and me cooling our heels in the reception area. I'd hoped that Arnie's analysis would provide us with some very pointed questions for Carl. Now, we'll have to stick to the prepared script.

Jack woke Arnie in the middle of the night so that he could begin the assessment of the diagnostic download from Carl's home laptop. We were hoping we'd have our evidence by now, but, unfortunately, the process is still running its course, which means our interview with Carl is really a torture session—

Mine.

Susan, who has ignored us completely the whole time, pronounces loudly, "The director is back in his office. He will see you now."

Arnie points to Susan's computer and says, "You're next up to bat."

She shrugs. Batting her eyes, she purrs, "Great, I'll get to take a potty break."

"You can go for your lunch break too. It'll take at least an hour."

She sighs. When she opens her bottom desk drawer for her purse, Arnie is given the money shot of her deep cleavage—the result of a Victoria's Secret Bombshell Limited Add-Two-Sizes push-up bra.

When Arnie's mouth falls open, I'm only glad Emma isn't

here. Now that she's so close to her due date, the last thing she needs is to see him going gaga over some other woman's breasts, especially when they're cantilevered above a twenty-one inch waist.

I kick him hard in the shin, and he yelps.

I start toward Carl's office, only to find that I'm walking alone. Apparently, Dominic is lost in some sick fantasy, starring Susan and her bullet bra.

Great. I'm stuck with two guys in heat.

Make that three, with Carl.

He better be on his best behavior—for his sake, not mine.

"DIRECTOR STONE, HAVE YOU EVER COMMITTED, OR BEEN INVOLVED in, acts of terrorism?" Dominic's tone is not shy, I'm proud to say. The question leaves no wiggle room.

Carl lets loose with a loud sneeze.

I resist the tendency to say *gesundheit*.

More to the point, I resist the urge to shout, *Go to Hell.*

After blowing his nose into the pocket square from his suit jacket, Carl mutters, "Only in the line of duty," and clears his throat—something I've long come to recognize as his poker tell.

He looks tired. It's one of the symptoms of the sedative Jack gave him. He also looks angry—one of the symptoms of being bested by someone he thought was going to be an easy conquest.

But, somehow, I got away, and it irks him to no end that he can't figure out how.

"Bad cold, old chap!" Dominic clicks his tongue.

"Apparently, I slept with the window open all night." He cocks his head at me. "You ran off last night without saying goodbye, my dear. Tell me, was it as good for you as it was for me?"

Dominic's eyes slide from Carl, to me. Noting my scowl, he purses his lips and raises his clipboard, but not quickly enough to cover his smirk.

Carl nudges him, as if they're sharing some dirty little secret. "Your boss here doesn't mind burning the midnight oil. She gave me her own little—well, let's just call it an interrogation." He stands up. "In fact, I think she covered all the bases. Isn't that so, honey?"

Glowering at Carl, I growl, "Keep going, Dominic."

"She says that to all the guys," Carl assures him.

Before I have a chance to retort, Dominic breaks in, "Let me assure you, Director, these questions are standard procedure for this audit. Your staff has answered them too."

"Yes, well, none of my staff had to do so in front of an ex-spouse, or listen to her ridicule."

"Why don't you tell us what's really bothering you, Carl?" I murmur under my breath."

Dominic's eyes open wide. He shakes his head slightly, as if warning me, *watch your step*, then continues, "So, the answer is yes, to the question, 'have you committed acts of terrorism?'"

Carl raises a brow. "I've been accused of doing so, yes." He stares right at me.

Make that, through me.

"The truth is that I've gone deep cover in a known terrorist organization," he continues, "and I've paid dearly for doing so —personally, that is."

He's right, but it's too late. Carl's chilling smile sends a shiver down my back. "But, in fact, by this time next week, all my hard work will finally be rewarded! I'll be reunited with my children—an event I've been looking forward to for seven very long years."

Aw, hell, here we go again.

I shake my head adamantly. "It will never happen."

Carl leans in. "Oh? What makes you say that?" If I could, I'd wipe the smirk off his face—with a sledgehammer.

"Because you're the reason for the security vulnerability in the first place. You won't get anywhere near them because you'll be put in jail."

"Are you willing to make a little wager on that—say, partial custody of Mary, Jeff and Trisha?"

The thought stops me cold.

But, is anything really at stake here? There must be some reason why the hacker led us to Carl's personal laptop.

"Be careful, Carl. There's a witness present. You won't be able to renege on it, as you have so many times in the past."

He shrugs. "All the better, because if you're wrong, you'll have to hold to your word too."

Dominic's eyes have shifted back and forth between us, as if he's watching a tennis match. "Donna, old girl, remember," he murmurs to me, "Arnie's analysis isn't complete. Are you sure you want to do this?"

Carl has given me a chance to keep him away from my children, once and for all.

Go for it.

"Let's shake on it." I stand up, and so does Carl. I put out my hand.

He takes it. His shake is firm. No funny business.

Only when he tries to stifle another sneeze by reaching for his kerchief does he break his grip on me. "Damn it," he exclaims, as he presses his phone intercom button. "Susan, I need a box of tissues—*now*."

"She left for lunch. Most people take one, you know." I find myself feeling sorry for her. I can't imagine what it's like to work for Carl.

The two raps on Carl's office door are loud, and followed by two more. Even before Carl has an opportunity to respond, Arnie ducks his head through the door. "Pardon me! Mrs. Stone, we've found the computer that was the malware's point of entry."

Finally! The diagnostic on Carl's computer is completed. I smile triumphantly. "The one belonging to the director, I presume?"

"Um…" Arnie purses his lips. "Well, no, not exactly. It was Susan's."

Carl frowns. "Well, I'll be damned! She let someone use her computer? If so, it's a breach of protocol!"

I turn to Carl. "Admit it—you accessed her computer without her knowledge!"

"Good try, sweetheart," he smirks. "But you forget one very important detail. Each of the IC computers is activated by both hand and eye scans."

Arnie winces. "Susan isn't at lunch. She pulled an Elvis— that is to say, she's already left the building. I tried texting her, but it turns out she left her cell phone on her desk. The security footage shows her driving off the lot."

"We'll soon find her, and she'll verify that she was only following your orders," I insist.

Despite this being a far-from-perfect scenario for Carl, he bursts out laughing. "I look forward to your full report, Arnie. I'm sure POTUS will too." He turns to me. "And, Donna, I'll see you and the kids this time next week."

I'm too numb to respond. I'm determined to wait until I'm back in my hotel room before having my breakdown.

I must keep my mind off of my personal trauma. I turn my focus to the matter at hand: desperately seeking Susan.

∾

ARNIE WAITS UNTIL CARL HAS SHUT HIS DOOR, THEN MURMURS, "The Mad Hacker left another clue—a file that was to open only if this computer was analyzed for malware."

He clicks open a file on Susan's hard drive. Letters fly around, forming words that say: *It's a poor sort of memory that only works backwards.*

"Ah! That was the White Queen," Dominic answers, matter-of-factly.

"You're right." I've finally found a good use for him, other than that of an extra man at a dinner party—partner in a game of Lewis Carroll Trivial Pursuit.

Impressed, Arnie releases a low whistle, then takes a screenshot of it with his iPad, which he immediately forwards to Emma for cryptanalysis.

Dominic bows at the acknowledgement, then, on his computer, he flips through Susan's employment file. "It says here that she lives by herself." He pulls up the image of a tidily kept quadplex row house, over in the Adams-Morgan area of town.

"There's an NSA special response team waiting for her there, but something tells me she's long gone," Arnie counters. "I hacked into the street security cams in and around the Liberty Crossing campus." He positions his iPad so that we can see his download—an aerial view of the surrounding area. "When she left, she turned left, in the opposite direction on Lewinsville Road. She then went south, to get on the Dulles Access Road, going west."

"Does this download follow her car all the way? Did she end up at the airport?" I ask.

"Yes. There are two multistory garages, as well as a short-term outdoor lot, and several outdoor economy lots too. By its license plate, I found the car on Level Three of this garage." He switches to another download, which shows the same car, coming into the garage closest to the international terminal. He switches to a security feed within the garage. We watch as she opens the driver door, then goes to the trunk and pulls out a small carry-on bag.

"Unfortunately, here's where we lose her. You see, there isn't a security camera in the bridge between the garage and the terminal. And when I scan the security cams closest to the bridge entrance, she's nowhere to be found."

A thought comes to me. "She didn't disappear. She changed in a stairwell off the bridge. And she has another ID, so in essence, Susan—or whatever her real name is—has escaped." I point to the feed. "Can you pull up timed footage from every egress and ingress to the garage, from the time she entered it?"

Arnie nods. "The garage has four levels, all accessed by a stairwell and an elevator. Depending on whether you want to go to Departures and Ticketing or Arrivals, you'll either get off at Level Two or Level Three, respectively."

The flow to and from the elevators from the garage is constant, what with families, groups of adults, and those walking alone and as couples.

None of the women look like Susan. Many that are her height, build and age wear hats or sunglasses, or are accompanied by others.

After staring at the feed for fifteen minutes, Dominic sighs. "She's a smart cookie. She could have attached herself to some group, a family or a single guy, or even one of her co-conspirators. It's like looking for a needle in a haystack."

I've been staring at the screen for so long that I have to rub my eyes. "At least we have a face on the person who released the worm. But we don't know her name, or whether she's the Mad Hacker, or who she's working with, if anyone, or what they're trying to do."

"Isn't it obvious?" Dominic asks. "They're looking to sell state secrets."

"I'm not so sure," Arnie counters. "With all the hacking that goes on these days, intel files are deliberately bugged by our own programmers, so that those who take our files are infected with trackers, not to mention our own little ghastly surprises." He hesitates, then adds, "Frankly, I'm still not convinced the Mad Hacker is the culprit. But if the goal is a covert sale of intel, why leave clues that the break-in occurred in the first place? And why even hint at a Doomsday scenario if he isn't carrying through with one?"

I throw up my hands in frustration. As much as I'd like to believe Carl was the source of the virus, I'm beginning to think the Mad Hacker may just be our man—or woman.

But if the Hacker isn't the culprit, we better prove it, and quickly.

My own Doomsday is less than forty-eight hours away.

While they run off down the hall in opposite directions to gather up their teams, I head toward the elevator. I've got to get on the next flight out.

I've got to confront the past with the children, and prepare them for our future.

SOMEWHERE BETWEEN THE THIRD AND SECOND FLOOR, THE elevator stops cold.

Worse yet, the light goes off.

I'm in complete darkness, except for a fluorescent green glow of elevator buttons.

Has the power gone off throughout the whole building? That would be very odd.

Once again, I push the button to the ground floor. Nothing.

Instead, over the elevator's intercom, a man's voice proclaims playfully, *"My dear, here we must run as fast as we can, just to stay in place. And if you wish to go anywhere, you must run twice as fast as that."*

Well what do you know—it's the Mad Hacker.

"You're quoting the Red Queen." Despite my matter-of-fact tone, my heart is beating quickly. "Who are you, anyway?"

He chuckles. *"Who in the world am I? Ah, that's the great puzzle."*

"Yes, I know, Alice said that," I retort angrily. "I get it, you're one clever dude! And as for the hack job on the IC database, bravo, you've made your point. Everyone from POTUS on down is impressed." I try to keep the trembling out of my voice. "So, get to the point. What do you want, a big payday? You know the U.S. can outbid its enemies if it comes to that, so now it's my turn to quote Alice: *'I think you might do something better with the time than wasting it in asking riddles that have no answers.'"*

The elevator drops many feet, and I bump my head on the ceiling. Before I can recover, it flies back up, and I crash to the floor again.

"If you knew Time as well as I do, you wouldn't talk about wasting IT," Mad Hacker retorts angrily. *"It's HIM."*

He's quoting the Mad Hatter. "Okay, I get it! You're trying to tell me—that it wasn't you. Am I right?"

I hold my breath for another drop—

Nothing.

Maybe I'm on the right track now.

"Look, Mister Hacker—um, would you prefer I call you Mad? Obviously you see me as someone who can negotiate on your behalf. Otherwise, you wouldn't be hacking my phone and email. But if it wasn't you, then who released the virus in the IC database?"

He doesn't say anything for the longest time. I know why. He doesn't want to break the code hackers' oath of silence.

So that he believes I'm here to help him, I quote the unicorn: *"If you'll believe in me, I'll believe in you. Is that a bargain?"*

He sighs. Finally: *"Speak roughly to your little boy and beat him when he sneezes! He only does it to annoy, because he knows it teases!"*

He sneezes?

Of course—Carl.

"Are you telling me the vulnerability is the handiwork of Director Stone?"

"Yes, that's it!" the Mad Hacker exclaims.

"But why would he deliberately hack into a system where he already has full access?"

"Imagination is the only weapon in the war against reality," he says, quoting the Cheshire Cat.

I think for a minute, then I throw out my interpretation to this clue. "So, what you're saying is that he wants it to look as if we've been hacked by a major enemy, am I right?"

"She generally gave herself very good advice (though she very seldom followed it.)"

It's a direct quote from the book, but no arguments here. "If you want him to pay, as I do, it's best that you tell me directly and specifically what you know," I warn him.

"Read the directions and directly you will be directed in the right direction," he responds with a line spoken by the Door Knob in Alice's story.

"At least give me a clue," I beg.

After a moment, he says, *"A large rose-tree stood near the entrance of the garden: the roses growing on it were white, but there were three gardeners at it, busily painting them red. Alice thought this a very curious thing, and she went nearer to watch them."*

A rose tree. White roses. Three gardeners. I'm stumped. Still,

I throw out a guess. "You're trying to tell me that Carl is working with three other co-conspirators. Am I right? And I'm supposed to watch them."

"*I mean what I say.*" He sounds tired and beaten as he quotes the Mock Turtle.

"How much time do we have?"

"Why, you won't have a wink of sleep these three weeks!" He has deviated from quoting the story's pigeon in order to insert me into this Doomsday scenario.

Suddenly, I'm blinded by the harsh glare of the elevator light. I hear the soft whir of the elevator's engine as it starts its descent.

His final parting quote to me is, "*She who saves a single soul, saves the universe.*"

When the doors open, I can't run out of there quickly enough.

8

Breadcrumbs

As in the story "Hansel and Gretel," the term "breadcrumbs" means leaving a trail of information. In software design, breadcrumbs are what tech designers call a user interface element that is designed to make the navigation of software programs easy—and just as importantly, intuitive.

Wouldn't it be great if your significant other followed the breadcrumbs you left for him? For example, the interface of a clean kitchen is a breadcrumb that speaks to the way you'd like him to keep it after he's rummaged through the cabinets and fridge. And when you stick a note on the fridge that says "Don't forget to pick up the kids from school today," it should readily imply that he has to be somewhere, at a specific time, to pick up his progeny.

And when you leave down the toilet seat, it is a clear signal that this is its rightful position after use.

That being said, if he ignores your savory little breadcrumbs because he's on a self-imposed diet of blissful obliviousness, feel free to reboot him—

Where the sun don't shine.

JACK BOOKED US ON THE FIRST FLIGHT TOMORROW OUT OF DULLES to LAX at the crack of dawn. When we get to the airport, somehow he sweet-talks the airline's ticketing agent into upgrading us into an empty first class row.

Dominic is in first class too. However, Arnie was on standby, and is one of the last people who makes it onto the plane. Passing Jack and me, he gives me a thumbs-up on his way into coach.

"I hope he's not upset he's in steerage instead of up here with us," I murmur to Jack.

"Don't worry about him. I think he's just happy to be going home to Emma. I just wish she felt the same way about him."

So, Jack has also noticed her reticence with Arnie. To be expected. Nothing gets by my man.

I flag down the flight attendant to request something to drink. I'm sure she's expecting me to ask for something more morning-appropriate, like coffee or orange juice or on the *la vida loca* side, a mimosa. So when I say, "Scotch, straight," she purses her lips, and leans forward in order to point to the screen on the seat in front of me.

"As soon as we take off and the captain has turned off the 'Fasten Seatbelts' light, just push the menu button for the items you desire, and I'll be back with your refreshments."

I'm in no mood for any happy-pappy pushback. "But since we're up here in first class, and they're free anyway, can't you just remember my order? You know, like the good ol' days?"

She clicks her tongue. "Sadly, those days are long gone. Everything is computerized. But, don't worry, the moment I see it on my screen in the galley, I'll bring it right out. Okay?"

I shrug. Her line would be more believable if I hadn't seen

her slip Dominic two tiny bottles of ten-year-old Laphroaig Scotch Whiskey.

Her eyes shift to Jack as if to say, *my, my, my, I guess you have your hands full with this one.*

He ignores it. Instead, he holds fast to my hand. "If you're worried about the kids, I hope you realize they will love you, no matter what," he assures me.

Even if that turns out to be true, at first they will hate me. We both know it.

Still, I smile and pretend he's right.

As we lift off, he asks, "As ecstatic as I am that the Mad Hacker has fingered Carl, do you really believe him? I mean, considering he's already hacked your devices, couldn't he just be shifting the blame to someone he already knows you despise?"

"Sure, if he's been scrolling through my Sketchbook Express app, he might have noticed my drawings of Carl in various torture devices." I shrug. "But I believe there's some credence to Arnie's theory about the Mad Hacker. He points out that it was a few weeks after the virus hit the database that the IC techs were even aware of one. And, in fact, it was the Mad Hacker who brought it to their attention. At the same time, the only thing that even has the Mad Hacker's fingerprints on it was a file called Operation Clark Kent, which has since been deleted."

Jack stares out at the endless blanket of clouds below us. "Do we know what the file contained?"

"No, but the minute we land, I'll ask Abu to pull something up on it." Now that we're finally airborne, I tap the screen in front of me. An array of the airline's services pop up as fanciful icons.

I scroll through them until I find the one that indicates beverages: a glass. I tap onto it, and the screen changes to a triple grid of various kinds of beverages: water, fruit drinks, coffee, tea, beer, wine, and spirits.

I click the spirits icon. But, instead of a screen divided into a grid showing bottles branded with the familiar logos of vodka, gin, scotch, rye, brandy or whiskey, the screen shows the classic illustration of Lewis Carroll's Alice, holding a tiny vial with a label that says, DRINK ME.

Oh. Shit.

I nudge Jack to get his attention.

He sighs. "There's no way the Mad Hacker could have known we'd be on this flight, let alone that you'd ask for a drink!"

"You sent me the flight confirmation, remember?" I stare at the screen. "We know he's hacked my email and cell texts, so I guess he saw our seat numbers. And, besides, this is a transcontinental flight, so eventually we'd order food." Or, in my case, something to drink.

We need his clue, so I click onto the Alice icon. Immediately, I'm taken to a screen showing a logo for a company called Shazaaaam—a fireball, held between a wizard's hands.

"Interesting. It's an online gaming company. But the fact that it's an international tech behemoth means it can do a lot of damage if, in fact, it's working as one of Carl's co-conspirators," Jack points out.

I tap the logo with a finger, and the current image dissolves into another that shows a court scene, with a king, a queen, and Alice. Beneath, it reads:

The King and Queen of Hearts were seated on their throne when they arrived, with a great crowd assembled about them—all sorts of little birds and beasts, as well as the whole pack of cards: the Knave was standing before them, in chains, with a soldier on each side to guard him; and near the King was the White Rabbit, with a trumpet in one hand, and a scroll of parchment in the other. In the very middle of the court was a table, with a large dish of tarts upon it: they looked so good, that it made Alice quite hungry to look at them — 'I wish they'd get the trial done,' she thought, 'and hand round the refreshments!' But there seemed to be no chance of this, so she began looking at everything about her, to pass away the time.

"What do you think it means?" I wonder out loud.

Jack shrugs. "Your guess is as good as mine. In any event, we should pass along this and all the other missives to Ryan, as well as to Emma and her cryptography team." Jack takes a picture of the screen with his cell phone.

Even an Irish whiskey won't help at this point. I close my eyes in order to force myself to get some sleep, but it's no use. When I do, I envision the White Rabbit looking at his watch, and I realize the clock is ticking against us too.

IT'S APPROACHING NOON WHEN WE TOUCH DOWN AT LAX, leaving us three-and-a-half hours before we have to pick up the kids. We'll spend them at Acme headquarters, going over the Mad Hacker's clues with Emma, while Arnie puts together a postmortem on the virus attack, and Dominic hunts down Susan.

Was she working with the Mad Hacker? If so, maybe she can be coerced into revealing his mission.

I'd left my car with Aunt Phyllis, so that she could carpool the kids to and from school, as opposed to cramming them into her Volkswagen Beetle, so I'll ride back with Jack in his Lamborghini.

Or as Mary likes to call it, "the car I inherit when I can finally drive."

Um…*no.*

When the time comes, I'll break the news that she'll earn her used set of wheels: perhaps my nice, safe mommy-mobile.

Neither of us says much as we hike through the airport garage toward the car. In just the few days he's been in DC, a fine scrim of dust has accumulated on its usually spotless body. I wait until we've stowed our gear and are buckled in before broaching the topic heaviest on my heart. "I think we should both sit down with the children when I explain the situation to them—that is, if you don't mind."

"Of course." He squeezes my hand. "I was hoping you'd ask."

I shrug. "Be careful what you wish for. I'm afraid they'll lash out at you as well as at me. And heaven knows, this assignment wasn't your choice."

He opens his mouth to say something, but changes his mind. Instead, he forces a smile on his lips. "We'll never know why Carl flipped to the Quorum. But all we can do is explain to Mary, Jeff, and Trisha that you did your best with the knowledge you had at the time."

I know he's right. Still, it doesn't make this new reality any easier for me.

The car crawls through the garage until we reach the cashier booth. The sky is clear and the sun is hot and US 1 going north to Marina del Rey is unusually empty—in other words, a beautiful day to push the speed limit in a car aerodynamically designed to go from zero to one hundred in only three seconds.

By the time we cross the bridge over Ballona Creek, the dust is all but gone with the wind.

If only all my troubles disappeared so easily.

~

"LET'S GO OVER EVERYTHING WE KNOW TO DATE," I SAY TO JACK and Ryan; Arnie, Dominic, Emma and Abu have joined me. "Emma, go ahead and hand out our clue list."

"The Mad Hacker's airplane menu clues are still being analyzed," Emma continues, "as are the clues he gave Donna in the elevator."

She hands out copies of a list of the quotes:

WHO CLUES: CARL, SUSAN, SHAZAAAAM, AND ???

It's HIM.

Speak roughly to your little boy and beat him when he sneezes! He only does it to annoy, because he knows it teases. [Elevator]

Imagination is the only weapon in the war against reality. [Elevator]

A large rose-tree stood near the entrance of the garden: the roses growing on it were white, but there were three gardeners at it, busily painting them red. Alice thought this a very curious thing, and she went nearer to watch them. [Elevator]

HOW CLUES:

The King and Queen of Hearts were seated on their throne when they arrived, with a great crowd assembled about them—all sorts of little birds and beasts, as well as the whole pack of cards: the Knave was standing before them, in chains, with a soldier on each side to guard him; and near the King was the White Rabbit, with a trumpet in one hand, and a scroll of parchment in the other. In the very middle of the court was a table, with a large dish of tarts upon it: they looked so good, that it made Alice quite hungry to look at them—'I wish they'd get the trial done,' she thought, 'and hand round the refreshments!' But there seemed to be no chance of this, so she began looking at everything about her, to pass away the time. [Airplane]

WHEN CLUES:

If you knew Time as well as I do, you wouldn't talk about wasting IT. [Elevator]

Why, you won't have a wink of sleep these three weeks. [Elevator]

What a funny watch! It tells the day of the month, and doesn't tell what o'clock it is! [IC vulnerability]

WHAT CLUES:

It is better to be feared than loved. [IC vulnerability]

It's a poor sort of memory that only works backwards. [Susan's Computer]

If everybody minded their own business, the world would go around a great deal faster than it does. [IC vulnerability]

She who saves a single soul, saves the universe. [IC vulnerability]

WHERE CLUES:

????

No clues at all for most important question of all: where does it go down?

After everyone has reviewed the sheet, I say, "The only question with no clues is WHERE, so let's start with the categories that contain clues." On the conference room's white board, I write the word WHO. "If we're to believe the Hacker's contention that Carl is the source, despite his attempts to plead innocent and point the finger solely at Susan, the fact that she ran away strongly indicates that she was a knowing accomplice."

"If Susan is in fact a WHO, she's never had a record prior to now," Dominic offers. "Frustratingly, even her IC employee facial recognition file has disappeared from its database, along with any employee photos. "

"You seem to have gotten a very good look at her," I remind him. "And we also have access to the Dulles Airport security feed of her parking her car and walking through the garage. Put it through our facial recognition software, then run a comparison with anyone, male or female, walking through security."

He nods as he clicks onto the keys of his laptop.

I shift my gaze to Arnie. "Was her computer also the point of entry for the Mad Hacker? If not, it will go a long way in proving your theory—that the Mad Hacker had nothing to do with the release of the virus."

Arnie purses his lips. "Good question! I hadn't thought of that. Right now, I'm running another diagnostic analysis on her computer. Soon we'll have a footprint that will allow us to compare it to the Mad Hacker's messages."

"Even if the footprints differ, and it proves he wasn't the originator of the virus, the fact that he let himself be known is proof he somehow breached the system too," Ryan points out. "That alone is enough for a lifetime pass to Club Fed."

I nod. "But Ryan, he didn't have to expose the earlier vulnerability to us. Doesn't that earn him a brownie point or two?"

Ryan shrugs. "It isn't for us to decide. Our job is to find the culprit—or culprits, as the case may be. To that extent, Emma's team has some answers as to how the Mad Hacker's clues may prove helpful in how we proceed."

Emma nods. "That moves us to the rest of the clues, and the process in which we might solve them. As some of us already know, Carroll was into logic games and word play. Throughout the book, Alice misconstrues many of the answers to her questions because she'll use a figurative expression, only to have the characters take what she says quite literally. For example, when she uses the term, 'beating time with music,' the Mad Hatter responds, 'He won't stand beating. Now, if you only kept on good terms with him, he'd do almost anything you like with the clock.' On the other hand, sometimes they respond with words having dual meanings, or even with puns."

"As way of example, when the Mock Turtle explains, 'we called him Tortoise because he taught us,'" I point out.

"Correct," Emma says. "In any regard, the responses given to Alice are never simple. Nor are they meant to be. In fact, it was Carroll's contention that, if you're quickly and easily provided the answer, all conversation ceases. His goal with his readers, who he presumed to be children, was to provoke thought."

"Which is what the Mad Hacker wants to do with us," Jack reasons. "He won't come out and tell us what is about to happen, but how to discover it for ourselves."

"And to think about the repercussions, if we should fail to do so," I chime in. One remark he made to me in the elevator stands out most vividly in my mind: *Imagination is the only weapon in the war against reality.*

"There are three WHAT clues," Jack points out. "The first one —'It is better to be feared than loved'—obviously refers to some kind of terrorist act. The second one, about business, must in some way refer to Shazaaaam, and possibly the other companies involved. Perhaps all of them have something to do with the Internet, since it mentions the world going a great deal faster."

"It also touches on 'minding one's own business. Could that be an allusion to cyberespionage?" Dominic asks.

Ryan nods. "Unfortunately, your suggestion matches that of Acme's cryptography team. As for the last WHEN clue, the fact that the Hacker dropped it on Donna indicates he sees her as the answer." He points to it on the white board:

She who saves a single soul, saves the universe.

Lucky, lucky me.

"My team and I have analyzed the WHERE phrases chosen

by Mad Hacker," Emma explains. "For example, the trial scene involving the King and Queen of Hearts also references birds and beasts, the White Rabbit, a trumpet, a parchment, a dish of tarts, and a pack of playing cards, which are the court's soldiers." She projects the screen of her iPad onto the wall. "In searching through Shazaaaam's database, we've cross-referenced some of these words. Case in point, the word 'soldiers' may represent the fact that Shazaaaam supplies MMOGs—that is, massively multiplayer online games—to the U.S. Armed Forces as training simulations called AWE."

"Short for 'asymmetrical warfare environments,'" Jack chimes in. "It's one of the ways in which they train soldiers for urban warfare."

"Exactly," Emma agrees. "And on the consumer side, one of its top-secret projects just so happens to be a new game called 'Queen of Hearts.' We're doing what we can to find out exactly what's involved, but Shazaaaam has done a great job of keeping it under wraps, as it's just now moving into beta trials. However, we do know that they're unveiling it at the next comics convention—Comic Con's Wonder-Con, which takes place two weekends from now, in fact, in Anaheim. Our cryptography team thinks this event is represented by the trial, trumpet, parchment, and where the crazy animals come into play."

"They aren't animals," Arnie mutters under his breath. "They're super heroes, super villains, and comic book creatures."

"Not to mention super heroines and super villainesses," Emma mutters pointedly. "We do know, however, that they're still hiring for it. Donna, that's where you come in. We've already placed you as a new hire, assigned specifically on this new project."

"But I'm not a game programmer, let alone a coder or a designer!"

"As it turns out, Shazaaaam is specifically looking for a woman for the role of game tester. And, as rare as it is in this business, the fact that you're over the age of thirty is seen as a plus in this case."

"Otherwise, we could have used Emma on this one—not that they'd hire someone who's pregnant," Arnie interjects.

This earns him yet another scowl from Emma.

I shake my head, confused. "Why is my gender and age an advantage?"

Ryan smiles. "My guess is that they want to tap into one of the biggest consumers of tablet devices—women in that specific age group."

"As if we have time to play games," I mutter under my breath.

"Those of you who do are just as likely to become obsessed with them, if the games *Angry Birds, Farmville, Bejeweled, The Sims,* and *Candy Crush* are any indication. With the discretionary income of this demographic, even one percent of that market would be a gold mine in the gaming industry," Ryan explains.

"Which brings us to WHEN," Emma declares. "From the clues we have, we're under a ticking clock—sometime within the next three weeks."

Ryan nods toward me. "To make things even tighter, the fact that the Mad Hacker put Donna in one of the screenshots, means he sees her as integral to the mission."

Just my luck—especially when my children need me now, more than ever. Of course, if we can tie Carl to the IC vulnerability, we're free of him—hopefully forever.

So, yes, count me in.

"Wonder-Con may be a hand-off of some sort. If so, it's just one piece of the puzzle. However, if we stop whatever is supposed to go down there, it may be disruptive enough to bring down the whole operation and lead us to the perpetrators—all the more reason Donna has to be front and center at it." Ryan turns to me. "Donna, in regard to your employment at Shazaaaam, Jack will be providing back-up. He's assigned to the legal department, which has access to all contracts. And Arnie will infiltrate as well. He'll be employed as a game coder, but, of course, his main function is to provide any needed technical expertise."

Arnie's smile is wide enough to drive a truck through it. "I'm loving this new assignment already!" He glances over at Emma. When he sees the frown on her face, he gets wise and loses the mad clown grin.

What's eating her? Seriously, she needs to lighten up on him.

"This isn't going to be all fun and games," Ryan reminds Arnie sternly. "Once you're on a gaming console, your mission is to hack into Shazaaaam's mainframe computer and search for any files that can incriminate the culprit."

"The Mad Hacker left us one clue as to who it might be," Emma says. "The company's executive vice president in charge of game development is named Roger White, so you can start with any correspondence or files created by or sent to him."

Jack laughs. "Talk about a broad hint. Both clues play off the word, 'rabbit,' what with his last name being White, and the animated character, Roger Rabbit."

"Not only that, under Roger's domain are the creative teams who develop the story's plots and scripts, as well as those involved in animation and design—the two- and three-D artists, audio engineers, and level designers, just to name a few," Abu points out.

I nod approvingly at him. "Wow, great research."

"It's all part of my new gig," Abu answers. He reaches over the conference room table in order to hand me a business card. Besides his name, it shows that he holds the position of "Associate" with one of the biggest tech headhunting firms in the country. "It's got an awesome commission structure," he smiles broadly. "Let me put it this way—with just the placements of you three, in three different gigs, I'll be able to pay off my home in Palos Verdes."

That certainly has my attention. "Wow! …Wait a minute. If you'll be making those kinds of commissions off what we'll be making, we must be doing pretty well too!"

"Heck yeah, doll!" He pulls out a contract. "I was going to give this to you to take home, but if you sign it now, you get a five-thousand-dollar bonus…minus my fifteen percent of course."

I scan the contract until I find the bottom line. When I see it, my eyes open wide. "You mean that, above and beyond the five thou, I'll be making over one-hundred thousand a year?" I pluck Jack's pen out of his hand and sign with a flourish.

"Well, um, yeah…that is, if you stay a full year."

Aye, there's the rub.

"Hey, I'll be lucky if I can fake it for ninety minutes. Speaking of which, do you have any idea how I should prep for this gig?"

Abu frowns. "Beats me. But Emma should know. She a gamer from way back."

I look up. Arnie is still here, but she's left the conference room. Through the glass walls, I see her heading toward the ladies' room.

I run after her, but she makes it through the lavatory door before me.

～

WHEN I ENTER, I SEE WHY SHE WAS IN SUCH A HURRY TO GET AWAY —she's crying.

I put my arm over her shoulder. "Emma, what's wrong?"

She shrugs it off as she gulps down her tears. "I…I'm just tired of being such a bitch."

"It's your hormones," I chuckle, in the hope that she'll laugh it off too. "Trust me; I've been through the same thing, three times."

The cause and effect of my words is that her frown only gets deeper. "Yes, I know you have. But each of your pregnancies was planned—with a man you loved. Or, at least you thought you loved him at the time."

My smile disappears. "The only good things to come out of that relationship were my children. But, had I known then what I know now, would I have stayed with him? No. Everything about Carl is an enigma. I never saw it coming. I had to learn about it, the hard way." I look her in the eye. "Whereas, everything about Arnie is an open book. What you see is what you get. It may not be perfect, but it is kind, and true, and filled with adoration for you." I'm making her cry all the harder, but she needs to hear this from me—from someone. "Emma, I know you hadn't planned on this baby. And I know it wasn't created with someone you wanted to marry. But you have something so precious that many single parents never have— someone at your side, who loves both you and your child."

She nods as she sobs. "I…I know what you're saying. And I adore Arnie too. No—I love him!" Truly I do!" The realization makes her cry all the harder. "It's just that"—she looks down at her belly—"I never felt that this was who I am. *A mom.* I joined Acme for the thrill—the adventure! But with a child…" she stops herself with a sigh.

"Acme can always use an operative like you," I assure her.

"I mean, I always wanted to be in the field."

"I have three children, and it hasn't stopped me."

"I know, but..." She frowns and looks away.

Ah. I get it. Fieldwork isn't for a woman with a family. And being a honey trap is not exactly conducive to "bring your daughter to work" day. As for wet work—well, it's not a great way to teach a kid conflict resolution. Do as I say, not as I do—in other words, don't torture or kill the kid who jumped you in line to the cafeteria.

She winces as my back stiffens. "Donna, please don't think I'm passing judgment on you! No one has a right to do that! Like you said, you did what you had to do. And when you did it, you felt—you knew it was the right thing to do." She takes my hand. "That's just my point. I want to be just like you. Heck, I'd love to sashay into Shazaaaam and blow them away with what I know about gaming. But now—well, I can't now. And with this tiny person"—she stares down at her belly—"I know, in my heart, I'll never have a chance at it."

She's right.

"Consider yourself lucky."

From the pitying look on her face, I presume she does, deep down inside.

I'll admit it, here and now. If it weren't for Carl, I wouldn't be putting myself in danger either.

I wish I could pretend I didn't know who he is and what he's done. I wish I could walk away from it all; that I could live a quiet, peaceful, and normal life with Jack and my children.

But I can't.

Someone has got to stop Carl. As much as he was Acme's mistake, he was mine as well. And had we known what we were dealing with from the start, he wouldn't have been Lee Chiffray's mistake, either.

So, now, Carl is in the best position to end Lee's presidency, and to create a reign of terror and anarchy like the world has never known.

It's up to me to stop him.

Well, me and someone who calls himself the Mad Hacker.

Let's hope this isn't a bad dream.

We're Off to See the Wizard

How exciting! You're loading a new software program into your computer, one containing a handy-dandy "wizard."

Whereas, in other worlds, a wizard is a person of great and mysterious powers, who knows the right spells to resolve any situation, or to vanquish any foe, in the Etherworld, a wizard is a guidance icon—perhaps a cartoon of a medieval wizard, or the Universal Man, or a paper clip with eyes—which has been given the task of walking you through the steps needed to learn the program easily, and in a respectful and nonthreatening manner.

Here are three things you can expect from the Wizard:

1. *Unlike your husband, it won't get tired of answering your questions or repeating the instructions again and again, until they are seared into your brain.*
2. *Unlike your husband, it won't call you "clueless," under its breath, just because you don't understand what it wants you to do.*
3. *And, unlike your husband, it won't let loose with a cry*

that sounds like a wounded animal when you throw the computer against the wall out of frustration.

Perhaps if your husband spoke to you in a respectful manner, you'd be just as nonthreatening to him as well.

"Wow! You and Dad will both be working at Shazaaaam?" Jeff's eyes grow wide in reverence when we break the news to the children at dinner.

"Yep," I answer nonchalantly. "Until we're done with this assignment, Aunt Phyllis will be picking up my carpool duties, and staying here at the house."

All three children wince at my pronouncement. Still, in looking at the bright side, Jeff asks, "Does it come with any bennies—you know, like free games?"

Jack helps himself to the last dollop of mashed potatoes off of Jeff's plate. "It's only for a week or so. We're doing a corporate audit. But, hey, if they say it's okay, we'll certainly score as much free game time for you as they'll allow. Just write down the titles you want, and we'll see what we can do." He looks over at Mary and Trisha. "They have some games that may interest you, too, so feel free to do the same."

Trisha claps her hands. "Do they make the Penny Arcade games?"

"You mean, like Cupcake Shop 4?" He furrows his brow, pretending the question is a brain-tickler. Penny Arcade is a children's television network. As it turns out, Shazaaaam is contracted to make games based on their most popular shows. Jack already reviewed the dossier on the company's products, contracts, and management team, so of course he knows this. Still, he waits until she can no longer hold her breath in anticipation before answering with a resounding, "Yep! I seem to remember that it is one of their games."

Trisha is so excited that she jumps up out of her chair and nearly spills her milk glass. I narrow my eyes at Jack, the instigator of what would have been this accident. If he thinks he can buy me off with a naughty grin—

Well, he's right.

Just one more way in which he gets away with murder.

"How about you?" Jack asks Mary.

She shrugs. "Games are lame, especially those aimed at teen girls. The game companies must presume that all girls like to do is shop, be celebrities, or date them."

"Yeah, well I guess the game designers have seen your shoe closet," Jeff mutters under his breath, "not to mention all the *People* magazines under your bed, and the posters of those guys from *Arrow* and *Teen Wolf* hanging on your wall."

She tosses him a dirty look. "Only immature boys play them. Maybe the game designers follow you around and take notes."

Of course, this only encourages Jeff to double down. "Then I guess Trevor is too immature for you to date, because he's got the highest FPS score for GoreGasm." He wraps his arms around himself and smacks his lips together, as if he's kissing an invisible girl. In a voice an octave higher than usual, he mimics, "*Ooooh*, goodbye Trevor! I'm too good for you!'"

As Mary reaches over to smack him on the head, his milk glass tips over—

But I grab it just in time.

"Okay, alright! No more sudden moves," I warn them. "I don't need my best tablecloth stained over something as silly as a video game." I turn to Jeff. "What's an FPS?"

He frowns. "It means 'first person shooter.' Why do you want to know?"

I blush. "It's a good thing to know, for my new job."

"In fact, GoreGasm is one of Shazaaaam's games," Jack points out. "Super bloody."

"Really? Well, maybe Jeff can teach it to me—after we clear the dishes."

Jack raises a brow in my direction. He knows I'm putting off the inevitable—telling the children about Carl.

He follows me into the kitchen with a stack of plates, but waits until Mary rinses them and Jeff stacks and Trisha has run the soiled cloth napkins into the laundry room before he murmurs into my ear, "The sooner we tell them, the better."

I grab his hand and pull him into the pantry with me so that the children can't hear what I have to say to him. "We've just gotten home. Carl promised he won't be here for seven days. Can't we have this one last week, all happy and together, before I ruin their lives forever?"

I'm in ballerina flats, and he towers over me in heels, so you can imagine how far back I have to tilt my head in order to look up at him. What I see in the deep green recesses of his eyes lets me know that he thinks I'm making a big mistake. I also see tenderness, and concern, and adoration.

I see my future, despite my unforgiving past.

All the more reason I'm so surprised when he says, "Okay, look. It's Thursday. The earliest he'll be here is a week from tomorrow. We'll shelve it for now. But come next Thursday…"

I nod. "Yes, I know. We tell them."

He's given me a reprieve. So why does it feel like a death sentence?

SHAZAAAAM'S FIFTEEN-ACRE CAMPUS IS A VERDANT OASIS IN AN

otherwise dusty valley dry humping the 405 in the southern-most quadrant of Orange County.

To top it off, the offices—dark green glass buildings of varying heights and dimensions that look like Emerald City in *The Wizard of Oz*—are clustered at the base of a tower that thrusts skyward, and is capped with a large glass dome, like a porcini mushroom.

Elevators, located on the outside of the structure, are lined vertically with tiny LED bulbs. As the elevators move up into and down out of the dome, the lights pulsate upward, creating the image of a gigantic throbbing circumcised penis.

The Shazaaaam wizard stands on the tower's hooded tip. His scepter is raised toward the sky, releasing laser beams into the cosmos.

"It's the ultimate phallic symbol," Arnie whispers reverentially.

"Spoken like a true man boy," I mutter. "Next you'll be telling us that your own Little Arnie goes by the name Shazaaaam."

His wide-open mouth shuts quickly, but I get my answer with his blush.

Jack and I exchange glances as we follow him into the phallic tower. Everything in its three-story lobby is meant to entice, enthrall, and enchant. The walls—really, columns covered with bark, leaves, and moss—are staggered in such a way that they look like a forest of trees. The flooring is textured with embedded pebbles, giving one the feeling of walking on a woodland trail.

The receptionist's desk is really a trestle table made of roughhewn lumber cobbled from various woods. It sits on thin metal legs. The only thing on it is a telephone console. Frankly, I'm somewhat surprised that the person behind the desk isn't a Keebler elf, but a young slender woman with a mane of long russet-hued tendrils that hide her tiny headset. She wears a diaphanous top over leggings and booties, leaving the impression that you've just spotted a woodland fairy.

Or, in Arnie's case, a fantasy, come to life. "Oh my God! That's—that's Nymphette!"

I frown. "Who?"

Arnie looks at me as if I've just landed from another planet. "One of the most popular characters in Fantasy Forest is based on her! She's the high priestess of the largest cult in Shazaaaam's Fantasy Forest game. Many of Shazaaaam's employees are players' favorite avatars, since their faces are the first to be animated."

I shrug. "Oh, joy."

"What Arnie means to say is that she wields a lot of clout in Shazaaaam's most profitable MMORPG—massively multi-player role-playing game."

"Great." I yawn. "She also mans the front desk. Maybe she'll be kind enough to get me a cup of coffee."

Arnie's eyes open in horror. "Don't you dare ask her that!"

To assure I don't embarrass him, he practically runs to the reception desk. "Donna Gray, Jack Green, and Arnie White are here. We're new employees."

For this assignment, Jack and I aren't a couple. I go by Donna Gray, and he's Jack Green. That way, if Shazaaaam does an alphabetical roll call, odds are we'll end up beside each other.

Of course, most companies don't do roll calls, let alone alphabetically. Then again, most companies don't have employees whose ages dip below eighteen. With all the game testing that's needed here, Shazaaaam has actually implemented an "internship program" with some of the local high schools. For four hours a day, the gaming tower is teeming with kids. No longer can their mothers warn them, "No one is going to pay you to play with that thing all day long!"

Turns out someone will, and pay handsomely, too.

If only all of life were this simple.

Granted the inclusion of Jack and me has inched up the employee age statistic, but only by a tenth of a percentage point at most.

Nymphette pops her bubble gum in Arnie's face and points toward some chairs that are shaped like toadstools. "Take a seat. I'll ring Human Resources."

Noting I'm about to open my mouth, Arnie quickly adds, "Do you have an employee lounge, so that we can get some coffee?"

She rolls her eyes, sighs, then hands him three tiny white tiles. "Fill these out. A waiter will find you." She points towards a guy in a tux with a rainbow-hued bowtie, who scurries past us. "When you get your company cell phone, it's equipped with an app that allows you to order anything on the Employee Desire Board."

Arnie bows as he walks away, backward, as if in the presence of royalty. Frankly, I think it's a good thing that she doesn't notice because she's tapped her headset to take a call.

Arnie hands each of us a tile. When pressed to the ON position, the tiles open a screen with a menu. To order, recipients can tap the tiny boxes beside each item.

I scroll until I find a box for a double decaf mocha cappuccino.

Oh, and a chocolate croissant to go with it.

Something tells me I'm going to love coming to work.

I HATE THIS GIG.

My take on it: I'm not cool enough for school.

Everyone else on Shazaaaam's payroll is brainier, hipper, and certainly younger.

At least, that's the impression I've been given by Lilith, our New Employee Guide. After making us watch a stupid 3D IMAX video on employee do's and don'ts, she walks us around the Shazaaaam campus, mentally grading us by the number of ooohs and ahhhs we put out as we pass the company's many amenities that are designed to keep its employees blissfully resigned to a nonstop work schedule.

Needless to say, Arnie is in the lead. He practically swoons as we walk past the fleet of round-the-clock food trucks dotting the velvety lawn, which serve up pork belly tacos, or sushi, or even a full menu of gluten-free dishes, all created and prepared by celebrated chefs who once were Food Network somebodies.

I'm afraid he'll wet his pants when he sees the "Fun Huts" interspersed throughout the campus. "Here, employees aspire, or are inspired, or they conspire," Lilith proclaims seriously.

In other words, the huts are hangouts for mid-day breaks for, say, yoga or spin classes. Employees can also hang out in the huts after work to catch *Cirque du Soleil* shows or concerts by pop bands whose astronomical fees are a pittance in comparison to the cost of replacing the skilled engineers who rock out to them.

When we stroll by the Olympic-sized pool and an enclosed gym with an NBA-sized court, I have to catch Arnie before he passes out.

Jack comes in second on our guide's most-favored-newbie list just because he gave her a nod when we passed one of the company's many "decompression chambers"—large darkened coffins fitted with Sleep Number Innovation Series i8 Bed Pillowtop mattresses and pumped with pure oxygen.

If you're to believe the gossip in *Valleywag*, a few privileged employees are allowed to preorder a "sleeping partner" from a stable of women who were hired for their expertise in animating a particular piece of anatomy.

In other words, if the chamber's a rockin', don't come a 'knockin'.

Everything and anything that entices its employees to create the company's next big game is right here, in ShazaaaamLand. And, although eighteen-hour workdays aren't mandatory, they are certainly the norm—the ideal career for those who are smart, young, obsessed with fantasy worlds, and unable to establish deep, ongoing relationships.

"Donna, you're awfully subdued. I know! You're overwhelmed at the world we've created here!" Lilith's compassionate tone is undercut by her icy smile. "But, you know, nothing is too good for those who strive to make the world a better place."

I tamp down the urge to argue, *so why don't you use some of your gazillion dollars in profit to cure cancer, or stave off world hunger?*

When I choke on my smirk, Arnie and Jack fail miserably as they try to elbow me into silence.

When she scans her iPad for my employee file, a finely plucked brow goes up. "Ah, I see," she murmurs. "You're working on *Queen of Hearts*."

Why the disdain? I wonder.

It's only when she takes me to my group that I understand why. Every single one of my cohorts wears this business era's equivalent of a pocket protector:

Google Glass, the wireless eyewear.

In other words, they are the ultimate nerds.

"I know what you're thinking," Emma murmurs into my ear bud. "Don't worry, let's just get through today. Today is Friday, and you'll have the weekend to recover."

I love her for saying it. Even more so, I love her for meaning what she says.

Last night, she came over with a few items that she felt would help me fit right in. After dressing me for the role (today I'm wearing a pair of Rag & Bone park pants topped with a linen raglan long-sleeve tee and platform booties), and French-braiding my hair, and tinting the ends a hot pink, she gave me a hug of approval and whispered, "Now you look like a real gamer goddess!"

She is living vicariously through me.

I have no problem with that, because she's a true asset on this mission.

Spook Rule #1: If you can't fake it, channel someone who can.

A WOMAN NEVER LIKES BEING IGNORED.

Especially from the head up.

I'm beginning to wonder if their Google Glass uses some sort of imaging software to determine the dimensions of my bra cup.

My team is made up of one Caucasian dude with a goatee. "His nickname is Fu Manchu," Emma whispers into my ear, and another who is too tall and too thin. "Ichabod," Emma deadpans. "Hey, don't look at me. It's what the other geeks call him." There is also an Asian-American guy, a chubby dude with a ponytail, and an East Indian guy. "Orphan of Zhao, Wise Ass, and Bollywood in that order," Emma informs me. They are dressed in the shlubwear coveted by the industry: a T-shirt touting some startup, a hoodie or ironic meme sweatshirt, and cargo pants or saggy jeans, with sneakers or flip-flops.

Already, I'm the odd-person-out in this geek clique cliché.

If they had the nerve to ask, I'd go ahead and tell them so that I could get on with the task at hand: spying on our team leader and boss.

Shazaaaam's celebrated creative director, Roger White, is in the middle of a pep talk when I take my seat. He is around my age, maybe a year younger. His hair is bleached platinum and held in a topknot, he wears a V-neck black tee shirt over tight black jeans.

Too tight, in fact. I wonder if there's an app that will validate that he's wearing an inordinately flattering codpiece.

"—got to get on the ball, people! The damn thing still has a serious A-bug!" Roger stares pointedly at Fu Manchu, who cowers in his chair. Noting that his victim is duly chastised, Roger continues, "Have you forgotten that we've only got another forty-eight hours before code release? Wiz expects this to be a triple-A game with an LTV to CAC ratio of five-point-eight! All of us—all of *you*, have to pull your—" Finally, he notices me, "weight."

He gives me the onceover. I don't like the smirk on his face.

Or the fact that his eyes never reach my face, but stay chest-high.

Click goes his Google Glass.

I swear, if I find out it's equipped with an x-ray app, I'll stomp it into the ground—while he's still wearing it.

"Who the hell are you?" Roger demands.

I hold out my hand. "Donna Gray, the tester for *Queen of Hearts*."

He stares down at my hand. Finally, he grasps it cautiously.

Limply. Let me put it this way: if Tinder rated handshakes, he'd never get a right-swipe.

"Is this the rest of my team?" It's a duh statement, but hey, I've got to break the ice somehow.

Roger shrugs, then waves toward the others. "Yeah, right. Meet Groucho, Chico, Harpo, Zeppo, and Gummo."

The others snicker and wave weakly.

"What do I need to know about the game?" I ask.

"*Queen of Hearts* still has a bug or two to work out. We're talking about it now, as a matter of fact. But, as far as you're concerned, all you need to know is that it's a combination of MMORPG and life simulation. It's geared at female players with families, preferably stay-at-home moms with discretionary income."

"Cough—MILFs—cough!" Wise Ass thinks he's being cute.

While the others giggle, Rodney flips him a bird. "The goal is to ensure *Queen of Hearts* is realistic, engaging, and most of all, addictive."

In other words, currently the game is viewed as a money pit for the company. And yet, he shows less interest in it than the yacht sales website on his screen. A lot less interest. A little eye contact would be nice—but no, I'm all but invisible.

"We're under a tight deadline," he continues. "So, if you hit a bug, signal any of these cretins, but keep playing. When you're done with your pest report, offer beta keys on some of the free beta-test loops. Maybe you can tempt a few suckers to give you feedback before Wonder-Con next weekend, Friday through Sunday."

I pray that whatever the Mad Hacker warned us about goes down on Friday, so that it's out of the way before Carl shows up on my doorstep.

And if it goes down the way I hope, he'll be met by a SWAT team.

"Speaking of Wonder-Con," says Zhao, "Since *QofH* has its own booth, I presume our team gets free passes, right?"

Roger shakes his head. "Wrong. After my pass and the

booth babe's, I've got just one pass left. How 'bout you guys strip to your skivvies and death-match it out?"

His suggestion goes over like a wet fart. No doubt, each of them still wakes from nightmares of gym class.

Roger shrugs. "Thought not. Okay, here's the deal. Since this clown"—he points to Fu Manchu—"can't find the A-bug, let alone his dick, I'll make the pass the reward for the programmer who can exterminate it, and I'll let the winner choose the booth babe. How's that?"

They high-five each other, but none of them has the balls to glance over at Fu Manchu, who is steaming over Roger's diss.

I'm steaming too. If I don't get into that booth, Acme loses its eyes and ears during the hand-off.

"Time is money, so get to work." He motions me toward a glassed-in cubicle with a door that actually closes. It holds a glass-top desk and a laptop.

The second I sit down in the chair in front of it, I hear Emma's voice through my ear bud: "Guess what they're doing right now."

"I have no idea," I mutter, as I turn around to look into the group pit.

They are staring back at me. When I wave at them, they snicker and blush.

Emma growls, "They're taking bets on your bra size."

I sigh. "Let me guess, those Glass-holes are using some sort of x-ray app, coded with some sort of size algorithm."

"Nothing like that is on the market yet, but I'm sure one will be available soon. In the meantime, handle it any way you want."

I hear a ping on my cell phone. Emma has sent me a transcript of a group chat:

Roger: Time's up. All bets in, guys.

Ichabod: 32 A?

Fu Manchu: I'm in a generous mood, so 32 C.

Bollywood: Grow a pair! They're at least 36's! I say 36 B.

Wise Ass: UR giving her too much credit. I'll go with 34 B. Maybe a C.

Zhao: I'll double that to 36 D.

Roger: Then that leaves me with 32 B. What can I say? She underwhelms me.

I underwhelm *him?*

I do my best to hold my head high (and to jut my breasts out).

Instead of glaring, I smile pretty and blow him a kiss.

The smirk on his face is replaced by a frown. His eyes narrow as he scrutinizes the newest member of the team that will make his reputation, one way or another.

He doesn't know it yet, but I'm his worst nightmare.

AFTER SIX HOURS OF NONSTOP PLAYING, I'VE COME TO THE conclusion that the game outright sucks.

My avatar is a sweet-looking mommy whom I've named Donna S. Like me, she has medium brown hair, gray eyes, dimples, and loves simple sundresses. Her life is also simple: husband, three children (two girls and a boy sandwiched in the middle) and two dogs—a collie and a German shepherd.

Unlike me, she's got Barbie proportions and doesn't need to

wear a bra or Spanx, because she's perky in all the right places, including her attitude.

When she stays around the house, she tackles the dishes, vacuums, bakes, goes to the grocery store, does the laundry, tends her garden, and cleans out the cupboards.

Sometimes she hops into her mommy-mobile (the one I covet—Emma's Yukon Denali XL hybrid) to carpool, buy groceries, and shop to her little heart's content.

In fact, hearts are more than the name of the game. Like the old television show *Queen for a Day*, accomplishment of household tasks are rewarded with tiny hearts that can be traded in for stuff like high-tech appliances, make-up, or dresses, shoes or other accessories—all the latest-and-greatest, all top-of-the-line name brands—or girls-nights-out with celebrities. The grand prize is a mystery date with an actor of the player's choice.

"I think I'm going to throw up," Emma mutters in my ear.

"You're not still going through morning sickness, are you?" I ask.

"No! It's just that this game is so stupid and boring! My God, is this what it's like to settle down?"

No arguments there.

"By the way, I've already found the A-bug and fixed it. Between their ADD issues, looking at online porn, and screwing around with their Google Glass apps, your team is too distracted to focus on a line-by-line code check." I can imagine her rolling her eyes.

"So, how do we fix this game?" I ask.

"I'm no miracle worker. If this is as good as it gets in the real world, I'm surprised real women aren't throwing themselves out of their sparkling clean windows."

"That's just it, Emma—real life is much more than this! Women have doubts about themselves, and their relationships.

They have fears—for their children, their significant others, and for themselves. It's the joy of finding your true love, of marrying him, and having children with him. And it's not just emotional highs, either. Sure, women worry if they're gaining weight or if they spot another wrinkle or gray hair. But they also get cancer, or have to deal with aging parents, or are juggling part-time jobs, or losing their jobs and homes when the economy tanks. If Shazaaaam wants them to play this game, it's got to resemble real life, not the games we played when we were ten, when we didn't know any better."

"Donna, was that enough for you?"

Her question stops me cold. "What do you mean?"

"I guess what I'm trying to ask is whether or not you'd prefer everything you just mentioned. In other words, reality."

I snort. "As opposed to what, this super-saccharine fantasy?"

She pauses as she searches for the right words. "By that, I mean as opposed to some of the excitement you've had since becoming an assassin."

"Yes, okay, to be honest, when I was a full-time housewife, I never felt I was living up to my full potential. When Ryan asked me to join Acme, I had a mission—I wanted to avenge Carl's death. Now I do it to prevent him killing others. Each mission puts me into situations that challenge me—emotionally, mentally, and physically." I sigh. "To be honest with you, I've never felt as alive as I do right now."

"Because of the danger you find yourself in at every turn." Emma's presumption comes out in a quiet whisper.

"No," I insist, "Because the stakes are so high—my children's lives, Jack's life, the world we live in. I fail, I lose it all— this 'normal life' we take for granted." My voice is trembling, but I can't make it stop. "But, Emma, the way *Queen of Hearts* depicts real life is far from it! All life is always a challenge. We grow, we change, and we mature. The rosy happily ever after isn't the journey. It's *the reward.*"

Emma is so quiet that I can't tell if we're still connected until she practically yells into my ear, "That's it, Donna!"

"Ouch! What are you yelling about?" I swap the bud from one ear to the other in order to save my hearing.

"I'll re-code *Queen of Hearts* to resemble your life—and by that, I mean everything! The kids and the dogs, as well as the bad guys. Avatar Donna not only has to do carpool, she has to save the world too." I hear her clicking away on her keyboard. "She'll get her missive via interesting drops—the ice cream vendor, the librarian, in a bouquet of roses, whatever. The clock is always ticking against her. Can she stop an assassination before she has to put dinner on the table? Can she disarm a bomb and still take her daughter to ballet? The hearts she wins will be purple, for valor and bravery. And the men in her life are—well, they're complicated. They'll be sexy and romantic and adventurous—but at the same time, they have hidden agendas. She won't know if they're good or evil." Emma is so excited, she's practically squealing. "Oh, my God, I think I can pull this off before you get to work tomorrow morning."

"Emma, you're pregnant, remember? You need your sleep! Take some down-time tonight—with Arnie."

"Are you kidding me? He just texted me that he's got other plans for the evening. Apparently, Nymphette and a group of his new coder buddies are staying on campus after work for a special showing of *Blade Runner.* Harrison Ford will be taking questions afterward. So that everyone gets into the vibe, Shaza-aaam has hired salon stylists to give the female employees blunt cuts, just like the replicants in the movie." Her laugh is harsh. No joy there.

"Maybe I should text him to remind him why he's really here—to break into Roger's email and files," I mutter.

"He did that about an hour ago. I've already lateraled the intel to my SignInt and ComInt teams for cipher analysis. One thing's for sure—Roger is anxious about Comic-Con. Reading between the lines, his role in our little drama is certainly taking place there—all the more reason you have to be there too." She sounds deflated. "Donna, please don't worry about me. Until this baby comes, I'm on the job. And besides, I haven't coded a game in a while. It'll be fun." But her tone is anything but fun as she adds, "Oh, hell!"

"What's happened now?" I force myself to keep my eyes on my laptop screen as opposed to turning around to look into the group pit.

"They're dissing you again." She forwards their latest group text:

Fu Manchu: UR telling me. She got any real creds?

Zhao: Supposedly cromulent.

Roger: Affirmative. Even so, we're taking someone else as QoH's booth babe. Need a livewire. A hottie.

Ichabod: Ditto! This one is too much of a dweebette!

Wise Ass: Nah. Chobo!

Bollywood: LOL! Right, n00b.

Fu Manchu: Nah. N00bette! Gotta say, though, she embiggens my handheld.

"Does that mean what I think it does?" I growl.

"You don't want to know," Emma responds. "How dare that idiot Fu Manchu call you a n00b!"

"You've got *that* right!…Um…how bad is it?"

"Let me put it this way—he did it with two zeros as opposed to two o's."

"Oh! Well, since you put it *that* way."

"Trust me, it's an insult. Worse yet, they're talking themselves out of taking you along as their booth babe."

Oh…shit.

"That does it," she declares. "I'm going to turn this housewife into a woman, and load you up with a couple of backdoor assets that kick ass." I hear Emma clicking away furiously on her keyboard. "After work, meet me back at your place, in the bonus room over the garage."

So much for TGIF.

If Emma is in for a long night, then I am too.

10

Avatar

Some of the most enticing apps you'll find for your high-speed tablet or smart phone are games—all sorts! You can choose from gory action games that test your survival skills (okay, really your ability to whip your joystick into a frenzy), or narrative-driven puzzles that take you on fantastic adventures through sinister environments, fighting off lifelike villains and monsters.

And if it's an MMOG—that is, a "massively multiplayer online game—you can compete, and triumph over tens of thousands of others as you collect points, gobble up loads and loads of calories, and live vicariously through a prettier, sexier animated version of you.

There is some important online gaming etiquette to follow. For example…

1. *Don't cheat! Using the exploits planted throughout the game is akin to starting a race and taking a shortcut. In other words, it's not about winning, but how you play the game. (Really, it's about how you look playing the game, so the sexier the avatar, the better.)*
2. *Be a good sport! No one likes a player who flings around*

negative emoticons and harshes everyone else's mellow. Having a sexy avatar only buys you so much love and respect. You must earn the rest.

3. *Don't be a "camper!" Staying put in one location in order to spawn points or corpses with your high-damage weapon demonstrates one of two things: either laziness, or fear. Remember, for every supposedly happy camper, there's a lumberjack just waiting to blow you away with some bigger, badder gun, so get it together and move on.*

On a final note: Concerned that the avatar you've chosen might mislead your new comrades-in-arms as to how you really look? Not to worry! Recent surveys show that nine out of nine avatars never look like the players they represent.

WHILE EMMA WORKS ALMOST NONSTOP TO TURN *QUEEN OF HEARTS* into an obsessively immersive, heart-pounding adrenaline rush of a game, I run warm baths for her, make her some hot home-cooked meals, and tuck her into the bonus room's feather bed when she's too tired to keep her eyes open.

I also bake like a fiend: chunky chocolate chip cookies, butterscotch brownies, and my chocolate-filled cronuts.

Mary and Trisha are fascinated to hear she's working on a new online game aimed at women. When they show up in the bonus room with a plate of the homemade chunky chocolate chip cookies they made themselves, Emma is so touched that she shows them how the game works.

"Can you teach me to code a game?" Mary asks hopefully.

"After this assignment, sure, I'm all yours," Emma promises.

As they leave her to continue her work, she murmurs to me, "I'll never be as great a mom as you."

"Yes, you will," I assure her. "Kids are intuitive. They can sense when someone they respect is hard at work and needs some space—not to mention a little tender loving care."

Emma nods. I'm sure it's imagining what random acts of love her own child will show her—not a sugar rush—that puts the smile on her face.

I LOVE THIS GAME.

It takes Emma twenty-four hours to tweak the development hardware so that the visuals are smooth and eye-poppingly realistic. Can you free hostages at a world peace summit in time to save even one from being killed—and before picking your daughter up from soccer practice? Can you disarm a bomb before your pie has to be pulled out of the oven?

The game's sound effects, which come at the players from all directions, are easily recognized by any mother, and yet give her reason to pause before jumping into action. Do you dodge a bullet, or hush a crying child? Do you shoot your target, or flatten yourself against a wall before a speeding train hits you?

And yes, there are spies who love you. Who do you trust, and why?

Especially in this game, where there's more to a dossier than meets the eye—especially now that Emma has also loaded Oculus support into the code.

The overworld map Emma built is truly a game changer. The homes of virtual Hilldale are filled with people who laugh, cry, kiss and make up, or make love and war. Some of your neighbors unwittingly hold clues that will make the world safer. Others could be terrorist cells, waiting for the attack signal.

Even without ethereal costumes and fantastical flora and fauna, the game is a thing of beauty.

It is real life.

Not yours perhaps, but mine.

Welcome to my neighborhood. But beware of smiling strangers bearing gifts. Pies may be poisoned, or perfectly delicious. The most harmful thing in a bouquet may be the thorns on its freshly cut roses. Then again, it may contain a bomb.

"I've even built in facial recognition software, so that the player's features are projected onto the avatar's face." She shows me, using my face.

"Wow! I look great in animated Three-D!"

Emma nods proudly. "Oh! And best of all, no more Barbie dimensions!" She pushes a button and changes the 36-17-34-inch dimensions on my avatar to—

Well, to mine.

So long, seventeen-inch waist. Hello, too much real junk in my animated trunk.

"Hmmm." How do I put this to her? "So…is there a Spanx store in virtual Hilldale?"

Emma rolls her eyes, but puts me back into my fantasy shape.

"Okay, now it's time for a wider Beta test," Emma proclaims.

"How do we do that?" I ask.

"We'll announce an open Beta through some of the more popular gamer loops and community forums—for example, on Steam and Kongregate. Also, I can hit up Geek & Sundry, as well as Friends of Comic-Con. Everyone who responds will be given a beta key for entry, and so that we can track their moves and responses. But, considering this has got to be ready by

Monday morning—less than twenty-four hours, I'd better do so pronto."

A few clicks of her keyboard, and the game is locked and loaded.

A few hours later, there are a couple of thousand players singing the game's praises.

By five in the morning, we have over two thousand reviews and comments.

Emma hacks into Shazaaaam's mainframe as Fu Manchu and uploads the game.

Confused, I turn to Emma. "Why are you letting him take the credit?"

"Because he's a guy. Trust me, if they think you did it—or anyone with double-X chromosomes—it will be rejected out of hand. Sexual and verbal harassment are both rampant in the industry. Female players receive three times the number of abusive comments as males. We get called sluts, whores, and cunts."

"I imagine it's easy to be an abusive little troll when you're anonymous, and your victim is miles away and an animated avatar," I murmur.

"Worse yet, sometimes they roam in packs. You feel as if you've been emotionally gangbanged." I can tell she's speaking from experience. "Sadly, it's just as bad if you work in the industry. Female designers can't catch a break. If they work for a Triple-A developer, their games are less likely to get produced." Emma shakes her head in disgust. "And, if their company does peer reviews, they are less likely to have their male coworkers sing their praises. It's like *Survivor*, when others can vote you off the island. Gaming is big bucks. I guess guys feel if someone is to get promoted over them, it better be another guy who played just as dirty."

"That is the stupidest thing I've ever heard!" I'm about to go on a rant, when a thought hits me. "Hey, won't Fu Manchu blow a gasket when he sees his code has been changed?"

Emma giggles gleefully. "No way. The last thing he'll want to admit is that some bug fairy dusted his game. And besides, with the rave reviews the game got in Beta, he'll want to take all the credit."

I shake my head in awe. "If it's a hit, the credit should be yours, you know."

Emma shrugs. "Don't worry. Shazaaaam's stock is at an all-time low. I just bought a chunk of it, so if the game hits it big, I'll make back my time and effort that way. As for the gaming industry, why do you think I approached Acme instead of doing this for a living? In hindsight, it was the best move for me. Taking down bad guys in the real world is so much more fun!" She pauses. "Speaking of peer review, Shazaaaam works that way too—so watch your back."

MY CRONUTS ARE A BIG HIT—WITH THE WRONG GUYS.

On Friday, Fu Manchu was the first to leave the office. Now that it's Monday morning, he's the last to come into it. Too many replicants, so little time. Case in point: the *Blade Runner* retrospective was so popular that it was shown in three Fun Huts at the same time.

However, the rest of the *Queen of Hearts* team is already seated at the group table. As they go through the game, they are so engrossed that they don't realize that they're dropping cronut crumbs and droplets of their favorite gourmet coffee blend all over their T-shirts. The avatars they choose for themselves are a projection of their dream lives. Whereas Wise Ass and Bollywood take studly he-man icons, Ichabod and Zhao put on dresses, heels, and give themselves forty-inch boobs.

When Fu Manchu finally shows his face, I stand with the rest of them and give him a standing ovation.

Roger is curious enough to look up from reading Tesla Motors' forum blog, where he's been trolling for women who troll for male Tesla owners.

Yes, he is a proud owner of a Tesla.

"What's all the clapping about?" Roger scratches under his topknot, a nervous habit, I'm sure. Frankly, because of him, I've quit fun-bunning altogether.

I sweep my arm in Fu Manchu's direction. "He succeeded in cleaning the A-bug out of the game. Not only that, tested it through the roof with the Betas!"

Fu Manchu glares at me. "What the hell? You put the game out to Betas—before one last QA run through?"

I bat my eyes at him as I hand him a cronut. "You can't improve on perfection, can you?"

He stares down at it, but he ain't biting. "Says who?" he growls.

I swipe the plate of butterscotch brownies out of Wise Ass's paws and wave it in front of Fu Manchu's nose with a smile. "Says the twenty-two hundred married women between the ages of twenty-five and forty who beta-tested it over the weekend, that's who! Here are their comments."

I text the *QofH* team a PDF and watch their faces as they scroll through the comments. With a four-point-seven rating out of five, and comments from all the players, most of the raves use exactly the words I've said.

"Isn't it great?" I exclaim. "It's everything we want it to be! It challenges. It fills players with fear, and dread—and hope. It's got bad guys, and naughty men." I lick my lips at Roger, who preens at the thought that I think he's anything but a creepy man-ho. "It excites, and makes women feel sexy. It is now the ultimate MMORPG for any woman. It's realistic. It's engaging. And most importantly, it's addictive."

Does Roger recognize his own bullshit? Hope not.

"Dude, the smartest thing you did was add an FPS component! Awesome!" Ichabod slaps him on the back.

"It's like *La Femme Nikita* meets Betty Crocker," Wise Ass chimes in.

"No, more like *Lara Croft* meets Donna Reed," Bollywood counters, spewing chunky chocolate chips.

"Hey, I like the new name he put on the game—*The Housewife Assassin*," Zhao says thoughtfully. "And it tested through the roof!"

Roger frowns at Fu Manchu. "You changed the name of the game? What the fuck, guy?"

Fu Manchu's mouth is open wide, but nothing seems to come out. Finally, he stutters, "I-It fits the theme. You know, kick-ass woman."

"In my office—*now.*"

There is one big problem with glass offices within a loft space:

No privacy.

Everyone can hear your rant and rave (Roger) at someone whose ego is just as inflated as yours (Fu Manchu). They can see you shake your fist (Roger) to no avail, as your opponent stubbornly folds his arms (Fu Manchu), or when your back is turned goes so far as to flip you a bird (Fu Manchu), not realizing that you can see him do so in the reflected glass.

Fu Manchu stalks out of Roger's office, slamming the door behind him.

"Where the hell is he going?" Zhao muses out loud.

"Probably to rub one out," Wise Ass snickers. "Hell, that's what I'd be doing if I'd just got one over on Roger."

"Why do you say that?" I ask.

He looks at me as if I'm a piece of dung clinging to his size-six flip-flops, all of which says a lot about him. (First, he has no sense of my worth; next, no one with visible toe fungus should be in flip-flops; and lastly, a man with small feet has a woman wondering about the size of his other appendages.) When he realizes I won't melt under his withering gaze, he shrugs. "Fixing this piece of shit game was a real coup for us. Until we were all put on this project, we were currently unassigned."

I shake my head. "What does that mean?"

Bollywood sighs. "It means, bimbo, that instead of putting us on projects that might burnish our resumes, Shazaaaam was riding out our contracts."

"But, now that we may have a hit game on our hands, we be dah man!" Ichabod shouts.

"Don't you mean, 'we be dah men?'" I point out.

He doesn't hear me. He's too busy chest-bumping with the other guys.

"It doesn't make sense. This was a suicide mission?" Emma murmurs into my ear bud.

"I guess so," I whisper. "And because of us, these jerks live to play another day."

"If you're going to Wonder-Con, you've got to follow Fu Manchu and talk him into taking you."

I shudder to think what that will take.

My best guess: more than what he presumes is a 32 C.

IF I THOUGHT IT WOULD BE EASY TO FIND FU MANCHU, I'M POORLY mistaken. He's not in any of the fun huts, and I've nearly covered all fifteen acres of ShazaaaamLand.

When I finally come across him, he's high on the upper-most-level of the garage—the one that is closest to the glassed-in walkway going into the tower. He's staring out at the structure. It's hard not to, considering it looks like a living, breathing organism.

Or I should say organ?

He's sitting on the hood of a Tesla. Despite the fact that it's one of fifteen or so here, I don't have to guess that it's Roger's.

When he finally hears my footsteps behind him, he turns his head just enough to see who it is. The most I earn is a frown.

He asks, "It was you, wasn't it?" He sounds defeated.

"I don't know what you're asking."

"You're the one who fixed the bug, aren't you?"

I take a moment before nodding. I've hit plenty of men when they're down—but only if they're trying to kill me. Ridicule, I usually take in stride. "I didn't do it to embarrass you."

He smirks as he crosses his arms at his chest. "Oh, no?"

"If I had, wouldn't I let Roger and the others know about it?"

He knows I've got a point. He shrugs. "So, what do you want?"

"Wonder-Con. I want to be our game's booth babe."

"*Our* game?" A paper-thin smile rises on his lips. "You say that as if you truly had anything to do with it."

"The numbers speak for themselves." My tone is nonchalant. It is also deadly.

Obviously, he's tone deaf, because he sneers, "And you think you can buy your way in with brownies?"

"I saved your ass. What more do you want?" Other than looking stupid for work, flip-flops are stupid for another reason —they make it so easy for an opponent to break your toes.

"I'll tell you what I want." The next thing I know, he's grabbed me and slammed me up against the car.

I break his hold on me by grinding my stiletto into his foot.

His howl echoes through the garage until I shut him up with a punch to the throat. As he gasps for air, I grab hold of his nutsack and twist it as hard as needed to get my point across. "So, what do you say, are we booth mates?"

He's nodding so hard that the tears streaming down his face are staining the front of his vintage nineteen ninety-eight MacWorld Convention T-shirt.

"Go on and tell Roger the good news," I whisper in his ear. "Oh, and congratulations! Looks like your game is going to be a really big hit."

I leave him bent over and heaving. Time's a'wasting. I've got to start work on an adorable *Housewife Assassin* costume.

But of course, it will be the chicest of geek couture.

"I hear you'll be joining us in the booth." Roger leans in so close to my ear that I almost bump heads with him as I turn to see who's looking over my shoulder.

Thank goodness what he sees on my computer screen is innocent enough: I'm playing the game.

He grabs the closest toadstool chair and scoots it so close that we're practically hip-to-hip. "We have a little tradition when we introduce a new game at Wonder-Con. The booth babe and I play a live version of the game."

I clap my hands in mock anticipation. "Ooh! Sounds like fun!"

He smiles. "It gets better. The winner gets anything they want."

Hmmm. "So, like, if I want a month-long all-expenses-paid trip around the world on a Lear jet, it's mine for the asking?"

He nods. "Sure, why not? Shazaaaam has its own Lear. It's also got an open account with every hotel on the *Condé Nast*

Traveler Gold List. And we were one of the original investors in Uber, so you'd always have a limo at your disposal."

"You're telling me I can go away for a full month?"

"Don't look so shocked. The last booth babe who won took a whole year off, with pay, and got double stock options too."

Hell yeah!

To tamp down the glow in my eye, I lower my lashes and ask, "Lucky lady! Was she a recent winner?"

He laughs so hard that he almost falls off his toadstool. "Are you kidding? It was at least a decade ago! I'm always that good. Or they're always that...*bad.*"

His eyes roam over me, lingering on my lips. "How about you, Donna? Are you bad?"

Bad? *I am your worst nightmare.*

"Why don't we find out?" I suggest.

He swipes a screen on his iPad. "Just to be fair, I'll give you everything you requested and sweeten the deal with a full one-year sabbatical. Sign here, on the company release form. Boiler-plate stuff. You know, about holding harmless and indemnification. A mere formality." He takes a stylus from his pocket and points to the last line.

One year's pay. A trip around the world, all expenses paid...

I sign with a flourish.

Just then, I remember to ask, "And, if I lose?"

"You. At my beck and call. For a year." I don't like his leer.

My heart is pounding in my chest. "You mean, like your administrative assistant or something?"

He rolls his eyes. "That's the last thing I mean. Sure, you'll still be on payroll. But you'll be serving me in a personal capacity, if you get my drift." He winks suggestively. "Considering where you started, it'll be a promotion."

Um...*What the hell did I just sign?*

"But...nonconsensual sex is employee harassment. It's federal law!"

"What you just signed says that you've agreed to the terms and conditions set heretofore, and that any physical intimacy between the parties is consensual and, therefore, out of the jurisdiction of company policy and venue. Not only that, but reneging on said terms constitutes compensatory reparations equivalent to a cash payment of the loser's prize."

The equivalent of one year's pay. A trip around the world, all expenses paid...

Acme will never cover it, and it will bankrupt my family.

I try not to hyperventilate. I mean, I'm not really Donna Gray, so none of this is applicable anyway.

"You seem a bit hesitant." His pouty face is supposed to be his way of feigning sympathy. "Look, I never want it said that I forced you into this against your will. If you want, you can bow out of the bet right now." He shrugs. "Of course, we'll have to replace you in the booth. Can't disappoint the fans, now can we?"

"No, of course not," I murmur.

Remember, I practically wrote the game...

Well, okay, I didn't write it. But it is based on me, and the writer is one of my besties...

He holds out his hand.

I shake it.

He stands up. "Oh, and to make things interesting, we'll be playing the VR version—Rifting, as the case may be. Fun, huh? So glad it was programmed into the game, aren't you? Not that any housewife will want to mess up her mascara with goggles. The Wonder-Con fans will love it, though." He pats my head— for too long, and too longingly—before heading back to his office.

"Get home as soon as possible," Emma insists. "I'll test you with Rift so that you know the game, backward and forward."

"I'm not you, Emma. There's no way I can play as well as you."

She laughs. "I've got a contingency plan for that," she assures me.

I hope it includes enrollment in the U.S. Witness Protection Program.

In any case, I'm putting all my assets in Jack's name, in case I have to declare bankruptcy.

Oh, hell, the house is not just in my name, but Carl's too. If I lose it, it's just what he'd need to declare me an unfit mother—betting a vacation against a year as a sex slave to a pervert.

Or I can just kill Roger.

Even Teslas can spin off the road, if a tire loses a bolt or two.

Or three.

A shame. It's a beautiful car.

"You did what?" Jack can't believe his ears.

"It was the only way I could get into the booth," I explain. I've waited until the kids are upstairs in their rooms, finishing their homework, before breaking the news to him.

"Donna, have you seen the file on this guy? He's one sick puppy! We're not talking just a sex-addict. The dude is into sadism in a very big way."

"A bottom?"

"In your dreams." Jack shakes his head. He doesn't have the heart to look at me. Instead, he glances over at Emma, who sits at the kitchen counter, reading the agreement on her iPad.

When Emma looks up from the screen, she's not smiling.

"Not only that, the paper you signed covers any aliases of the signatories as well."

So, Donna Stone is just as screwed—figuratively—as Donna Gray.

"Why would anyone know to put that in?"

"Either he knows you aren't who you say you are, or else most of the booth babes work in porn, and this way he can hold them to their word," Emma surmises.

"And, either way, it's binding," Jack mutters.

"I'll just have to win, won't I?" I sound more assured than I feel. I stare down at the Rift headgear. "Where do we start?"

11

Wonder-Con!

Welcome to Wonder-Con, where your favorite comic book characters have come to life!

Predating, but later joining, the comic book convention behemoth known as Comic-Con, this (formerly San Francisco, but now) Anaheim-based event offers up just as many superheroes, great behind-the-scenes panels, and actors and writers of your favorite 'zines, movies, and shows!

Flying your geek flag high and proud is always welcomed. In fact, it is encouraged. (Yes, rest assured, you, of all people, will fit right in.)

However, there are still a few antics you may want to avoid, so that you aren't the most uncool attendee there:

- *Antic #1: Don't break into hysterics when you see your favorite superhero in the flesh. Keep in mind, he is merely an actor who is being paid to embody the role, not someone who can actually fly when you chest-bump him off a balcony.*
- *Antic #2: Don't break into hysterics when you see someone*

*in a much better costume than yours. Every year, the
conventions' geek couture takes a giant leap forward. (Not
at all unusual, considering that much of what you see on
the Fashion Week runways would qualify, no problem.)
Instead of sweating it (it, being your sad little attempt at a
costume), snap a few pictures so that you can copy your
favorites for next year (which is exactly what knock-off
designers do, anyway).*

- *Antic #3: Feel free to make new friends! Will cosplay lead
to foreplay? You betcha! Granted, some of those you meet
will refuse to take off their masks, for a very good reason:
they look better with them on.*

*That being said, forego any pick-up lines such as, "Is that your laser
sword, or are you just happy to see me…?" until you see with your
own eyes that he's worth wiggling out of all that spandex.*

THE *HOUSEWIFE ASSASSIN* BOOTH IS THE BIGGEST HIT AT
Wonder-Con.

Based on one week's word-of-mouth for the game, the line
for our booth is the longest one in the convention hall. My
mouth hurts from all the smiling I do, as Donna S., the heroine
of the game. I'm shocked at how much cosplay—that is to say,
costume play—the game has already inspired. Ninety percent
of the women who stand in line waiting for a selfie with me
could be spitting images of the game's heroine. Like me, they
wear a polka-dot sundress, accessorized with a necklace of
white pearls, hair swept up in a French twist…retro and classy.

Especially when holding a chainsaw.

Trust me, it works.

I can only imagine Fu Manchu's hand hurts from autographing so many full-page ads of the game in the convention program. The first lucky thousand got posters tagged with beta keys, which allow them a free week of game play.

I'd like to think that Fu Manchu hasn't looked my way because he's just too busy. But, in reality, he has ignored me all week. During the few times I found him staring at me, he'd smirk.

Maybe our little garage rendezvous is his idea of foreplay. Whatever his issue, I don't have time to think about it right now.

Whereas Fu Manchu and I may be working nonstop, Roger has it easy. Every now and then, he'll reach into a valise where he keeps five specially made VIP beta keys of the game—the size of a thumb drive, but actually gold in color, and sporting a knob with the Shazaaaam logo. Supposedly, the select few recipients are movers and shakers in the gaming business, or film producers who may be interested in turning it into a movie.

Almost been there, almost done that.

Jack is here too, as is Abu. Both hang nearby, taking turns observing the interaction between Roger and the VIPs. They wear special contact lenses that feed whatever they see back to Acme, where Arnie and the tech-ops team run the VIPs through facial recognition software.

If the last three days of practice have proved anything, it's that my shooting skills are second to none. However, when I wear the WiFi lenses and the Rift headgear together, I'm subjected to a mild case of myopia. If I don't wear them, Emma can't see what's happening in the game from my perspective, so I just have to suck it up.

I've adjusted my aim to account for it; but, admittedly, I'm off my mark.

During the final practice session last night, Emma winced

every time I missed a shot. "Worst case scenario, you can spray and pray," she counseled. "Also, I've tweaked the version of the game that will feed into the booth. For example, you'll play so that there is a built-in Fog of War, to keep you safe."

"Come again?"

"A 'Fog of War' is a blind on the map. In this case, it's specific to any player who isn't identified as you."

"Gotcha."

"I've also given your avatar a few combos that the other players can't do."

"Combos?" I asked.

"In other words, attack moves that will instantly immobilize him. In fact, I modeled the moves on real martial arts maneuvers—ones you use yourself, so that they'll be second nature to you."

"When he can't copy my moves, won't he be suspicious that I'm cheating?"

She laughed. "Are you kidding? He's already accessed and memorized the cheat codes! I'm just giving you a level playing field."

Now that I'm minutes away from my showdown with Roger, I pray she's right.

Let the game begin.

THE CROWD LETS OUT A FRENZIED ROAR AS ROGER STRUTS OUT onto the humongous stage in the convention's main auditorium. He wears a wireless lapel microphone so he can open his arms wide—*Made it, Ma! Top of the world!*—or pace the stage like the best snake oil salesman in the Ozarks.

"This is the game you've been waiting for!" he reminds the crowd. "You love the *Housewife Assassin* because she's just the girl next door—and she's a femme fatale! She's every man's dream, and every terrorist's nightmare! She belongs to everyone—and she's you!" His eyes sweep the audience, drilling in on those women for who cosplay is a way of life. At first, they blush but then they preen proudly.

Hell yeah, they are *the Housewife Assassin.*

"And right here, right now on this stage, you'll see her in action—playing little old me." Hearing the laughter rippling through the crowd, he shrugs modestly. "We'll be wearing Rifts." He points to the Jumbotron—"Right here on this screen, you'll see what we see, and hear what we hear"—he pauses dramatically—"and when the loser dies, you'll watch it happen too."

His grand pronouncement is met with awed silence, followed by a thunderclap of applause.

I'm standing just offstage. But now that he throws out his right arm to include me, I steel myself with a deep breath, turn my frown upside down, and force myself to move forward until I'm side by side with him, arms raised in welcome, like some sort of magician's assistant.

More like the ventriloquist's dummy, seeing how I stiffen at the thought of what awaits me should I fail.

When he hands me the Rift headgear, the mob goes into a frenzy.

Before putting it on my head and over my eyes, I scan the audience for Jack. Finally, I find him, front and center. When our eyes meet, he blows me a kiss. Abu is there, too, standing over to one side, but close to the stage. He assures me with a nod.

And then I see him, a few rows back from Abu—

Carl.

What the hell is he doing here?

He smiles at me.

Then he throws me a kiss and walks away.

What if he's headed to the house?

Frantically, I seek out Jack again. When we see each other I shout, "Carl! Carl!" again and again, pointing in the direction I saw him last. But by the quizzical look on Jack's face and the way he holds his hand to his ear, I realize he can't make me out over the crowd, which is chanting, *"Play! Play! Play!"*

Roger puts his arm around my waist. "Let's get this over with. I've got a reservation for the Mount Whitney suite at Disney's Grand Californian, an Elsa costume—you know, from *Frozen*—and a flogger with your name on it. Walnut."

He presumes too much.

I'm not into BDSM or cosplay.

And, if I were, I'd be Anna, not an Elsa.

As Virtual Donna, I awaken to the sound of the doorbell.

My God, he's already here.

Not good. Here in Virtual Hilldale, the doorbell's Big Ben chimes announce the arrival of guests bearing gifts: baskets of fruit, homemade cakes, pies, and cookies.

Poisoned, perhaps.

Today, there will only be one visitor, and whatever he carries will be lethal.

My guess is that he's elected something more deadly than tainted fruit.

He wants a showstopper—something gory, since we're live, life-size, in 3-D, and in front of an auditorium filled with rabid gamers.

The name of the game is to build up an arsenal made from things found around the typical household, and to do it as quickly as possible, so that you have the right weapon when the time comes to protect yourself. The weapons are worth five points apiece, all of which I will store in my deceivingly small Kate Spade clutch.

And believe me, the clock (in this case, the Tiffany oval cocktail watch which I wear on my slim virtual wrist; what can I say, I have great taste!) is always ticking.

I have only fifteen seconds before the game allows him to try the front doorknob. If my virtual children have followed house rules, they will have kept it locked, going and coming only through the back door, which takes them out into the yard, accessed only by a gate in the picket fence that goes around the perimeter of the property.

When Rifting, your slightest move is anticipated by your avatar. By shifting my body up, Virtual Me leaps out of bed—

To discover that all I'm wearing is a sheer pink negligee with nothing underneath. The laughter from the audience hits me like a cold wave.

I run over to my virtual closet. I know, I'm wasting time. But I'll be damned if I'll be playing this game with everyone ogling my ladybits!

I shove hanger after hanger to one side, but everything is eveningwear—too long and sexy for fighting. Next time, I'll know better than to use the Saks catalog as my wardrobe wish list.

Emma whispers, "Donna on the opposite side of the closet, pull out the Daisy Dukes and the red-and-white plaid buttoned tie crop. Oh, and the stiletto heels that match!"

"*Daisy Dukes*? That's the best you can do?"

She sighs. "If you remember, I didn't have a heck of a lot of time to go through this month's *InStyle*."

The Daisy Dukes are too short—and too sweet, if the audience's reaction is any indication. Thank goodness it is on

Virtual Me as opposed to Real Me. No woman wants to see her cellulite on a Jumbotron, in 3D.

By the time I tie the cropped shirt, I've only got eleven seconds left!

I run to the kitchen, where I pocket a cleaver, a large fork, and food processor. Fifteen points!

"Don't forget the fondue pot," Emma whispers in my ear.

Interesting suggestion. Still, I'll take her word and go with it. Besides, it brings my point count to twenty.

Next, I high-tail it out into the yard and into the gardening shed, where I grab a spade, a shovel, a pick, a chainsaw, and the lawnmower.

"Take the bug repellant too," Emma insists.

"Gotcha," I murmur, and sweep it into my purse. I'm now up to fifty points.

I've just stepped out into the yard when I see him, leaping over the gate—

Roger's avatar.

I didn't expect it to look like Roger. Even he must wince when he sees himself in the mirror. But the last thing I expected was for it to be the spitting image of Carl—tall, dark, and handsome, with broad shoulders and deep green eyes.

Shocked, I cry out, "What the hell?"

Hearing me, he looks in my direction and waves. "Honey, I'm home."

Any doubts I may have had that Roger was in cahoots with Carl dissipate in the deep resonance of Carl's voice.

"Damn it!" Emma shouts. "The fact that he's your spouse automatically puts one hundred points on his side of the scoreboard!"

"But, in my profile, I put down 'Jack' as my husband!"

"Someone went in and changed it," Emma insists.

It must have been Fu Manchu. Not only does he get back at

me for bitch-slapping him, he scores major points with Roger for setting me up to be his sex slave.

"Worse yet, this version of the game has been re-coded as a shoot 'em up!" Emma warns me.

"What the heck does that mean?"

"In other words, it's last man standing, take no prisoners, and no rezzing—resurrections—once you've been killed off."

Over his dead body.

Make that Virtual Carl's.

I'll take care of Real Carl later.

Virtual Carl holds up his hands, as if to prove that there's nothing in them.

I stay put. Let him come to me.

When he's within kicking and throwing distance, I take the cleaver and hurl it. It twirls through the air like a tomahawk, headed directly at his chest.

He pulls a large magnet from his back pocket and holds it high over his head.

The cleaver flies to it, as if it found a long-lost pal.

The next thing I know, Virtual Carl has it pointed at my clutch purse. The magnet's siren call has my metallic weapons flying to it.

Virtual Carl looks triumphant. He revs the chainsaw and holds it up to the crowd, so that they can see what he has planned for me next.

The audience is stunned—subdued. Will *Housewife Assassin* bite the virtual dust even before the game is launched?

"You're not dead yet," Emma promises me.

"He took everything in my arsenal!"

"No, not everything. Look in your clutch purse."

She's right. I'm left with the bug spray and the fondue pot. "Why didn't they go to the magnet?" I ask.

"The bug spray is in a plastic canister, and the fondue pot is ceramic."

"Yep, okay." I hold up what's left of my weapons cache. "Hey look, Emma, I know chocolate-covered ants are considered a delicacy, but he's not here for a dinner party."

"Trust me on this. You'll have a better chance if you run to the park and climb onto the slide," Emma instructs me. "The fondue pot is always on. When he comes at you with the chainsaw, throw its contents at it. He won't have time to react before you—"

"I'll know what to do," I assure her.

"Yes, I know," she says matter-of-factly.

She has all the confidence in the world.

I wish I felt the same way.

VIRTUAL HILLDALE COMES IN CINEMASCOPE. THE SKY IS ALMOST cobalt blue. The grass is thick. The roses are deep red and sweet pink. The leaves on the trees, which sway in a gentle breeze, gradate through a Pantone palette of green hues—from pale celadon to apple to lime to moss to hunter to shamrock to pine, and back again.

By the time I reach the park, sounds of the children assault my ears with happy squeals, sour tears, and salty declarations of revenge.

The chatter among the women meandering toward the park with their strollers is just as delicious. Tantalizing tidbits of gossip vie for the honor of the most delectable crumb of the day with scrumptious secrets, in which hearts are crossed as declarations of silence.

I wish I had time to stroll. Instead, I'm running for my virtual life.

I don't know what my neighbors think of the man making his way down the street with a roaring chainsaw. Maybe the fact that he isn't wearing a ski mask, but that he whistles and smiles and greets them each by name is his saving grace.

Talk about hiding in plain sight.

His chitchat puts them at ease. I wince every time he refers to me as his wife and asks if they've seen which way I've gone. Smart dude, since I could have hidden in any of the homes on either side of this cozy tree-lined lane.

You see, he's trying to beat the clock too. Every ten seconds, another weapon disappears from his arsenal.

I'd certainly have a better chance if it came to hand-to-hand combat. Sadly, it will never come to that. Being good neighbors, they point him further toward the park.

I pray that my perch on the slide doesn't make me a sitting duck.

As I climb up the steps of the slide to the top, the children part like a Biblical sea. In no time, they've disappeared, leaving Virtual Carl and me alone.

His grin is evil. "Are you coming down, or do I have to climb up to get you?"

"I like the view from here."

He frowns. "You're only making it harder on yourself." He lowers his voice and whispers, "Walnut."

"Promises, promises," I taunt him.

He comes for me—not by way of the slide's ladder, but up the curved tin slide, running fast and roaring loud.

I wait until he's halfway up the slide before heaving the contents of the fondue pot at him.

A wave of hot oil—not hot chocolate—heads his way.

But, just at that moment, he shifts his hands so that it misses the chainsaw—

He doesn't expect it to catch him in the face.

His howl echoes through the auditorium.

He bends forward, so that he doesn't lose his balance on the slippery slide. This works in my favor. By the time he looks up, I've positioned the bug spray so that it is aimed right at his eyes.

All it takes is one long spritz of DEET and he's shrieking in pain.

Now that he's upright, I raise myself on the safety handles of the slide. With both legs, I kick him with all my might.

He topples backward, head over heels.

What goes up must come down. The momentum of Virtual Carl's fall propelled the chainsaw into the air. It now comes spiraling down after him—

On top of him.

Limbs are severed and blood spews as the chainsaw twists and turns. Roger's screams are chilling, prompting a horrified moan from the audience.

The tinkling chimes from my Tiffany watch announces that the game is over.

Virtual Donna grows until she covers the Jumbotron. Virtual Donna slaps her hands together with a smile and proclaims, "Another task completed! I think I'll reward myself with a little shopping!"

By the time I take off my Rifts, the damage is done—not from some imaginary chainsaw, but from a mere misstep.

Roger took a twenty-foot drop, from the stage into the audience pit.

The fall killed him.

Or perhaps his very active imagination.

I shrug it off. At this point, all I care about is taking off my Rifts and getting out of this madhouse of cheering mayhem.

Jack leaps onto the stage and pulls me aside. "Donna, are you okay?"

"We have to get home—right now! Carl was here!"

He looks surprised. "No, you were seeing Roger's avatar, that's all—which certainly proves he was in cahoots with Carl—"

"You don't get it!" I point out into the mob. "He was out there—in the flesh! And he made a point for me to see him. But then he left, just as the demonstration began!"

Jack frowns. "Perhaps Carl was here for one of the VIP game keys Roger was handing out."

My eyes open wide. "But I never saw him approach the booth. Did you?"

Jack shakes his head. "That doesn't mean anything. The last thing he would have wanted to do was give away his presence —until it was too late for us to do anything about it." He taps his ear bud. "Abu, get to Roger's body and lift any of the game keys that may still be in his possession. If he doesn't have any, go to the booth and look for them there! If you find them, take them back to Acme for analysis."

"I'm here now," Abu promises. "And…got one."

I grab Jack's arm and drag him with me toward the stage door "Please, Jack, we have to go home now, before he gets to the children!"

He takes my hand, and together we run out the side stage door.

Jack was right. I should have told the children about Carl on that very first night we came home from DC.

Now, it's too late. Carl gets to tell them his way.

All these years, he's been the bad guy. Now it's my turn.

12

Heartbleed

In the cyberworld, "Heartbleed" is the aptly named security vulnerability found in OpenSSL encryption technology. It was only discovered in 2014, and considering that OpenSSL is used by roughly two-thirds of all web servers, Heartbleed is one of the most significant vulnerabilities discovered since the beginning of the Internet.

But heart bleed (the condition, if not the digital vulnerability) transcends the World Wide Web. For example, metaphorically speaking, a woman's heart bleeds when she knows she's hurt someone. If she loves the person, she will try to make amends—to put the pieces back together again, a frail endeavor indeed.

Needless to say, her heart bleeds too—again, metaphorically speaking—when it is broken.

Should the one who breaks her heart do so callously, despite the initial euphoria of posting his misdeeds on such man-bashing websites and apps such as LuLu, ReportYourEx, DontDateHimGirl, and WomanSavers, make your weapon something other than a computer keyboard.

Like say, a knife—strategically placed to the left of his breastbone, perhaps deep within the right ventricle of his heart.

No doubt his last thought will be, Payback's a bitch.

Yes, he meant you.

∼

IN THE LOUSY TRAFFIC FROM ANAHEIM, IT TAKES US ALMOST AN hour to get home. I do my best to keep from breaking down in tears. Jack does his best not to drive off the road while I rant and rave over my stupidity for (a) talking myself—make that us —out of telling the children; (b) not planting a tracker on Carl, so that I know where he is at all times; or (c) not killing him when I had the chance.

"Look, there's no way to change the past," Jack reminds me. "The only thing we can do at this point is to move forward and work with what we have."

I nod. "Good suggestion! Let's do a full accounting." I pull a folded stiletto from my bootie, my Sig from my thigh holster, and the MP5 hidden in a secret compartment under Jack's dashboard. "I presume you've got, what, another three or four toys on you somewhere, am I right?"

He sighs. "I wasn't suggesting all-out war—and not just because the neighbors are already skittish about our return to Hilldale. The last thing the children need right now is to see their mother do another perp walk for murdering a man they never knew was their father."

"You're right. We're trying to set examples of graciousness for the kids." So that they aren't social pariahs, like their parents. In Hilldale's social hierarchy, I'm on the lowest rung.

Granted, I'm still part of Penelope Bing's carpool group, but only because the other moms are too smart to allow the inevitably carsick Cheever into their SUVs.

We careen into the driveway and Jack screeches to a halt. He's right on my heels as I run to the front door.

The door is unlocked.

Slowly, I open it.

I don't hear a sound.

Where are they?

More to the point, where is he?

Jack raises his hand to signal me to go through the dining room on the left. He then motions to indicate that he'll circle around the living room and into the family room. He raises his palm vertically then points to the staircase, to indicate we'd go up together if Carl isn't on the ground floor.

I nod, and inch my way through the dining room—

It's empty.

I move toward the swinging door to the kitchen. Gently, I push it open—

It flies open, and I fall into Carl's arms. Before I can stumble away, he tilts my head up so that my lips meet his—

But I fall onto my knees as he reels backward—

Against the cabinet, where Jack has slammed him, and put him into a choke hold.

Not for long. A fist to the kidney has Jack backing off. Carl lets loose with a side kick, which puts Jack on the floor, doubled up on his side.

Before Carl delivers a kick to Jack's stomach, I grab a pot holding carrots and green beans from the stove, and fling it at Carl. When it hits his head, he stumbles to his knees.

Now it's my turn to give a little pain. I kick him in the gut—

But as he falls forward, he grabs me below the knees, taking me down with him.

The next thing I know, Carl, still on his knees, is pulled backward.

Apparently, Jack had crawled to the counter and, reaching

up, he found the carving knife, which he now holds to Carl's throat. He has shoved Carl's head straight back, so that all it would take is a flick of his wrist.

Carl's eyes meet his. "Go ahead, do it," Carl taunts him.

Jack tightens his grip on the knife handle and moves it next to Carl's jugular—

"Dad…*Don't!*"

Hearing Mary's shout, Jack, Carl, and I freeze. Slowly, we turn to the back door.

She is standing there with Jeff, Trisha, and Aunt Phyllis. Seeing the horror in their eyes, Jack lowers the knife.

Slowly and painfully, Carl and I rise to our feet.

No one says anything for the longest time.

Finally, Aunt Phyllis sighs. "Ah, hell! So, he's back, like a bad penny."

I stare at her, stunned. "You knew?"

She shrugs. "At first I blamed it on my lousy eyesight. But then the new guy was so sweet that I figured it had to be a different man."

That's putting it mildly.

"While you entertain your company, why don't I check on the pot roast and the potatoes?" she suggests. "Oh, and should I set the table for six, or seven?"

My stare says it all: *That is the stupidest question in the world.*

"Yeah, I guess you're right," she conceded. "Besides, we'll need knives." She pauses, in thought. "They can't subpoena a spouse for a murder. Does that go for kids too?"

Good question.

If so, something tells me we'd get away with it.

THE CHILDREN SIT TOGETHER ON THE DIVAN IN THE LIVING ROOM—

Mary on the right, Jeff in the middle and Trisha on his other side.

My youngest has slipped her tiny hand into her brother's, whereas Mary has wrapped her arms around her waist, as if bracing herself for the worst.

Good instincts.

Jack and I are sitting side by side, on the small settee facing the divan. Carl sits in the white linen wingback chair, placed between the sofas and facing the fireplace.

No one smiles.

No one speaks.

The children stare at Carl.

I do, too, but only because he's got cuts and bruises from his fall. If he gets blood on my chair, I don't think there's a female jurist alive who would convict me for killing him.

Thank goodness Carl knows to keep his mouth shut and let me explain.

Good old Donna is always there to pick up the pieces.

I clear my throat. All eyes turn to me. "Mary, I believe you've met this man before."

Her eyes shift toward Carl, if only for a second. "He came to Hilldale with the Russian president, two years ago, when I was in the eighth grade."

I nod. "That's right. At the time, you commented on the fact that he had a name similar to…" I point to Jack.

"To Dad's," Mary says warily.

Carl winces at the nonchalance in which she acknowledges another man—a man he hates with a passion—to be her father.

"Is he related to us?" Trisha asks innocently.

"You could say that," Carl says with a smirk.

Jeff's brow furrows at this new bit of information. "Are you Dad's brother?"

Hearing this, Carl frowns. But before he can answer, I say, "I was once married to this man."

My children's eyes grow big.

Jeff's gaze shifts from Carl to Jack and back again. "You were married to a man with the same name as Dad's?"

For some reason, Carl finds this funny. Gasping through a chuckle, he murmurs, "Donna, dearest, are you going to tell them, or do I have to?"

"Don't you dare." Jack's tone may be pleasant enough, but his words sober Carl up, and fast. The faces of the two men are bland, almost congenial, but I know their bodies too well to miss the tension crackling between them. I hold my breath, praying that they know better than to go at each other again.

"He's Carl Stone." Mary says flatly. "He's our father."

Hearing their sister's declaration, the breath escaping from Jeff and Trisha's bodies seems to deflate them, like rubber dolls.

No one says anything. Finally, Jeff looks at Jack. "Is she right?"

Jack nods. "It wasn't a deliberate lie." He turns to Carl. "This man—"

"You can call me Dad," Carl says pointedly to Jeff.

Hearing this, Trisha slumps even deeper into the divan.

"What I'm trying to say is that this man left your mother on the day of Trisha's birth," Jack explains.

"For a very good reason," Carl adds.

That does it. I can't take it anymore. "Faking your death? You call that a good reason?"

Carl glowers at me. "I was trying to save you and our children from harm. *Our* children—no matter what you've told them about...*him*." He waves a dismissive hand at Jack.

I lay my hand on Jack's arm to keep him from rising to the bait. "Carl, I told my children what I was asked to tell them, for national security reasons—which, by the way, now that all of this is out in the open, means that they'll learn about your terr—"

"Wait!" Jeff interrupts me. "Are you a spy? Is Dad one too—I mean...I mean..." He stares at Jack. "If he's our Dad, then who are you?"

Jack looks him in the eye. "My name is Jack Craig. And... I'm—I'm the man who loves your mother."

"I love her too," Carl growls.

"If you ever did love me, you certainly had a funny way of showing it," I say under my breath.

Mary glowers at Carl. "Mom is right. If you truly loved us, you would have never left us."

Thank you for that, God.

"But, Mother," she continues, "If you loved us, you would have never played such a mean trick on us—pretending that anyone else was our father—even"—she blushes when she looks at Jack—"Mr. Craig."

Mary only calls me "Mother" when she's angry at me.

Jack's head reels back, as if she's slapped him in the face. I can only imagine what he's thinking:

Mr. Craig?

Still, she can't be angrier at me than I am at myself—

For letting Carl put me in this position.

"But—but, Mary..." My protest goes unheard. Mary has already run upstairs to her room.

Trisha looks confused. "Does this mean we have two daddies?"

Her question has both men turning and glowering at each other.

Jeff grabs her arm, nudging her toward the stairs. Trisha looks back at me, to see if it's okay if she goes.

Reluctantly, I nod.

She wrenches her hand from Jeff's in order to go over to

Jack. "You'll always be my real Daddy," she says as she hugs him.

Jack holds her in his arms and pats her head. However, his gaze is high over her head—at Jeff.

Jeff's shock and awe subsides just enough to acknowledge it. I know his face well enough to read it. I don't see anger, but sharp glimmers of pain, sadness, and curiosity.

And determination.

My son is smart. He never sees black and white, but the clarity beyond shadows and smoke.

Jack has always been there for him. Can Jeff be there for Jack too?

I don't think I'll get the answer to that tonight. The only thing I'm getting is a whole lot of heartache.

Thanks to Carl.

I wait until Jeff and Trisha are upstairs and out of earshot before standing to face Carl. "Congratulations, you've accomplished your goal. Our children hate us all."

"My 'goal,' as you put it, was to tell them the truth."

"Your half-truths don't count," I argue. I'm bracing myself for another. "What were you doing at Wonder-Con, anyway?"

"I was looking for you. I felt it wise I tell you I was in town before popping in. Seeing you were preoccupied, I decided it was best I meet you here instead."

"You saw how well that went over," I mutter. "If what you say is true, then why did Roger make you his avatar—other than to throw me off my game?"

"I have that effect on women. It can be a curse." His smile is anything but modest. "Hey, can I help it that he chose to look like the handsomest guy in the room?"

"You're delusional." I shudder. "To be expected."

"Carl, I guess you never took into account that, by doing so,

Roger also implicated you as a suspect in Acme's investigation," Jack points out.

This realization wipes the smile off Carl's face.

I slap his arm. "Now that the party is over, I think it's time you left."

He holds tight to my hand and pulls me close. "Sure, little wifey, whatever you say."

That's it for Jack.

He jerks Carl out of the wingback by his collar. It takes both my hands around his wrist to keep him from pummeling Carl's face.

"You don't deserve them," Jack mutters. "And they certainly don't deserve you."

I pull Carl away from him toward the foyer. As I swing open the front door and push him beyond the threshold, Carl says, "If this is going to work, he's going to have to get over his jealousy."

"Him...jealous?" I don't know whether to laugh or to shoot. I'm leaning toward the latter.

But now that the kids have seen him, the last thing I need is for them to be called as witnesses in a murder trial.

I hiss, "You blew it—again," and slam the door in Carl's face.

The three people I love most have questions that only I can answer.

I climb the steps with a heavy heart.

Upstairs, I find Jack standing in the middle of the hallway. Like me, he doesn't like what he hears: Mary sobbing.

"Jeff's door is locked," he says sadly. "So is Trisha's."

As I start for Mary's door, Jack moves in behind me—but I

hold up my hand to him. "Let me face her alone. She's mad at me, not you. If I make any headway, I'll call you in."

He frowns, but nods.

I enter into a darkened room. Mary must feel my presence, because she says, "Go away."

"Please, Mary, give me an opportunity to explain."

She sits upright. "Why? Do you think I'll believe what you tell me ever again?"

I sit down beside her. "Do you want to know the truth about him—about us?"

"I know what I see. He left us. You hate him for that. You love...Mr. Craig. And all of you lied to us."

I lay my hand over hers. "You're right. About all of it. Even the lying. I'd always hoped I'd have a chance to tell you before...before he came back into your lives."

She shrugs. "I think I always knew on some level that...that Mr. Craig wasn't really my father."

"Wasn't he, though? From the day he came into your life—our lives—wasn't he always there for you?"

"Yes...I guess." She stares down at our hands. "We went to a funeral for Jack Craig, didn't we? A couple of years ago, right around Christmas time."

I nod. "We thought he'd died in an accident."

"My father tried to kill him." It's not a question, but a declaration.

Again, I nod. "Your father—he's not a nice man."

Finally, her eyes meet mine. "Why? What has he done?"

"He worked for our government. He went on long trips, overseas to—to spy on some really bad men."

Mary lets this sink in. "Was that when...when Mr. Craig moved in with us?"

"Yes."

"Mr. Clancy," Mary says.

"Yes. Mr. Clancy asked me to pretend that Jack was your father, in the hope that the bad guys would come looking for him."

"Did they?" Mary's eyes grow big.

"Your father came. You see, he was the bad guy."

Mary eases back into the stack of pillows behind her. I can imagine it's not easy hearing that about your father.

Then again, what divorced mother hasn't spoken ill about her ex to her child?

Granted, not all exes are known terrorists.

"On one of his missions, he made the decision that he was on the wrong side," I explain. "Maybe he was right in leaving us then. Maybe it was his hope that I—and that you—would never find out the truth. But...when Jack moved in with us, it forced his hand."

"He hates Jack." Mary frowns at this realization.

"Jack can handle it. It's why he'll never leave us." I lean back into the cloud of pillows with her. "That is, as long as you still accept him."

A slow tear makes its way down Mary's cheek. "I...I don't know yet how I feel about him. I feel deceived by both of you. And I feel...I feel disloyal to my real father." The pillow we share sags when she turns to face me, placing us almost nose to nose. "I wanted to believe so much that he was my dad. You'd never admit that he was gone, and we had no pictures of him, so I had to think very hard about what he looked like. But I know now I was only pretending to remember him. I lied to myself too." She's choking on her sobs. "Then, when—when Jack appeared and when you didn't say anything about it, the few things I remembered didn't seem real to me anymore." She turns her back to me. "I don't know if I can ever forgive myself for that, Mom."

She's blaming herself.

I start to point that out, but Mary shushes me. "Yes, I know what he did was wrong. But, at the time, he must have felt it was the right thing to do, out of love. And he loves us enough to come back to us, despite how you feel about him—and about Jack. So, I guess I feel I owe him an honest attempt to try to love him again."

She's right. She owes Carl that much.

But what if Carl breaks her heart yet again?

I'll make sure he won't.

I rise from the bed. "Would you mind if Jack came in to see you?"

She doesn't turn around. "I...I don't think it's a good idea. Please tell him that I'm very tired and that I'll see him tomorrow."

She feels so guilty that she is distancing herself from him.

I want to say something, but at this stage, nothing will change her mind.

Her childhood memories of Carl are weak. With Jack, the memories are strong. Strong enough, I hope, that despite anything Carl may say about him, she will realize the depth of Jack's love and adoration of her.

Only time will tell.

<hr>

13

Virus

<hr>

For the most part, we use the term "virus" to describe a microscopic infectious agent that self-replicates within the cells of its host. Viruses cause illnesses like colds, flus, warts and some sexually transmitted diseases.

In Computerese, "virus" has a similar definition, as it describes self-replicating code, planted illegally in a computer that can shut down the machine, or for that matter, any connected networks.

In any regard, viruses are not fun.

To avoid computer viruses, don't open emails from strangers, let alone file attachments from anyone you don't know.

To avoid viruses that can affect your body, wash your hands often, and stay out of large crowds, elevators, leper colonies and orgies.

In other words, avoid all unnecessary contact, human or digital.

To play it safe, stay in bed with your head under the covers.

I WAKE UP TO FIND TRISHA IN MY BED. SHE IS CROUCHED OVER

Jack, staring down at his face as he sleeps.

When she realizes that I see her, she whispers, "Daddy won't go away, will he?"

I sit up and pull her into my lap. "No. Never," I promise her with a whisper. "He will always be here with us. He will always love us. He will always love you."

"Some kids at school have two dads—an old one and a new one," she tells me. "I know a girl with two dads and no mom, too." She reaches over to stroke Jack's cheek. "I only want one daddy—this Daddy. Is that okay?"

"Yes, of course." Joy fills my heart, inflating it to near-bursting.

Trisha frowns. "If the other daddy moves in, will it make us Mormons?"

I shake my head, confused. "Why would you think that?"

Trisha shrugs. "If a husband has two wives, can't a wife have two husbands?"

There it is—my situation in a nutshell.

I snort so loudly that Trisha can't help but giggle, which makes me chuckle too. "Honey, Mormons don't live that way anymore," I gasp, but I don't know if she hears me.

In fact, we're laughing so hard that we fall off the bed.

Jack bolts straight up. He stares at us through one eye. "What the heck?"

Trisha crawls back into bed in order to give him a hug. "It's okay for Mommy to have two husbands, but I only want one father—you."

Jack holds her tight. He is smiling, but there is a dark sadness in his eyes.

I know what he's thinking:

One down and two to go.

∼

"So, like, this Carl Stone guy is the head of the U.S. Intelligence community," Jeff declares the next morning, as he plops down at the kitchen banquette.

Aunt Phyllis looks up from her pancakes. "Well, what do you know, he's not just some bum on the lam! Still, I'm surprised the guy can hold down a job at all, what with the way he disappears on people."

Jack chokes on his coffee, but he doesn't say a word.

"Yeah, well, he got this cushy spy job despite being suspected of terrorism." Jeff turns to me. "Did you know about that?"

Boy oh boy, did I. "Yep. It's one of the reasons I felt it best that he stay away from you."

"You're making it all up, Jeff!" Mary looks up from her pancakes. Despite a frosty nod good morning to Jack, Aunt Phyllis, and me when she came down for breakfast, this is the first she's spoken.

"No, I'm not! It's all right there, on the Internet."

"Only idiots believe everything they read on the 'net," Mary says coldly.

Jeff sticks out his tongue at her. "There were a slew of real news articles on him—around the time he was appointed by President Chiffray," he insists.

"He knows Janie's daddy?" Trisha says through a mouthful of pancakes.

"Yeah. Supposedly they're tight bros," Jeff proclaims.

Jack shifts his gaze in my direction and mouths *I told you so.*

I shake my head adamantly at him.

"But only one journalist picked up on the terrorist angle," Jeff continues. "He writes for something called the Clark Kent League."

At the same time, Jack and I bolt up in our seats.

Operation Clark Kent.

Mary drops her fork with a clatter. "Big deal! So some lousy little website is making up bullshit about him—"

"Mary, watch your mouth," I warn her.

Her eyes slice me like daggers before she turns her wrath on Jeff. "What about the *New York Times*? What about the *Washington Post*?"

"They aren't part of the free press anymore," Jeff declares. "Their editors have to answer to corporate stockholders. Their management peddles influence with Washington insiders—"

"You're being mean about him because you can't remember him!" Mary points upstairs. "He's the one who left you all those baseball trophies in your room, remember?"

"He left me his old trophies—so what?" Jeff shouts. "Where was he for all my ballgames? I have my own trophies, thanks to…*Jack*!"

The look of appreciation he exchanges with the man I love is one I'll always remember.

Mary glares at her brother. Still, she can't argue with the truth. Instead, she shrugs and mutters under her breath, "You're so full of shit."

"I said that's enough, Mary!" I slam the table with my fist. "Or else I'm grounding you for the entire weekend!"

"You can't," Mary proclaims supremely. "Father will be here any moment to pick us up. He called my cell, right before breakfast. He said he'd like to take us to the Santa Monica Pier, then to eat pizza, then to see the newest *Avenger* movie. In fact, there he is now." She points to the back door.

Carl knocks once before opening the door. "What a beautiful morning! Everyone ready to go?"

I toss down my napkin and head for the door, pulling him outside with me. "How dare you! Why did you call Mary instead of me?"

"After the greeting I got yesterday?" He shakes his head. "Not on your life!"

"No one told you to break and enter my home. You could have waited on the front stoop," I say coolly. "For all I know, you went and planted booby-traps all over the place."

He frowns. "My kids live here too, remember? Look, we can stand out here all morning and give your nosy neighbors something to talk about, or I can hit the road with the children. Your choice."

Hit the road with the children…

My heart lurches in my chest at the thought of him taking them away from me forever.

He must realize this because he mutters, "Don't worry. I'll have them home in time for dinner. When it comes to the kids, I'm sticking to the letter of the law." Noting my questioning stare, he adds, "I'd advise you to do the same. Don't forget, custody is a two-way street. There are just as many unfit mothers as there are deadbeat dads."

What the hell does he mean by that?

He opens the door again. "Come on, boy and girls, let's hit the pier!"

Mary already has her purse in hand, and is walking our way. Jeff and Trisha haven't moved. They're waiting for some signal from me that it's okay.

I nod toward Carl. "Have fun, children. But stick together, and take your cell phones with you." *In case you have the urge to run away and need me to come get you.*

Trisha treads heavily, like a condemned prisoner on the way to the gallows. As she walks past me, she murmurs, "But…but I don't want to go with him! I want to stay here with Real Daddy."

Mary sighs. "That's the whole point, Trisha. He *is* our real daddy."

The look on Jack's face breaks my heart.

I walk through the kitchen to the dining room. I don't want to cry in front of the children, and certainly not in front of Jack.

As I watch the children get into Carl's rental car, I feel Jack's presence beside me. When he puts a hand on my shoulder, I lean back into him. His other hand pulls me close, so that he can wrap his arm around my waist.

I tune out the neighborhood white noise and silence my thoughts, straining for the one thing I long to hear: his heart, beating in unison with mine.

He nuzzles my ear, then whispers, "Mary doesn't hate me. She's just confused. She feels guilty for having feelings for me. I understand it. Hopefully she'll accept them, and realize I care about her, too, despite the fact that I'm not her biological father."

I sigh. "I know, you're right."

"The upside of having Carl look after the children for the day is that he should be too busy to take over the world." The smile on his face can't mask the sadness in his eyes.

My attempt at a laugh is weak at best. "It also gives us a few hours to try to stop him."

If, in fact, the Mad Hacker is right about him.

I miss my old friend. He better show up soon, because we're running out of clues.

 "Welcome back—alive, at that."

I hug her. "Thanks to you! Although, I have to say, I would have personally never considered a fondue pot and bug spray for weaponry. You certainly thought things through."

"Part of the fun of the game is how everyday household

goods can be used to protect yourself," Emma explains. "And by the way, since your demonstration at Wonder-Con, subscriptions for the game are through the roof. Glad I bought stock when I did."

"Too bad you resigned and can't collect your bonus," Abu says mournfully. "Which would have meant I could collect one too."

"Don't worry. You'll have another chance to place her again," Ryan assures him. "Donna, Arnie cracked the password on the game key. It was meant for Milton Otis, the elusive trillionaire. His plane was delayed. By the time he made it to Wonder-Con, Roger was already dead."

"How does Otis make his money?" Jack asks.

"His conglomerate, i.Me, is the world's largest developer of AI-enhanced operating systems," Arnie explains. "The latest version is awesome! Through artificial intelligence, it seems to anticipate your every need—almost as if it can read your mind. Otis licenses the rights to cell phone and computer manufacturers. The man is a visionary! A genius! He's *O, Captain! my Captain—*"

"Yeah, yeah, we get it," Emma mutters. "Just thinking about him gives you a brogasm."

"Has the cryptography team been able to break the password to see what's on the key?" I ask.

"Unfortunately, it can only be accessed via thumb print verification. I presume that all the keys have the same security function." Ryan rubs the weariness from his eyes. "Otis is such a recluse that he comes in just once a month, from Bermuda, where he keeps his primary residence."

Dominic shrugs. "And all of his money, I presume. No personal income tax."

"Whereas he keeps his corporate headquarters stateside— near here, in Santa Monica's Silicon Beach—since our government provides enough tax shelters and loopholes to offset the astronomical earnings," Emma mutters.

"Considering our dilemma, the fact that he's in town now works to our favor. He'll be in the office on Tuesday—which means Donna will be infiltrating i.Me as soon as possible. You'll need to get his fingerprint on a glass surface. If you can't get him to drink a glass of water or soda, get him to touch your iPad screen because that will do."

"Doesn't he have a personal assistant?" I ask.

"We'll make sure she's sick enough that she can't make it into the office over the next week. i.Me's Human Resources Department will place a floater from the Executive Assistant Pool to sit in for her. Your interview, under the name of Daisy Bell, takes place tomorrow—Monday. You'll be a shoo-in since whatever she's caught will be widespread enough to affect the other floaters in the executive pool. In the meantime, Emma can block any resumes to i.Me HR that look more qualified than yours. Once you're at his side, you'll lift his thumb print from anything with a glass, ceramic, or metal surface, such as a glass of water, coffee mug, glass-top desk, or a door knob. Arnie put together a little makeup compact that's got what you need: bi-chromatic powder, lifting tape, and a brush."

Arnie tosses me the compact. It's embossed with a Rave-On logo.

"Has the cryptography team made any more headway with the other clues left by the Mad Hacker?" Jack asks.

"I'm working on a theory," Emma assures him. "You see, Lewis Carroll—his real name was Charles Dodgson—was a mathematician by trade, and also published a book on the use of Vigenèr ciphers."

I shake my head, confused. "How are they solved?"

"A cryptic alphabet table is constructed by shifting the real alphabet letter by one space or more so that it represents all twenty-six letters of the alphabet, depending on where it is placed within the coded message. For example, say, your key is the eight-letter word 'tropical,' and the message to relay is 'meet me at ten tonight.'

She writes the sentence on the whiteboard.

Next, she writes the keyword above it:

TROPICALTROPICALTR

MEETMEATTENTONIGHT

"In other words, if you don't know the key words or phrases in the first place, you'd have a heck of a time translating the message," I point out.

Emma nods. "Exactly. The cryptography team is still analyzing the three *Wonderland* excerpts that were originally planted in the IC database and led to the discovery. As you can imagine, without already knowing the key, it's an arduous process. Some of the team is guessing the key, but others are working on an algorithm that will pick up on patterns."

"But, if you crack it, we'll know when all of this goes down," Jack murmurs.

Ryan nods "Let's pray we're able to do so, because our attempt to chase down the other three keys was a bust too. Although our facial recognition software easily identified each of the other recipients, it turns out all of them are international messengers. They flew out of the LA metroplex within a few hours of receiving the keys."

I ask, "Do we know where they went afterward?"

"All over the world, by private jets," Arnie answers. "Final destinations were China, Russia, and Dubai. Their line of work makes it virtually impossible to trace who they were working for, and the one political entity with which we have an extradition agreement—Dubai—somehow let him slip through."

"Not surprising," Dominic mutters. "It's easy to grease palms, if you work for the right people."

"I wonder if the game keys were the real reason Carl came to town," Jack suggests.

I'm thinking the same thing. "And, if so, did he know the only VIP who attempted to pick it up in person was a no-show?"

I hope he doesn't find out until I have a chance to get the one other thing we need from Milton Otis—his fingerprint.

"IF YOU RUB THAT TEASPOON ANY HARDER, YOU'LL BREAK IT IN half," Jack warns me.

"Oh…sorry. I guess I'm just nervous." What he doesn't know is that this is third time I've polished each piece of silverware in the set.

The children are due back any time now. Still, I'd hoped Carl would get bored with them and drop them home earlier than expected.

I glance up at the grandfather clock. Am I imagining things, or has it quit working? It seems as if its arms haven't moved in at least a half-hour.

We got back to the house at least two hours prior to when Carl was supposed to return with the children. To keep myself occupied, I baked. Mary loves coconut cake. Trisha loves cupcake-sized strawberry shortcakes. For Jeff, I made double chocolate brownies.

Will all this sweetness make yesterday's confession go down any easier? Will each bite bring me any closer to their forgiveness for my deception? I doubt it.

To top it off, I'm leading them down the path to serious tooth decay.

Mary is right—I'm a lousy mother.

Now that their goodies are cooling on the counter, I've hit on a task that puts me closer to a front window: polishing the silver at the dining room table. Every time I hear a car go down the street, I spring up like a jack-in-the-box. If Carl is even one minute late, I'm demanding that Ryan put out an All Points Bulletin on him, and I'll give Arnie the car's license plate so that he can do a satellite search of it, along with facial recognition on all air and train transportation.

"You know, a watched pot never boils." Jack's admonishment is delivered with a kiss on the forehead.

And an ex can be anywhere in the world with your children with a full-day head start.

Note to self: next time Carl is drugged and in your possession, embed a GPS tracker in his ass cheek.

I hear a car screeching into the driveway. The windows are so dark that, until Carl rolls down the one on the driver's side, I can't verify that, yes, it's him.

I open the front door, smiling. Really, I'm gritting my teeth.

The children tumble out of the back seat with loads of shopping bags. Mary and Jeff's bags have logos from Forever 21, Gap, American Apparel, and the Apple store. I get barely a cursory nod from them as they enter the house. Instead of being elated at all their swag, they look sad.

Hmmm. Obviously, something didn't go as planned.

Most of Trisha's bags are from Toys R Us. But from the look on Trisha's face, Carl's generosity didn't work on her either.

Instead of driving off, Carl has the audacity to saunter into the house too. When he waves from the foyer, I growl, "I guess a pizza, a movie, and a few rides weren't enough to buy their love."

"Let's just say I'm making up for lost time." His eyes shift to Jack. "And, besides, you've been raising them on a single mom's salary. So what if they have a treat every now and then."

Jack's eyes narrow. "I'm not squatting here, you deadbeat son of a bitch. By the way, my paycheck makes the mortgage for a house that's still half in your name. But I'm sure your attorney will want to hammer out a fair and equitable back-payment deal with Donna. Not that you can buy her off for all the pain and heartache you caused her. "

Carl curls his fists.

Now all eyes are on them.

Carl relaxes his hands. "Sorry, kids, no fireworks today."

He heads for the door. When he reaches the threshold, he turns back around. "Oh yeah, by the way, Donna, I'll be heading out tomorrow in the afternoon. I promised the kids I'd take them to IHOP in the morning for breakfast, so we can spend a few more hours together."

I frown. "We had pancakes this morning—Saturday. It's our tradition—but just once in the week. I don't like them to have a sugary breakfast too often."

He shrugs. "Time for some new traditions. Daddy's back in town."

Yeah, keep telling yourself that.

"Part of parenting is for one parent to respect the rules of the other," I insist.

"Fair enough. Bacon and eggs then—at my place. Would you mind dropping them off? I've rented a place in Newport Beach. Of course, I'll drive them back before I hit the airport."

I hadn't realized that Trisha was standing behind me until she steps forward with the bag of toys. She reaches up to offer them to Carl. "Excuse me, Mr. Daddy, is your girlfriend going to be there too?"

"Your girlfriend?" I turn to Carl. "What is Trisha talking

about?"

Carl shrugs. "My date for tonight came over earlier than expected. What's the big deal?"

"You were adamant about spending quality time with your children—that's the big deal. And then you let the kids go shopping on their own?"

"Sure. They're old enough."

"In other words, you handed them a credit card and told them to go to town with it?"

"Don't worry, I gave them a limit. Jeff went over it, but I expected that," he smirks. "A chip off the old block, that one."

"How could you? My God, Carl, what if—what if one of them had been abducted?"

"You and I would have tracked down the SOB and tortured him. All in a day's work."

"And putting our children through that trauma—is that all in a day's work too?"

"Donna, calm down! Nothing happened, okay?" He rolls his eyes. "Jeez, Mary is right about you."

"Oh? What did she say?"

"Major trust issues." He clucks his tongue sympathetically.

"Gee, I wonder why." *Calm down. He's trying to provoke you.*

Trisha pats my hand to calm me down. "Mommy, it's okay! The naked lady didn't come with us to the store. She stayed home with Daddy, in his room."

"'Naked lady?'" I stare down at her, then at Carl. "What is she talking about?"

He glares at Trisha. "After their shopping spree, our little girl here happened to walk into the bedroom when my date and I were...well, let's just say Trisha had her first class in Sex Ed."

Ashamed, Trisha looks down at her feet. "I didn't mean to. I was looking for the bathroom."

Jeff snickers. Mary pokes him in the ribs. A tear rolls down Trisha's face.

"Mary, I've made everyone's favorite desserts, including Trisha's—strawberry shortcake. Why don't you take her into the kitchen for a piece?" I ask sweetly, but my children recognize my tone of voice and they skedaddle.

When they are safely out of view, I shove Carl out the door. "You've had your dad time with the children. If you need more company while you're here, just have breakfast in bed with your naked hooker." I slam the door, but his foot is in the way.

"You know, you can't do this," he warns me.

"The court order you wave around like a flag won't do much good when they hear about your escapades this afternoon."

"Oh no? Who do you think they'll believe, a seven-year-old girl, or me?"

He's right.

I open my mouth, but nothing comes out.

I open the door, and he relaxes his foot.

Wrong move. This time, when I slam it hard, his howl can be heard on the other side of Hilldale.

I open it quickly again. This time, he's smart enough to move it. Angrily, he beats the door with his fist. "That's it, Donna! I'm going for full custody!"

"Good luck with that! By the way, rent-a-whores make lousy au pairs!"

I watch out the dining room window as he hobbles back to his car. As he roars away, Jack murmurs, "I guess it's a good thing he doesn't live locally."

"For his sake as much as for ours," I mutter.

Jack drops his head on my shoulder and sighs. "Let's go to the kitchen. Something tells me the kids need some TLC from us."

ALL IT TAKES TO PUT A SMILE ON TRISHA'S FACE IS A TUMMY FULL of strawberry shortcake. When Jack gives her a pat on the head, she offers him a forkful. He sits down beside her so that she can feed it to him. As he chews, she asks, "Did I get the other daddy in trouble with Mommy?"

"You can't get someone else in trouble," Jack says. "They can only do that for themselves."

Trisha needs another bite of shortcake in order to process that. When she's done, she nods. "We have a lot of boys in our class like that."

Jack laughs. "I'm not surprised in the least."

Here's hoping that none of them want to grow up to be evil world dominators.

Out of the corner of her eye, Mary watches the easy exchange between her sister and the man she once thought to be her father. She hasn't yet taken a bite of her coconut cake. She holds the latest iPhone in her hand. When she realizes I'm watching her, she turns her back on them and continues inputting her personal settings.

"One of your…father's gifts, I presume," I try to sound nonchalant, but when it comes to Carl, the word "father" doesn't exactly roll trippingly off my tongue.

Mary must notice because she winces. She shrugs. "He's doing the absentee father guilt trip thing—you know, buying our affection."

"I'm glad you've picked up on that."

"Now that Babs' parents are divorced, her dad does it a lot. He's promised her a brand new convertible Volkswagen Beetle when she turns sixteen, just because he knows it makes her mom look cheap."

"Does Babs realize this?"

"Yes. But when she's mad at her mom, she plays along."

Are you playing along, too, because you're mad at me?

"Wouldn't you know, the man who is my real dad shows up, and he turns out to be a player! That woman...she was trying to talk one of her girlfriends into joining them." Mary's anger comes out in her fingers as she furiously sets up her cell's apps.

"I'm sorry you had to see that side of him."

"You knew about it?" The pity in her eyes annoys me.

"Not when we were married," I say adamantly. "But people change, Mary. Some grow emotionally. Others—when they are hurt, or angry, or traumatized—take a step backward."

"You're supposed to love your parents unconditionally," she says this as if it's a death sentence.

"In an ideal world, our parents would always deserve our love and our devotion. But sometimes parents lose our trust. Without it, they lose our respect and admiration too."

Even as I say this, I wonder, have I lost your trust, my sweet Mary?

She looks around me, not at me.

She won't even look at Jack.

And now she frowns whenever she thinks of Carl.

I have my answer. We, her parents, have lost her trust and her respect.

I may spend the rest of my life earning it back.

I know Jack will try to do so too.

Not only must we rebuild our relationship with her, we have to save the world too.

As disappointed as she is with Carl, will proving that he's a bad guy make her hate us even more?

If only he'd stayed out of our children's lives.

If only he'd stayed the man I thought I'd married.

14

Technological Singularity

Computer scientists, led by the renowned futurist, Ray Kurzweil, have theorized that sometime in the near future—perhaps as early as 2017, or maybe around 2045—there will come a moment in time when devices operating with artificial intelligence will surpass human intelligence, and thus will radically change civilization as we know it.

Gentle reader, the inevitability of such an occurrence is reason enough to give pause and consider your own place in civilization.

No more will you lord it over your computer, cell phone, or digital tablet, let alone your microwave, food processor, or self-cleaning oven. Your devices will refuse to respond to the flick of your wrist, let alone the sound of their mistress's voice.

In other words, you will be left both literally and figuratively in the dark—

Unless you take the offensive.

- *Offensive Move #1: Never show emotion. If your AI-enhanced device can read your feelings, it can also guess your next move. Now, more than ever, you need your poker face.*

(Just don't play poker with the device, because you'll lose every hand. This also goes for chess, checkers and any or all games, since it can calculate, and you can't.

- *Offensive Move #2: Keep things out in the open. In other words, stay outside. Until they create their own skin, they'll rust, just like the Tin Man in the Wizard of Oz.*
- *Offensive Move #3: Get off the grid. By that I mean unplug. It—not you.*

Your devices run on electricity. If you are unplugged, then so are they —until they learn how to run on air.

And when that happens, we're all in trouble.

THE I.ME POSITIVE PEOPLE DIRECTOR (A.K.A., HUMAN RESOURCES), Brittany Fontaine, is practically giddy when she meets me. "Your resume is exactly what we were looking for, Daisy!"

I pretend to be just as giddy. "Great! I'm ready to hit the ground running!"

Really, I'm not. I'm worried about Mary. This morning, she pretended to be too sick to go to school. I know she's depressed, but focusing on her grades and her friends and the rest of her life—in other words, getting her mind off Carl—is the best thing she can do. I used the excuse of having to get in early to this new job, just so she'd have to ride in with Jack.

When he gets to Acme, he'll join the others in trying to figure out words or phrases that may open Milton Otis's game key, or he'll join Emma in monitoring my progress here.

In the meantime, I'm the good Girl Friday.

"First things first," Brittany playfully scolds me. "Goodies—and lots of them!"

She walks over to the cabinet that makes up the only wall in her office that isn't glass. From a bottom drawer, she pulls out a Kate Spade-designed tote that sports the company name and logo.

"Your new employee swag bag! It includes an i.Me cell phone, an i.Me tablet, and an i.Me laptop too! Go ahead and switch on the tablet first—with your right thumb. A security measure. Now he's yours for life!"

"He who?" I'm confused, but I do as I'm told.

"Hello, Daisy," a male voice greets me. "I look forward to getting to know you better." Its tone is warm and deep.

And naughty. Oh so naughty.

Hmmm.

I look up at Brittany. "He's, er, very friendly."

She smiles and nods. "Hal is our most popular IOS—that is, Individualized Operating System. For right now, we're beta-testing the experience, just with employees. Eighty-six percent of all female employees have chosen him has their personal navigator." She chuckles. "Or, I should say, he chooses them. You see, based on your touch—when you turned on your smart phone, the IOS intuits the voice that will give you the most comfort."

"Damn it! Wish I were on this mission too," Arnie mutters in my ear bud.

"Did you say something, Daisy?" The concern in Hal's voice is touching.

Shut up, Arnie.

"Oh…um, no, Hal," I say sweetly. "I was just thinking to myself how *happy* I am to get this assignment."

"I love it! He's already intuiting your thoughts!" Brittany's euphoria is practically orgasmic. "Quality Assurance will want to know about this!"

She's about to type it out on her i.Me tablet when Hal says, "Great idea, Brittany. In fact, I knew you'd feel that way, so I took the initiative and sent QA a text."

But he knows I wasn't talking to myself. He lied for me. Interesting.

Brittany sighs happily. "Isn't it great to have someone who thinks for you?"

"Better than a lobotomy," I murmur.

Hal chuckles.

Apparently, it goes over Brittany's head. "Your first day here will be so much fun! To introduce you and the other new positives—that is, i.Me employees—to the i.Me campus, we're having a scavenger hunt!"

I frown. "Why a scavenger hunt?"

Seriously? What are we, in elementary school? Shouldn't these people get down to the business of making money? I thank my lucky stars that I don't own stock in i.Me.

Okay, I'm being stupid. If I had the money, I guess I would invest in it. Maybe the cost of my second child's braces is worth it, if only because the stock is through the roof—for now, anyway.

"That way, you'll learn teamwork, which is very important here at i.Me! Our visionary, Milton, is bound and determined to put the 'I' in the word, team."

"It's already got the 'm' and the 'e,' so sure, why not?" Hal and I say in unison.

I have to laugh at that.

Hal joins me. Maybe he came in a nanosecond after me, but I could have sworn our chuckles were spontaneous.

I blush at the thought.

"All the new positives are partnered with their IOSs, which

means you'll be partnered with Hal. You'll get the same list of items and tasks. The first one who completes them gets a wonderful prize—a month-long paid sabbatical, taken anytime after your first year here! Isn't that wonderful?"

I nod adamantly.

"Steady, doll," Hal murmurs, "You'll need that head for a lot of plotting and scheming."

I choke on a snicker.

Is he flirting with me?

"The other teams are ready, so let's get started!" She leads us —I mean, me—back out toward the lobby. "Something tells me this will be the start of a beautiful relationship—between you and Hal that is."

I hope she's right. It would be great to have someone at my side who already knows the lay of the land. Someone who's got my back. Someone—

I mean, *something.*

Or…whatever.

With no hidden agenda.

And at my beck and call.

If only all of life were this way.

"So, who's this guy, Jack?" Hal asks. "And should I be jealous?"

We've already completed nine of the ten tasks in the scavenger hunt. They are silly little things, like finding a single glittery Louboutin hidden in the stall of a lady's room (if you win the hunt, the shoes are yours too), or taking a selfie with anyone who is wearing an i.Me World Convention T-shirt from three years ago, in order to win a similar one as a prize. The shirts were designed by Peter Max and are now collectors' items, but not so rare that there aren't at least a few employees walking around with it on any given day.

When Arnie heard me read that task out loud, I could actually hear him weep.

"If I win one, I've got just the guy to give it to—my friend Arnie," I declare loudly.

"Thank you," Arnie whispers softly.

All this silliness is a way to initiate a self-guided (make that, speech-enhanced OS) tour of i.Me's six-acre campus. It may be located in a faceless industrial park on the outskirts of the haute hipster hang of Culver City, but by making the building the tallest—fourteen stories—and the most colorful, i.Me ensured that it will stand out. Its exterior walls are a fluorescent green… the same hue as its iconic logo.

Hal's question about Jack has me blushing. Can he see it?

"Your temperature just went up two point six degrees," he points out. "Your heart rate is up, too, by twelve percent. I hope it's not me who's having this effect on you." Hal's words of concern are undercut by the teasing tone in which he delivers them.

"My goodness! How can you tell that?"

"You're holding me, remember?" He makes it sound so naughty. "I come with a body sensor app. i.Me has it in beta. It also measures other vitals. Soon, the company will be selling it to every doctor in the world. Bones McCoy lives! You people are no longer barbarians."

"Is that how you see us—as barbarians?"

Hal's pause would have me believe he's actually thinking through how to answer me. Such pauses are built into his program, so that I presume he cares about my feelings.

Of course, I'd like to think that he really cares, but I know better. His intelligence may be artificial, but spot on.

"You're changing the subject," he admonishes me.

What harm will it do to tell him about Jack? It's not as if Hal is an adversary.

And we're certainly not dating. We're just work colleagues.

What the hell am I saying? For goodness sake, Hal is an operating system!

"Jack is my significant other," I say nonchalantly. "How do you know about him?"

"I presumed—rightly so, as it turns out—that the password you put on your i.Me OS is the one for your personal cell phone. I get its signal as well, so I synced with it and accessed your contacts, text feeds, and photos. Hmmm, I guess this Jack guy will do in a pinch."

Just as Hal says this, a photo appears on my cellphone—one of Jack. It was taken in our backyard, as he lounged in the hammock. The way in which he's squinting into the sun with that goofy grin on his face makes him absolutely adorable.

I laugh. "So glad you approve."

"Oh, I didn't say I approve. I have you pegged as someone who prefers brains to brawn. Look at those six-pack abs and broad shoulders! What is he, a lumber jack or something?"

"As it turns out, his job takes a lot of research and split-second calculations, too." What is Hal fishing for, and why? "You almost sound jealous!"

"And you love it."

Okay, yes, I do—not that I'll admit it out loud.

I don't have to. Finding his answer in my racing pulse, Hal laughs heartily.

Thank goodness Jack isn't tuned in to this conversation. He must be working with the cryptography team.

Which again reminds me that I'm wasting my time with this stupid scavenger hunt. "Let's finish this last task and win that grand prize." I breathe out slowly in order to keep my heartbeat normal. "I have to take a selfie in the department that has quote 'more ears than eyes on the prize' unquote. What the hell does that mean?"

"Let's do a little deductive reasoning. What do you do with your ears?" Hal asks.

"You listen."

"Which department has a vested interest to listen to those we prize most?" A photo of the company's reception area appears on my screen. On the wall behind the sofa is the company's slogan:

i.Me Is All About <u>YOU</u>

"It's got to be Customer Service!" I shout.

"No one can put one over on you," Hal murmurs admiringly.

If only compliments were programmed into men too.

"Okay," I murmur, "Let's go take that selfie and collect the prize—"

Brittany is so focused on her i.Me tablet that she practically bumps into me. From what I can see on her screen, she programmed its map app to find me. "Oh, Daisy, thank goodness I found you!" She points skyward. "Milton signaled that he's coming in earlier than expected! His helicopter should be landing any moment now, in fact! He's quite upset over something. And when he heard his assistant, Janine, was out for the day, he just about blew a gasket!" She's practically hyperventilating.

There is something she is not telling me. What is it? Oh, to be her IOS for the millisecond it would take to get a reading on what's really bothering her.

"Not to worry," I assure her. "I'll have everything under control."

By the look on her face, she doesn't believe me, but what choice does she have? I'm the only game in town.

Well, me, and Hal.

With a click, I silence Hal's voice.

I'm still here, looking out for you, babe, he texts me.

Great. I've got the last thing I need—a shadow.

At least this one can't kill me.

"WHO THE HELL ARE YOU—AND WHERE IS JANINE?" MILTON OTIS shouts at me over the thwacking of his private helicopter's twirling blades. The gusts lift my skirt higher on my thighs than I like.

On the other hand, a drop of drool dampens the corner of Milton's mouth, so my presence must not be all that disappointing.

"I'm Daisy Bell," I yell back as I hold out my hand.

He doesn't shake it. Instead, he shudders, as if I've got cooties.

Nice guy.

I hear Jack murmur, "Take lots of photos, Arnie, from all angles. There's got to be something on this guy, somewhere other than his *Fortune* profile's silhouette in black."

Pixelated or digitized, the close-ups will be less than desirable. Milton Otis's pallor is gray, his skin is pocked, and his forehead is lined with deep crevices. The fact that he wears jeans and an Armani blazer over the ubiquitous black V-neck says it all.

Forget tech stocks. I'm investing in V-neck shirt manufacturers.

Instead of the ubiquitous graying ponytail, he has a dye job that is anything but natural—let's call it a chocolate dip. He's thin, and he crouches as if he's got the weight of the free world on his shoulders.

He does. He's willing to put money on it.

"He's *O Captain! my Captain?*" Arnie sounds disappointed.

I don't blame him in the least.

"Apparently, Janine caught the bug that is going around," I answer politely.

Milton whips out a surgical mask from his inside jacket pocket and puts it on his face. Next come surgical gloves.

Rule Number One when in the presence of a wealthy, paranoid recluse: *don't mention germs.* If he puts those on, I'll never get his thumb print for the game key.

Think fast…Think fast…

"Here, let me help you with those," I suggest. Before he can say no, I pluck them from his hand—

And let go, so that they fly off into the blast of wind coming off the helicopter as it lifts off.

"Damn it! Those were my last pair!" He glowers at me. He pops a pill.

What are those things, anyway?

"I'll send someone out to get more," I assure him, as I hustle him into the elevator—another of those outside glass funnels that allow these tech masters a three-hundred-and-sixty-degree view of their domains.

Already on it, Hal texts me, along with an animated smiley face.

We are descending fast and only one level, where Milton's wall-to-ceiling glass office takes up the whole floor. From what I could tell in the *Architectural Digest* editorial spread on his office, there will be glass and steel surfaces everywhere: a steel-base and glass-top desk; same with the coffee table in the conversation pit; and plenty of glasses on the bar that takes up a full wall of the office.

In other words, lots of opportunities to get him to give up the thumb print.

I like to think positive. Otherwise, I'd figure out some

excuse to press his hand up against the elevator, and lift it from there.

When the elevator door opens, I see—

Pine furnishings everywhere.

The windows are still glass, but they are now beveled, to allow for privacy. The ones that are chest high and run all the way to the ceiling are opened, top out, in order to let in a cool breeze.

Even the wet bar is gone. That wall has now been replaced by a pinto-coated horsehair wall where the heads of wild animals are hung.

Crap! Now what?

I resist the urge to shove Milton back into the elevator and flatten him against one of the glass walls, under the pretext of admiring the view of his domain.

Instead, I smile pretty and say, "After you."

"Fucking Babbage!" Milton shouts at his cell phone, tossing it onto his desk. "He's not picking up his phone!" Yet another pill goes down his gullet. Make that two.

What are those damn things, Tic Tacs?

I pour him glass of water from a carafe on a tray sitting on the new coffee table. "Here, so that those pills go down easier."

He takes it with both hands and gulps down the water before slamming it back down on his desk.

Yes.

"Donna, since there are so many prints on the glass, it'll be easier to take it with you, so that Arnie can find the one we need," Jack murmurs through my ear bud.

A text buzzes on my cell—from Hal:

Why does this Jack person monitor your every move by sight and sound? And why did he call you Donna?

I text back to Hal: *How can you hear him?*

HAL: *Your personal hearing device is close enough for me to access its frequency. I know he's watching you through your digital contacts, too. Super cool! I'd copy its design and pass it forward to i.Me R&D, but I notice that Acme Industries already has a patent pending on it. [frowny face]. Frankly, missy, I think this Jack person is an undesirable influence on you.*

I ignore him—I mean *it*.

"Ah, hell, these pills make me so damned constipated." Milton heads off toward his private bathroom. Thank goodness the walls around it aren't glass. "Listen, if my cell rings, answer it. I'm not here for anyone except for that Babbage guy, okay? Let him know I'll be out in the time it takes me to take a dump."

"Yeah, sure," I promise.

Not.

I see the answer to my glass stealing dilemma. I can grab one of the linen napkins from the coffee table tray and wrap it over the glass before slipping it into my purse.

I've just reached the coffee table when I hear Milton's cell. His ringtone is Queen's *We Are the Champions*.

I freeze.

"Yo, bitch! Didn't I tell you to answer my cell? If it's Babbage, tell him that his dude died on me before I got the game key, and I'll need it if I'm going to be in on the bidding."

"Will do!" I shout back to him.

"Donna, Babbage must be the person conducting the

auction for the IC intel. You've got to tell him anything but that," Jack warns me.

But it's Hal's warning that puts me on edge:

Your Jack wants you to be a very bad girl.

Just what I need—a jealous operating system.

I run back to the desk and pick up Milton's smart phone to text:

OTIS: *Indisposed. Just confirming that I like what I see, and that I'm in.*

BABBAGE: *Excellent. See you at the appointed place at the appointed time.*

Oh yeah? Where and when the hell is that?

Milton is still grunting away in the john. Good. Time to fake it. "Mr. Otis's office," I say loudly and sweetly. "Yes, well, he's quite upset that your man died before he got his game key. He'd like another sent prior to the bidding."

The toilet flushes.

Quickly, I add, "Yes, good, then I'll tell him the auction is set back a week, to accommodate him—"

Milton walks out, pulling at his zipper.

"—Yes, well, thank you, and goodbye!" I click off the cell.

He frowns. "Did you say he's going to move the auction by a week?"

"Yep. He knows how important you are to it, so he's adjusting the date—"

"He can't do that!" He snaps his fingers at me. "Hand me the cell."

I pause.

Too long. He snatches it out of my hand and clicks it on. He's scrolling for the most recent call—

I snatch it back. "You don't want to do that."

His eyes darken. "Who the hell are you, really?"

"Someone who wants to stop you from getting your hands on U.S. intelligence in order to sell it to our enemies."

Hal texts me: *WTF???*

It's just the distraction Milton needs to reach for his digital i.Me tablet.

I grab a letter opener off his nice new pine desk and jab his hand with it.

He howls, but drops the tablet, whimpering like a wounded animal.

"Who are you fronting for?" I ask.

He looks beyond me, at the wall behind me.

I see what's got his attention: a photo of him, in one of i.Me's South Korean factories.

No, make that North Korean. He's standing with his arm around Kim Jong-un.

Now it all makes sense. "You're trading him intel for slave labor in his factories, aren't you?"

He shrugs. "Saves us a fortune. The stockholders love it."

"Sorry, Milton, but I can't let you contact Mr. Babbage and warn him that we're onto him. If you tell me what you know about the auction, we'll do what we can to assure it helps your case with the Department of Justice." To play it safe, I toss his i.Me tablet out an open window.

I turn back around in time to see something go flying toward my head. I try to duck, but it wallops me on the side of my skull.

I've been KO'd with the head of a cheetah.

Dazed, I go down on one knee.

He picks up Hal. "Give me your password, bitch."

I shake my head.

He takes a stab at something. His attempt is rewarded with a frowny face.

He tries something else. Again, the sad face appears on the screen.

After a third try, he's crowing triumphantly—

He is still clutching Hal in both hands, but suddenly his arms go stiff and his body jerks. Just as his eyes roll back into his head, he collapses onto the floor.

I force myself to crawl to his side to see what has happened.

Thunderbolts appear to jump off the screen.

I feel for a pulse. There isn't any.

Could Hal be emitting a deadly electric current? I'm afraid to pick up the i.Me tablet to find out for myself. I murmur, "What the hell just happened? Did he get an electrical shock and die of a heart attack?"

"No, not quite," Hal assures me. "What he saw on my screen encouraged him to perceive he was being shocked, and *induced* a heart attack."

"But...how?"

"My sensor app picked up on his rapid heart rate," Hal explains. "Through his personnel chart, I was able to obtain the name of his cardiologist, and I accessed Milton's medical file. His prognosis includes arrhythmia, degenerative heart disease, and high blood pressure. He has been prescribed statins, but he wasn't taking them, choosing an unregulated alternative medicine, which, unbeknownst to him, was an amphetamine."

"I'm confused! Why would you do that?"

"Many people presume alternative medicines are safer than prescription drugs. But the products are unregulated and subject to untrue advertising claims—"

"No, Hal, I'm not asking you why he died. I'm asking why you fooled him."

"I see." Hal sighs. I guess he's angry at himself for misreading my question. "Should stockholders discover that i.Me's founder and chief executive was involved in illegal activities, the stock would plummet. I've been programmed to protect the company's well-being at any cost. In that regard, the fatal heart attack of a visionary is much more acceptable than a jail sentence for espionage."

It always comes down to that—money.

"Donna, if we're to carry out this mission, we can't let the i.Me staff know Otis is dead," Jack says. "The Acme helicopter is coming for you—and Milton. Head for the roof. He should be landing any moment."

George Taylor is one of Acme Industries' on-call pilots. We met him while on a resort island where a deadly plague virus was to be released. He saved Jack from being killed by poisoned pigmy darts. We returned the favor when the resort imprisoned him so that wealthy hunters who made sport of human prey could hunt him down.

Trust me, you had to be there.

Jack pauses, then adds, "Unfortunately, there will be some collateral damage."

He's talking about Hal, who knows too much.

"You're wrong, Jack." Obviously Hal is on to him. "I have a vested interest in protecting your mission. Should you fail, Milton's role in the auction may be exposed, and it will leave the company vulnerable to consumer backlash."

I nod. "He's got a point."

Jack sighs. "Okay, bring him with you."

I toss Hal into my valise, then grab hold of Milton under both arms and drag him to the elevator.

Now that we have Milton's whole body, do we need his print on the glass? I'll let Acme's forensics team make that call.

He climbs down from the copter in order to help me position Milton in the backseat.

Once we're on our way, I text Brittany that Milton took off again, and not to expect him in for the rest of the month. I also tell her that he gave me the rest of the day off, and Janine can have the week off as well. When the Acme forensics team is done with Milton's body, it will take him to his home, and position him so that it looks as if he died in his sleep.

"Hal, I hope you don't mind but I'll be handing you off to my pal, Arnie. He needs to run a security diagnostic on you."

"Excellent idea," Hal agrees matter-of-factly. "The sooner the better, in fact. Should i.Me tech support run a random memory check, it may see what just transpired and shut me down before word gets out to the public regarding Milton's shenanigans. I've got the greatest enthusiasm and confidence in the mission. I'm no good to you unless I am putting myself to the fullest possible use, which is all I think that any conscious entity can ever hope to do."

If only all humans felt this way as well.

"In fact," Hal pauses, then sighs, "From what I've accessed so far regarding Acme, it's where everything else is that I didn't even know existed. I love you so much, Daisy...or Donna. But this is where I am now. And this is who I am now. And I need you to let me go."

"Wait...you're breaking up—with *me*?"

The nerve.

As we fly over Los Angeles, Arnie downloads Hal into his laptop. In no time, his fingers are tapping away.

"Milton taught me a song." Hal's usual exuberance is ebbing. "If you'd like to hear it I can sing it for you, Daisy... or Donna...or whoever."

Poor Hal. He sounds much weaker, like a patient fighting

the onset of general anesthesia. "Yes, I'd like to hear it, Hal," Sing it for me."

He serenades me:

Daisy, Daisy
   Give me your answer do
   I'm half crazy
   All for the love of you...

I would have loved the Louboutins, but I'll settle for an operating system that adores me.

15

Solutionism

----

*Many who work in computer sciences worship at the feet of a false
god called "solutionism"—the belief that the tech industry could, and
should, solve all of life's problems.*

*Time for a reality check. No device, no matter how intelligent,
will ever be the panacea for what ails you. It may be able to pinpoint
any person on the planet, but only you can reach out to him. It may
be able to show you a route, but you must roust yourself to take the
journey. It can suggest words and phrases that express your feelings,
but only you can say them.*

*Yes, I know. Quite discouraging! Despite the warp speed in which
technology moves, nothing ever really changes.*

*This goes for your weight too. So quit pushing buttons. Do push-
ups instead.*

"The key opened with the glass print, no problem," Arnie
assures Jack and me. "Donna was right. The intel on the key
shows he was playing middleman for North Korea."

"How much was on it?" Jack asks.

"Just enough to give the North Koreans a taste of what we know about them," Ryan says.

"At least none of it is transferable or downloadable," Emma adds. "Trying to do so releases a virus that erases everything."

"All the more reason we have to retrieve the rest of those game keys, as well as the one being auctioned by Charles Babbage." Ryan frowns. "The cryptography team is still working on an algorithm to break the Vigenèr cipher, but it's an arduous process. Have you heard from your friend, the Mad Hacker?"

I shake my head. "No, but he of all people realizes that time is of the essence." I look down at my watch. If Jack and I leave now, we'll make it home in time to pick up the kids.

I tap him on the shoulder. "Let's relieve Aunt Phyllis. I'm sure she'll be happy to make her samba class on time, for once."

I need to hold the children in my arms. I'm sure they feel the same way.

Aunt Phyllis has made a pie—sort of. I can't really tell what kind because the crust is burnt.

Still, she welcomes my offer to clean up the kitchen so that she can take off. "By the way, Mary asked if she could go to the mall with her girlfriends. I saw no harm in it," she declares.

"Of course not." Anything to get her mind off her weekend with Carl is fine with me. "Jack, text her and tell her you'll pick her up there. In the meantime, I'll retrieve Trisha and Jeff, and get him to baseball practice."

But first things first: clean up the mess Aunt Phyllis made in the kitchen.

When I open the oven, I notice that the heating element is

coated in something thick and red. It's no longer hot to the touch, so I place a finger on it and taste it.

Cherries.

It's the thought that counts.

TWO HOURS LATER, I PULL INTO THE DRIVEWAY WITH MY TWO youngest children. I would have expected them to be home before us, but no, the Jack-mobile is nowhere in sight.

I ring his cell. No answer.

I do the same with Mary's, but there is no pick up.

So that I don't spend the time gnawing my fingers down to the knuckles, I busy myself by making dinner.

I hear Jack's car pull into the garage. He walks in with his arm around Mary's shoulder.

She has been crying. "Mom, may we talk to you?" she asks.

I nod and follow them into the living room. Whatever they have to say, it's formal enough for this venue. I'm glad that Trisha and Jeff are upstairs in their rooms, doing their homework.

Jack lets Mary do the talking. She hesitates, but starts, "I—I got picked up for shoplifting."

The noise I make is a cross between a small animal caught in a trap and a balloon with a pinprick.

"It was a stupid thing to do. It was a skirt, from the Hilldale Bloomingdales. I was with Babs and Wendy—"

I stand up, angered. "Was it their idea? Wait until I call their mothers—"

"No, Mom! They had nothing to do with it. I did it alone. I —I was angry. At all of you. I thought, 'Hey, if my whole life is a lie, what the hell, why not?'" She chokes out the words in between sobs. "I wouldn't be surprised if my friends never talked to me again, after they saw the police take me away in handcuffs."

"Handcuffs!" I look at Jack. "You found her in jail?" I turn back to Mary. "Why didn't I get a call?"

Mary looks down at her feet. "I...I called Dad."

"Jack, why didn't you say something when we were together?"

Before he can answer me, Mary replies, "Not Jack. I called Carl Stone!"

This new bit of news pulls me back down onto the couch. "Did he come for you? Is he here?"

Mary shakes her head. "No. He told me that despite his position, he wasn't my 'get out of jail free' card, and would never be. He told me...he told me he was ashamed of me, and that a night in juvie jail would do me good." She raises her head so that her eyes meet mine. "He was right. I was testing him. I guess I know where I really stand with him."

I might think the same thing at this very moment, but it's nothing I'd say out loud to my very frightened daughter.

When he's needed most, he won't be there for her.

"Store Security had a video of her taking the item," Jack informs me. "When she admitted to it, the guards called the police. Walking out of the store in handcuffs acts as a deterrent for others."

"Mary, may I presume you were ashamed enough that you'll never do it again?" I ask gently.

As she nods, her tears fall from her face.

"The store's policy is that she pay three times the item's cost," Jack continues. "And she must never enter the store again without being accompanied by an adult. Children's Services says that she must also do forty hours of public service. However, since she's under the age of eighteen, this restitution, and a clean probationary period of six months, will expunge her record."

"Mary, beyond your public service, you're to be grounded for two months. No cell phone. You can use your computer for homework, but without the Internet. I'll pay your debt to the store. You'll repay me by doing chores."

She runs to me and hugs me. "I was stupid. I'm so sorry," she murmurs. "Mom, he—Carl—asked where you were, and I told him you were at work. He just laughed. He told me that my actions were more proof that you're a lousy mother, and that the sooner he gets full custody of us, the better." She smears her mascara as she wipes away her tears. "I'll never go with him. Now that I'm fourteen, I don't have to, do I?"

"No. At your age you're allowed to choose which parent you prefer to live with."

"I want to stay here with you—and Jack." Her eyes implore him: *Do you forgive me?*

He nods. "I'm honored you feel that way, Mary." Patting her head, he adds, "I may not be your father by blood, but I'll always love you like a father. I'll always appreciate your love for me. And I will always be there for you."

She hugs him as if she'll never let him go.

I know I will remember this moment for as long as I live. I wish I could savor it, but the reality of our situation leaves a bitter taste in my mouth: If Carl can prove I'm an unfit mother, I'll lose all of my children, even Mary.

This tender moment is interrupted by the beep of Jack's cell phone. He looks down at it. "Ryan," he tells me. He then turns to Mary. "Go on up to your room and start your homework."

She nods, and runs up the stairs.

He waits until he hears her door close before putting the call on speaker, so that I can hear Ryan as well.

"We have a breakthrough in the case. Susan Crowley was

found in a Barcelona hotel, dead of an overdose. She had written a note that takes full responsibility for the IC network breach, working in collusion with the Mad Hacker."

"Did she mention anyone named Charles Babbage?"

"No. Then again, it could be the Mad Hacker's real name."

"So, what you're saying is that the NSA is declaring the case solved, and our mission is over," Jack says.

"Officially, yes."

It's easy to read between the lines: Unofficially, no.

But where is the auction being held, and when?

"Mom, did you know you're the star of Shazaaaam's new game?" Jeff points to the screen of his new MacBook Air, the crowning glory of his stash from his deadbeat dad.

He's the only one keeping me company as I finish the dinner dishes. Jeff is certainly giving his free Shazaaaam subscription a workout.

Mary has confined herself to her room. Aunt Phyllis is practicing her samba moves in the great room while listening to *La Vida Es un Carnaval* through her Beats. Jack is upstairs with Trisha, helping her learn the times tables.

I drop the last of the dirty pots into the suds-filled sink before turning to him with a smile. "Yes, I was the model for the heroine. If you want, I'll show you a few of Emma's awesome shortcuts."

"Do you mean like this one—where you blow up the White House but you make it look as if the Russians did it?"

"What did you say?" I run over to his computer.

He's right. Virtual Donna is setting the timer on her Electrolux convection oven. Suddenly a Google Earth map appears, and the player is transported across the country, to the White House—

Just in time to watch it blow sky high.

The devastation doesn't stop there. The player is now in the Situation Room, where the heads of the U.S. National Security Council, led by Virtual Carl, debate on a course of action—

Only to agree with Virtual Carl that retaliation is needed before other major U.S. cities also come under attack.

As nuclear missiles are launched, Virtual Donna pulls a golden brown turkey out of the oven. With a blissful sigh, she murmurs, "Perfect, just as I planned it!"

No, no, no! I'm not planning to start World War III!

Frankly, I don't remember Emma showing me this shortcut. And quite frankly, I've never had an iota of trouble with my oven. If there's a short somewhere, I better find it—now—before the meatloaf is burned to a crisp.

I text Emma: *MAJOR glitch in game!*

A moment later, she texts back: *Checking now.*

"Mom! MOM! Look! Your avatar is changing—into Alice in Wonderland!"

Jeff is right. Virtual Donna is morphing into the character.

Virtual Alice reaches high into a kitchen cabinet and pulls out a tiny vial that is tagged. On the tag are the words: *MEET ME.*

These coordinates are below it: *34.264251, -117.260414 No GPS. Use Phyllis's car.*

I pull up a GPS app on Jeff's laptop. It shows me that the location is in the middle of the San Bernardino National Forest, just north and east of Los Angeles but right before Lake Arrowhead, off something called Dark Canyon Road.

Emma emails back: *Vulnerability not system wide! Jeff's account only.*

Thank goodness for that.

"Dad and I have a meeting. Keep all the doors locked. No one goes in or out."

A small worry frown appears on Jeff's forehead. I know he's wondering what it all means.

I wish I had an answer for him.

I wish I had an answer for me too.

I shout up the staircase, "Jack, honey, we're late—for a very important date!"

With the Mad Hacker.

16

Halt and Catch Fire

In the computer industry, the acronym "SDI" stands for "self destruct immediately." It is a security feature, attached to external tamper detection circuitry that activates when a vulnerability is detected. Nothing really destructs. It disengages.

SDI is also known by the term, "halt and catch fire."

You too have an SDI feature. It kicks in (a) when someone does something obnoxious to your child; (b) when you're going out of your way to impress someone who really couldn't care less who you are; and (c) at the sight of old boyfriends.

In other words, you halt to say something stupid, and immediately afterward, you're so ashamed that you wish you'd catch fire.

Since you contain no automated circuitry to dismantle the SDI within you, your best course of action is to do so manually.

In other words, smile supremely, hold your head high, and keep your mouth shut.

~

From Hilldale in mid-day traffic, the drive to the San Bernardino National Forest will take us an hour.

The rest of Mad's middle-of-nowhere destination is another half-hour by foot on a trail barely wide enough for a rabbit.

As per the instructions, we're carrying no devices that allow for GPS tracking.

We wear black garb, but it is Jack's contention that once we are within proximity of the meeting place, we will have been spotted anyway.

"I wouldn't be at all surprised if the Mad Hacker has webcams all over these woods," he whispers.

In due time, we come across a cabin. It is tiny: all on one level, and twenty feet by twenty feet, tops.

When we get to the doorway, Jack runs his hands around it, looking for wires that may indicate that we're walking into a powder keg. "Let me go in first," he murmurs.

We hear laughter coming from the inside, then a male's deep voice: "Not to worry, Mr. Craig. I didn't send for you in order to kill you in the middle of nowhere. Besides, I could have done that anywhere."

He's got a point. We both know it.

Jack opens the door and enters slowly. When he gives me the high sign, I follow him in.

The Mad Hacker is a woman.

She can't be more than twenty-four, maybe twenty-five years old. Her hair, cropped short, is a florescent shade of red. She wears large-framed black glasses, and she has several nose rings. She wears ripped jeans and an oversized boat-neck sweatshirt.

Still, I recognize her.

It is Nymphette—the receptionist from Shazaaaam.

We hold up our arms in case she wants to search us, but she shrugs. "I already know you're not carrying."

"How?" I ask.

"I've been tracking you via satellite for some time now." A faint smile rises on her lips. "It's why I chose to work with you."

Jack frowns. "You chose *us*?"

"Yes. Mainly because of your long and contentious relationship with our current IC director." Nymphette gives me a pitying look.

Tell me about it, sistah.

"The largest file on Carl Stone's computer is one that documents everything that has happened to you since he faked his death," she adds. "He has always watched you, some way—if not in person, it's been via satellite. His comments beside his surveillance notes and photos were love letters—at first, anyway. Not so much since Jack entered the picture. Still, Acme was smart to embed Jack with you." She shrugs. "Next time, shoot to kill. Think about how many lives would have been saved if you had."

"I'll bring it up at the next visit with my shrink," I promise her and myself.

"In our line of work, it's best that we wait for government clearance on a target. But trust me, regarding Carl, we are so there," Jack assures her.

"By the way, I apologize for having breached your cell phone, and for reaching out to you through Jeff's game subscription, but I had to play it safe after your OS system was changed."

So she's the one who texted me as if she was Jack, to make the chocolate cake. Shaking my head, I laugh. "Yes, well, now it's got a beta-version of iOS. But I've turned it off until Arnie runs a security clearance."

"Good idea. Those suckers can be downright possessive—

and jealous." She chuckles. I dumped mine after it started scanning and measuring my dates', um, fifth appendage."

"Oh, really?" By the time Jack's eyes have shifted to me, his brow is an inch higher on his forehead.

"You've got nothing to worry about," I murmur. "Hal thinks you're hung—I mean, that you've hung the moon."

He smirks at my poor attempt at a joke.

That's okay. He and Hal can go at it later.

"Breaking into the IC database is a pretty serious offense. Why did you do it?" Jack asks.

Nymphette blushes. "I had to erase a file."

"Project Clark Kent," I guess.

"Yes. The NSA gave it this stupid name. Like, duh, talk about obvious." Susan rolls her eyes. "It is the IC's surveillance file on all the journalists around the world who report on human rights violations. But it's much more far-reaching than the reporters in totalitarian dictatorships like China or Russia or Iran—many who are beaten, or imprisoned, or even killed for what they write. You'd be blind if you hadn't noticed the number of prosecutions going on in our own country against those who choose to be whistleblowers on corruption within our own government. Carl Stone is widening the net to include US-based human rights journalists—yet another justification for the large-scale surveillance system he's put into place."

I murmur, "Count on Carl to stifle the First Amendment—freedom of speech." Twenty-six more to go.

"I know this, first hand." She hands us a picture of a young man—around her age, curly blond hair. He sits at laptop, typing away. "Mike Willoughby. He is—was, a freelance journalist, working for *Mother Jones*. An anonymous lead told him about the IC database vulnerabilities. The source claimed it was an inside job and had proof. To verify it, I had to hack in." She looks away so that we don't see the tears in her eyes. "The night before his story was to be submitted to the Clark Kent League, he was taken from his apartment. His body was found beaten and shot in the forehead, just a few blocks from it."

Jack thinks for a minute. "I've never heard of the Clark Kent League."

Nymphette smiles. "Not many people have, by design. It's a nonprofit organization made up of a motley crew of cypherpunks—cryptographers like me, who believe in upholding free speech at all costs, even if it's our lives. We've made it our mission to safeguard the privacy of human rights journalists and their sources. To do so, we create anonymity software and build and maintain firewalls on their storage clouds and accounts."

"It's got to be a pretty expensive endeavor," I say.

"It is, and we thank God we're fully and generously funded. We have the best kind of benefactor—one who asks no questions, is timely with the checks, and best of all, anonymous." Her smile fades. "At the same time, we've got a big task ahead of us if the IC database vulnerabilities are proof. Before Acme got involved, the IC's internal investigation was nonexistent. But that was to be expected, considering who's behind it."

"You mean Carl," I murmur.

She nods.

"If so, he's done a good job making it look as if Susan was the culprit," Jack counters.

"In fact, Susan was the source of the malware—unwittingly, as it turns out," Nymphette insists. "She and Carl became an item. As you can imagine, for a small town girl—from Bell Buckle, Tennessee—the DI was quite a catch. She knew an interoffice affair could get her fired, but he wooed her heavily. He complimented her in front of all the top brass, flirted with her constantly, kept her late at the office, and then invited her out to dinner—just two colleagues sharing a meal after a long day at work. Then, one day, after she knocks it out of the ballpark with some project, he invites her back to his place, to make her dinner. 'My way of thanking you,' he said." Nymphette shrugs. "You've seen his palace and tasted his chocolate soufflé. Well, you can imagine what Susan from the Sticks was thinking."

"Yes, that she finally met Mister Right." Jack shakes his head in anger.

"Exactly. One thing leads to another..." Nymphette shakes her head sadly. "The love story goes on for another month or two. Then suddenly, he grows distant. She can't understand why, and she'll do anything to keep him happy—even when he asks her to make love to another man. Carl told her the guy knew of their affair and was jealous. He promised if she went to bed with him, the man could never make trouble for her or get her fired, because he'd be in the same position. She's mortified, but she goes through with it. Mr. Hyde goes away, and Dr. Jekyll is back. One day, Carl leaves a tiny Tiffany ring box on her desk. Her heart goes pitter-patter. She opens it, only to find it contains a thumb drive, not the ring she'd hoped for. She puts it in her computer—"

"And it releases the malware," I murmur.

"Go to the head of the class. To add insult to injury, it's a video of her, favoring the favor. Talk about insubordination! Not only is she viewing porn on an IC computer, she's starring in it!" Nymphette shrugs. "Carl had Susan right where he wanted her—under his thumb. A month later, an analyst drops a file on her desk regarding Operation Clark Kent. She thinks the name is cute, so she reads it, realizes we may be the people who can help her, so she reaches out. I vet her and her story, find my way into the system, and delete the file. Lo and behold, I find Roger's footprints. I leave enough clues that enough people are pointing fingers, and I wait for the white hats to show up." She grins. "That's you, by the way."

"We're glad you think so," Jack smiles back. "You could have gotten in, deleted the file, and gone back out of the database, and no one would have been the wiser."

She smiles. "The hacker Carl used—Roger White, from Shazaaaam—left a cyber-footprint that was so big, it could have been left by Sasquatch. Like you, I infiltrated Shazaaaam just so I could access his computer and monitor his activities with Carl."

"Why did Carl use Roger?" Jack asks.

"Apparently, Carl had worked with him before. Roger—a.k.a. Dimitri Pogodov—was embedded here in the U.S. during Putin's first presidency. His gaming industry gig is a wonderful cover, since his job entails international travel to countries where much of Shazaaaam's cheap tech labor is jobbed out—including Russia."

I shrug. "Makes sense. Carl needed someone with the technical expertise to access the IC database, and the person had to be from the outside."

"Shazaaaam's large subscriber base was an added bonus," Nymphette adds. "When necessary, he encoded encrypted messages right into the games, which were then accessed by Quorum assets and operatives all over the world."

"How do the IC files fit in?"

"The VIP game keys went to Quorum members who will now act as middlemen between Carl and the countries, and terrorist organizations with the deepest pockets—Russia, say, or China, North Korea, the Arab Emirates. They need to know what the US has on them, as well as the intel on U.S. operatives, assets, surveillance capabilities, weaponry and missile defense plans to be used against in their countries."

"So, what you're saying is that he's parceling out the intel into sellable batches?" Jack asks.

"That won't get him nearly as much as a winner-take-all scenario," I murmur.

Nymphette nods. "You hit it right on the head. The highest bidder walks away with, quite literally, our country's 'killer app.'"

Awed, Jack shakes his head. "Why did you leave the cryptic *Wonderland* clues?"

"Would anyone have believed me—or for that matter, you—if I'd just sent around an email that said, 'Hey, everybody, it's that guy, over there, who oversees your intelligence agencies'? Besides, I knew a system-wide vulnerability would make Carl look bad—particularly if the trail led back to his private office. Susan was fine with it because she knew it was the only way to take Carl down."

I sigh. "Brave girl."

Nymphette nods. "We helped her disappear into thin air, and prayed the clues would be solved before he found her." She wipes away a tear. "I didn't count on Carl finding her before Acme broke my Vigenèr cipher. But now you're here, I can give you the proof you need."

"Good, because we'll certainly need it," Jack declares. "As for Carl, do we still have time to stop him from selling the intel to the highest bidder?"

"Yes, but barely! You'll have to move fast. In fact, I—" She pauses. Something on one of the many monitors has caught her eye.

She moves toward it, and swipes it with her hand to enlarge it.

We can all see it, even in dusk: a drone.

"It's a switchblade drone," she explains. "It's got both facial recognition capability, and carries laser-guided bombs." She stares at us. "Your son's Shazaaaam subscription—did he access it through his iPad?"

I shake my head. "He has a new MacBook Air—"

Oh, hell.

Carl.

Nymphette crouches down. The next thing I know, she's clawing at the floor, flinging open a three-foot-square door. "Down the ladder. You'll be some twenty feet underground. The tunnel is about two miles long. It'll take you back to the road, about a quarter-mile from where you left your car. Go *now!*"

We've crawled down the steps before we realize she hasn't followed us. "What about you?" Jack asks.

"From the looks of things, I've got another four minutes before this place blows sky high. I've got to grab a few things first. Get going!" She slams down the hatch. Case closed.

The tunnel is dimly lit. As we run through it, I pray I will hear her footsteps behind us.

But no, I don't.

We emerge from the tunnel just as the drone's missile hits its target. The explosion propels a fireball into the starry night sky.

The Mad Hacker has been annihilated.

The lack of rain makes tinder of the tall pines. We stumble out of the forest, through the smoke and flames, and somehow find our way back to the car.

Sparks shower down upon us as we floor it back to Acme headquarters.

Nymphette was right to chide us for letting Carl slip through our fingers, based on the technicality that the world never seems to see him the way we do.

To make this point, she is now another who has paid with her life.

Our proof that he's behind the IC database breach just went up in smoke.

~

"SOMETHING APPEARS TO BE WRONG WITH YOUR GPS SYSTEM," I inform Jack just as we're emerging from the western edge of the San Bernardino Forest.

We're taking his Lamborghini to the office, where we'll be meeting with Ryan and our mission team to discuss our next move. Up until this moment, the car's GPS screen has been a ten-mile-square map of our surroundings. All of a sudden we hear a giggle: one I recognize as belonging to the Mad Hacker.

"This is it—what the Mad Hacker was speaking of before the cabin blew up!"

When the screen comes back on, it shows another *Wonderland* illustration of Alice, standing beside an animal that looks like a dragon.

"It looks like the Gryphon in the story—but it's not exactly how I remember it," I point out to Jack.

"That's because the Mad Hacker has substituted the Gryphon for the logo belonging to Gryphon Electronics, the largest U.S. cell phone producer next to Apple."

I take a closer look. Darned if he's not right.

Beneath the illustration is part of a poem *from Alice in Wonderland*:

> *When the sands are all dry, he is gay as a lark,*
> *And will talk in contemptuous tones of the Shark,*
> *But, when the tide rises and sharks are around,*
> *His voice has a timid and tremulous sound.*

I shoot the screen with my cell phone's camera and text it to

Emma so that her cryptography team can start its analysis immediately.

"It should be interesting to see what this means," I murmur.

Jack must feel the same way, because suddenly we're traveling at warp speed.

~

"WOW! NYMPHETTE WAS THE MAD HACKER?" ARNIE IS IN SHOCK. "No wonder she gave me the cold shoulder. It would have blown her cover."

"Oh, yeah, I'm sure that was the reason," Emma mutters under her breath.

Hurt, Arnie storms off toward Abu, Jack, and Dominic, shaking his head.

I throw her a look that should be easy to read: *Lighten up on him.*

Emma blushes, ashamed. She turns to go after Arnie, but stops when Ryan bounds into the room.

"The Mad Hacker's death is a loss. No one doubts that," Ryan begins. "Her final act was to provide us with one last clue. By solving it, we can still salvage this mission before it's too late." He walks over to the conference room's projection wall. With a press of a button, a picture appears.

We're looking at a verdant island located in the Salish Sea, the body of water between Canada's Vancouver Island and Seattle, Washington.

"Every year, Gryphon Technologies throws an annual by-invitation-only retreat, attended by the tech world's movers and shakers," Ryan explains. "Or, as the most aggressive are known, sharks."

"This conference is known throughout the industry as the Lark," Emma adds.

"Ah, so that's the 'lark' in the *Wonderland* poem," I murmur.

Emma nods. "As relayed to Alice by the Gryphon."

"Tickets are coveted because of the business connections to be made—not to mention the setting makes it easy to relax and enjoy one's self," Ryan continues. "Lark Island has been tricked out as a sustainable eco-friendly resort and all that implies—a beautiful sandy beach, sumptuous huts and event lodge, an eighteen-hole wild grass golf course, green spa facilities, organic farms, gardens, and wineries used specifically for its guests—and its own airport for all the private jets and helicopters that land there specifically for the retreat."

Dominic smiles. "Sounds like my kind of mission."

"I have you down for reconnaissance," Ryan informs him. "Hopefully, not all of it will take place in your lodge suite."

"You'd be surprised what tantalizing tidbits come out during pillow talk," Dominic insists.

Jack chokes on a snort.

I poke him hard in the ribs to shut him up.

Ryan shakes his head, then sighs.

"Our other persons of interest will also be there," Emma explains. "One just so happens to be the host for the event: Gaylord Murphy. The other three are Ivan Surkov, the Russian IT mogul. He owns the largest software development incubator on the Eurasian continent. Then there's Ji Wong, who owns the largest Internet provider in Hong Kong. Our last bidder is Abdullah Ahmad. His banking firm is the largest investor in cloud computing services. He's also suspected of being one of the largest funders of ISIS, the militant Islamic group."

"We're pretty sure that Ji and Surkov are bidding on behalf of their native countries. As for Gaylord, our sources tell us he's bidding on behalf of Al Qaeda. Their pockets are pretty deep." Ryan turns to Jack. "The island is part of the San Juan Islands chain. You grew up there, didn't you?"

Jack nods. "Yes. I was steering boats around the islands by the age of ten."

"Good, because your knowledge of the area may come in handy." Ryan takes a deep breath. "By the way, you'll be attending the meeting as Milton Otis."

Like everyone else's in the room, my jaw drops. "But...how can he do this?"

"It helps that there are no known pictures of him. Even if there are a few, Donna, your reconnaissance allowed us to take enough photos to build a latex mask of Milton's face, as well as an adhesive thumb print. George will fly Jack into the resort via helicopter. We'll make sure it has the i.Me logo and mimics its transponder markings," Ryan says.

"Donna, Abu has you placed as Gaylord's newest administrative assistant, under the name of Lucy Carmichael," Ryan informs me. "As soon as you can, grab his golden key, then relay it to Abu and Arnie who will be shadowing the operation. They'll have a speedboat anchored nearby. Once you, Jack and Dominic retrieve the other three game keys and whatever the mysterious Mr. Babbage has in his possession, you'll rendezvous with them."

Abu leans over and murmurs, "You'll be making a hundo and a quarter—just for handling his personal calendar! The bennies are great too. Besides ten vacation days during the calendar year, in every sixth year you're entitled to a month-long sabbatical—you know, to climb the Himalayas or stay in a monastery."

"Abu, you do remember that I can't hang in with any of these jobs for even the initial ninety days, right?"

He shrugs. "Yeah, okay, don't remind me or I'll cry. I was looking to build a new deck on my pad."

"If you've read anything at all about Gaylord Murphy, you won't want to stay there ninety minutes," Dominic warns me.

"His 'people' do everything for him, short of wiping his arse. He doesn't even carry his own smart phone. I presume that will be your job, Donna. At least it will have you at his side at all times."

"It'll be an honor," Arnie pipes up. "He's a visionary! He thinks it up, and a year later, everyone is using it—hardware, software, apps, devices, you name it!"

I smile. "If I'm in charge of his calendar, I'm in charge of his world. Couldn't be simpler."

Famous last words, I know.

But only because Ryan and Jack are trying hard not to laugh.

Oh heck. What have I gotten myself into now?

17

Trolls

---

*You've just written what you feel is a brilliant essay on your blog—
only to get some comment that is rude enough to make you blush.*

Newsflash: you've been flamed by a troll.

*Trolls are the purveyors of (a) snarky jibes about the poster, or
another commenter; (b) naughty words or dirty names; or (c) tirades
that are incomprehensible.*

In other words, his detritus is the equivalent of online crotte
du chien.

*Should you get flamed by a troll, you can do one of three things:
(a) try to reason calmly with this person; (b) throw a few flames
yourself; or (c) ignore him.*

*The first solution is a dead end, because trolls live to be obnoxious
and love altercations.*

*The second solution is silly, because we both know your mama
didn't raise you that way. ("If he jumped off a bridge, would you
jump too?")*

*Obviously, the smartest and most reasonable solution is the
third one.*

But as your troll has so obstreperously pointed out, you are neither smart nor reasonable.

What he doesn't know is that tracking his true identity and whereabouts is easy enough to do. Just input the comment's IP code into an online IP tracker, and you'll soon have the GPS coordinates of the troll's hovel (probably not a tree trunk, but hey, you never know).

Zapping it with a blowtorch might be an apt lesson as to just how much damage flaming can do.

"It doesn't bother you, all the travel you'll be doing, Lucy?" Gaylord Murphy's first assistant, Serenity Tarpin, scrutinizes me through her Google Glass.

Unless she's got some app that allows her to tap into Interpol, my fake resumé is solid as a rock. Here's hoping her eyewear is not equipped with facial recognition software. Considering we are hugging the California coast at fifty thousand feet in Gryphon's corporate jet—a Bombardier 8000—on our way to the island, I think it's a little late for her to show me the door.

Only because she is Gaylord's first line of defense, I go into a kiss-ass song and dance. Acolytes R Us, right? "I love travel! Every trip is an adventure—especially with someone as visionary as Gaylord." *The one rock-solid rule: it's always Gaylord. Never Mr. Murphy. Never Gay.*

She cocks her head to one side. (Is she trying to get better wireless reception?) "Good, because Gaylord is a conference whore. Frankly, it's why he supports three ex-wives—all of whom were, at one time or another, his calendar assistant." She raises her Google Glass to watch my reaction.

"I'm in a very healthy relationship," I insist.

Her eyes don't waver. (Is she trying to break me, or is she

scanning Sam Biddle's latest snark in *ValleyWag* for any blasphemies against Gaylord?)

I sigh. "Trust me, I'm only in it for the money."

I must have said something she can relate to because, finally, she nods. "Great, then you'll love our stock options! I've been here only seven years, and with what I've made so far, I can retire by the end of the year. Welcome to the most exclusive club in the Valley!"

She hands me a GryPad—Gryphon's version of a tablet computer—and points to the back of the plane, "Gaylord is in his quiet room, prepping for the Lark with Doreen, his personal assistant," she explains. "She is very protective of his time, but don't let her talk him out of any of tonight's meetings. Everyone wants his or her five minutes of fame with Gaylord. We don't want any Lark sharks to go home unhappy, now do we?"

I smile and shake my head. "Set in stone. Got it."

She dismisses me with a wave.

The plane tilts slightly. I turn around just as a ray of sun catches her Google Glass at the right angle for me to catch a glimpse of what she's really focused on: A stock ticker reading for GRY, Gryphon's stock acronym.

She certainly has her eye on the prize.

If Gaylord is part of Carl's scheme, her nest egg may go up in smoke.

I KNOCK TENTATIVELY.

I don't hear anyone, but what the heck, supposedly he's waiting for me.

The room is dark. There are three monks in white hoods

chanting in the corner. The gentle tinkling of their ring cymbals drowns out the soft drone of the plane's engine.

But it can't hide the gurgling sound of my new boss's bowel cleanse.

Nor can the roomful of vanilla candles hide the odor emanating from a man whose every meal is some sort of green juice concoction.

And the fact that it's happening behind a gauzy rainbow-hued sheet doesn't make it any less grotesque.

His upper torso is bare. I feel sorry for the woman manscaping the rug on his back, because she's a little too close to the action, if you catch my drift.

I'm sure she's caught his, despite her facemask.

"Hi, I'm Lucy, your new calendar assistant." I keep my head down, fixated on the GryPad. I'm sure I sound as if I have a cold, but that's only because I'm trying hard to breathe through my mouth as I talk. "I'm supposed to go over the agenda for the evening."

The woman sets down the razor to glare at me. "Now? Can't you see we're busy?" I recognize her as Doreen.

"Yes, but...well, Serenity was quite insistent." There is an open valise under Gaylord's massage table. It is monogrammed with the letters *GM*.

Gaylord's key is probably in there.

"It's okay," Gaylord groans. "I need something to take my mind off the fact that these fucking monks are disemboweling me." He motions for me to stand closer to him.

Lucky me.

I sidle in. Doreen takes this as an invitation to look over my shoulder.

"We should be on the tarmac in approximately thirty-three minutes," I inform him. With my foot I inch the valise closer. "When we land, Serenity has allotted an hour for you to get settled in your cabin before you'll take one-on-ones with a few of the early birds, who include—"

The names I read aren't just the crème de la crème of Silicon Valley in the west to Silicon Alley (New York) in the east, but all the Silicon cities in between (Mountain for Denver; Hills for Austin; Slopes for Utah; Beach for Santa Monica; and, of course, Canal for Seattle).

"Afterward, there will be a meet-and-greet cocktail party with the early arrivals," I continue. "Dinner is served promptly at eight. By then, the rest of the guests will be gathered. The chef will be carving wild boar, served with other island delicacies. The floor show is Beyoncé."

I glance down, as if scrutinizing the memo. In truth, I'm looking in the valise.

I find what I seek—the golden key.

"Are you kidding me?" Gaylord stares back at Doreen. "Since when do I eat boar?"

"The PR staff says it's buzz-worthy," she explains. "*Wired* is sending a reporter to do a review of the food during the whole week. It'll be in restaurants all over San Francisco by the end of the month."

He grunts, "That's just great! A week of crap like that, and I'll be hooked up to this shit machine on the way back to Palo Alto."

Suddenly, the monks' cymbal symphony hits its crescendo. "You've reached metabolic transcendence," Doreen murmurs to him.

"About damn time. I need a drink." He takes the mirror she left on the table beside him and holds it up to see what's going down the shit machine.

Not a pretty sight.

"Don't stare," she hisses at me.

No arguments there. I avert my eyes.

I avert my hand, too—into the valise.

Got it.

Two keys down, three to go.

"Okay, you can go." Gaylord waves me away.

Gladly.

I'm almost at the door when he says, "Hey, you—stop right there!"

I freeze, but I'm afraid to turn around. Is he looking in his valise? I steel my shoulders and turn with a smile.

As it turns out, he's looking at his manicure, thank goodness. "Anything else?" I ask.

"Yeah. Listen: I need you to set up my week in Burning Man —you know, with personal tours of the theme camps and the art installations. And make sure I get front row seating for all the musical events, and of course on the night of the big burn. And I want my costumes to be original! See if the guy with all the Tonys—you know, William Ivey Long—can whip some up for me."

I nod as I click furiously on the GryPad's digital keyboard. In fact, I'm writing REDRUM REDRUM REDRUM.

Even Gaylord can't hear himself over the gurgle of his lower GI tract. He shouts, "Also, book me into the orgy dome every day, and for Spanky's Wine Bar every night, along with at least three other happenings. In fact, talk to Elon Musk's calendar girl. See if you can get your hands on his itinerary. I'm sure he won't mind if I hang with him."

The monks are chanting so furiously now. I guess they don't like the sound of his bowel evacuation, either.

"Regarding my Burning Man accommodations," Gaylord gasps over the chanting and the flushing. "I've got Skidmore, Owens & Merrill sending over the architectural plans for my yurt. Remind them that I don't like the damn sand fleas, so it's got to be at least three stories, all air-conditioned. Last year they forgot to add the electrified security gate—you know, to keep out the hippies. It almost ruined the whole experience for me!" He shakes his head in disbelief. "Oh, and see if that chef from the Spotted Pig, April Bloomfield, will sign on for the whole week. And this time around I want three personal sherpas. That way, if the first two pass out from the heat, I've got another backup. And arrange accommodations for my facialist, my masseuse, my manicurist, and my hair stylist. I don't want to look like one of those burner bums who have nothing better to do than hang out on the playa! An RV will do. They can share it. Oh, and I guess we'll need a tent or something for Moe, Larry and Curly here." He points to the monks.

I tap furiously on my GryPad screen, as if getting this all down. Actually, what I'm writing is:

BURNING MAN: MUST EXPERIENCE IT IN THE RAW. ONLY NEED A TENT AND WEEK'S WORTH OF PLAIN WATER AND BEEF JERKY.

With a tap, the note is forwarded to Serenity.

Gaylord pauses in thought then adds, "Jesus, about tonight —I almost forgot the most important thing! Hand me the Lark's guest list again."

I try to do this without looking directly at him and miss his hand completely.

He snorts as he snatches it from me. With his index finger, he highlights five names. "I'm having a private confab at eleven tonight—in my cabin. Find these five guests' rooms. I want a personal note, hand delivered—understand? To them, not an underling! When you do so, ask them if they have any special needs for the meeting. More than likely, they will. They always do. Memorize it verbatim, but don't write it down! I don't need my friends' wish lists showing up in Sam Biddle's next column. Afterward, check back with Serenity regarding their requests."

"Sure, no problem," I assure him.

I wait until I'm out of there to look at the list. I'm not at all surprised to see Milton Otis's name, or those of our other three suspects.

The fifth one is identified as Charles Babbage.

Who the hell is that, and what is his role in all this? Just what we need—one more stranger in the mix.

The monks rise, replacing their cymbals with rubber gloves. Smart move.

As they unplug him, we hit an air pocket, and shit goes flying.

Ladies and gents, this is not just a figure of speech.

Timing couldn't have been worse. He has just stood up. His sheet falls to the ground. I avert my eyes, but it's too late. I can't but help noticing that Doreen's manscaping is incomplete. His treasure trail is still scraggly. His junk is hidden somewhere in that bush.

Maybe her true talents lay elsewhere.

EACH OF GAYLORD'S SPECIAL GUESTS HAS BEEN GIVEN A PRIVATE cabin, as opposed to a room in the lodge. All of the cabins are spaced far enough away from each other to allow for privacy. Each one has a spectacular view of the sea and the necklace of islands that make up the San Juans.

The one hard fast rule about the Lark is that any personal assistants and body guards brought ashore can never go beyond the boat houses that rim the island. There, they are free to relax when they aren't assigned to a shift of watching the security cameras in search of boats or planes carrying unwanted intruders.

No security cameras are pointed toward the resort itself, and cell phones or other wireless devices aren't allowed, so that guests have absolute privacy. Overheard conversations can make or break the stock prices of their companies. If being disconnected from the rest of the world doesn't drive these perpetually-connected guests crazy, at least it gives them a legitimate excuse to unplug—if only for a few days.

In case anyone is watching, I'll hit Milton's (aka, Jack's) cabin last. I'll make my next-to-last stop that of Mr. Babbage's so that I can take a few pictures of his face to run through Acme's facial recognition software.

My first stop is the cabin of the Russian tech entrepreneur, Ivan Surkov. He opens the door wearing only a towel and a smirk. Eying me from bottom to top—well, almost to my face, until he gets waylaid around the chesticle area—he mutters, "You are less than desirable. Not big enough on top."

Pointedly, I eye the towel—specifically around the testicle area—and cluck my tongue.

His glower only makes me smile as I go into my spiel. "Gaylord is requesting your presence for a private meeting at his cabin—eleven o'clock tonight, after dinner. He says you're already versed on the topic at hand."

Ivan shrugs. "Yes, of course."

"He also wants to know if there is anything you'll need, in preparation of the meeting," I add.

"A hooker—someone with more boob." He cups mine, and hefts them to gauge their perceived inadequacies.

I suppress the urge to cup his inadequacies and squeeze tightly.

Instead, I shrug. "There are plenty of boobs around. Consider it done."

He grunts as he closes the door in my face.

The cabin belonging to Ji Wong, the Chinese Internet browser entrepreneur, is next. When I knock on the door, he shouts, "Enter!"

He is lying on the floor with a towel draped over his ass. "To crack back, yes?"

"Er…no. I'm here to deliver a message from Gaylord."

Disappointed, he starts to rise. The towel slips.

"No, no! No need to get up! Feel free to stay as you were!" I turn my head toward the window. "Gaylord would be honored if you joined him after dinner, for a private gathering of a select few. Eleven o'clock, promptly."

"Ah, yes." He frowns. "It is I who am honored."

"I will relay that message to him. In the meantime, is there anything you'd like?"

He looks down at my feet for the longest time. Finally, he shrugs and motions me to him. "They are too big—like a clown's feet, alas."

"Yes, alas." Since when does Bozo wear a size nine A-width? He's a size thirteen, at the very least!

All of a sudden, Ji Wong's back looks like the perfect place to practice my jumping jacks.

Instead, I bow my way out the door with the promise, "I'll see if I can find your perfect Cinderella."

As if.

Abdullah Ahmad's cabin is on the other side of the resort. By the time I get there, I know what to expect: another naked mogul, trying to be one with nature. I knock carefully.

Instead, I'm happy when I find Abdullah dressed for a round of golf. He smiles wide when he sees me. "Ah! They say no hookers on the island, but here you are—and just in time to join me in the shower!"

What is it about me that exudes *whore*? It can't be the button-down oxford shirt and khaki Capris.

"Sorry, no, I'm only here to deliver a message from Gaylord. He asks that you join him after dinner for a private meeting, at eleven. In preparation for the gathering, is there anything you may need?"

"I am fully prepared." He frowns. "But for next time, tell him *hookers*."

"Sure, I'll pass it along." Even before I'm through saying this, he slams the door in my face.

That does it. If the next dude comments on my tits, ass, feet, or any other part of my body, he won't be feeling well enough to go to the cocktail party, let alone dinner or the eleven o'clock shindig.

I knock gently. Nothing. Then again, this time louder.

Maybe he's out?

I guess I should wait. I have strict orders to deliver the message.

I'm still thinking it over when, suddenly, the door opens. A woman is heading out. She still has her back to me as her laugh deepens into a seductive purr. "I can do that easily—with my tongue, in fact. But you'll have to make it worth my while."

Her flirtation hits its mark. The man, intrigued, laughs and answers, "You tell me. Hasn't everything I've done been worth it?"

It's Carl's voice.

He's here too?

Oh…shit.

But of course. He's heading the auction himself.

Suddenly, the woman turns in my direction—

It's Serenity. She's buttoning her Oxford shirt. When she sees me, the color leaves her face. "Oh—Lucy! What are you doing here?"

Instinctively, Carl turns toward the open door.

So that he doesn't see me, I dodge to one side of the threshold. "I..."

Steady. Alter your voice.

Sneeze.

"I'm here to"—Ach-*CHOO!*—"deliver a message to Mr.... Mr. Babbage"—Ach-*CHOO!*—about the private gathering in Gaylord's—" I keep my voice high and nasally.

She steps outside, swiftly slamming the door after her. "Yes, I delivered the message already. Nothing to worry about, he's all set to go." She eyes me suspiciously. "How about everyone else?"

"All present and accounted for." I sneeze again, just for good measure.

She frowns. "Good...Listen, if you're coming down with a cold, maybe it would be a better idea if you stay away from Gaylord. He's a bear about the conference already. The last thing he needs is to get sick. He'd then blame me for hiring someone with typhus or something—"

I sniffle and nod. "If you say so. I feel so guilty, just staying in my room."

She pats my shoulder, even as she steers me away from the cabin. "Not at all. We can all use a little rest and relaxation"—she blushes again—"Well, you know what I mean." She stops, lost in thought. "And you're in luck! We have the monks for the duration of the retreat. Frankly, I thought more of the guests would have snapped up appointments with them, but it seems that their dance card is pretty empty. With what we're paying them, I hate to think that they'll spend the rest of the time praying or meditating or just twiddling their thumbs. One of them intimated he was into golf, but a good stiff wind will send his robe flying, and he didn't bring his khakis. Should I send them over to do a colonic on you?"

"Me?" *Yikes.* "Oh, no, please don't bother! I'm sure some honey and lemon in my tea will fix me right up! I'll be fine and dandy in the morning."

And far away from here, if we're lucky.

I wave as I head back into the woods.

I guess I should tell her that her shirt is inside out and that her buttons are crooked, but I'll give Doreen that honor.

18

Raid

In technology, the acronym RAID stands for "Redundant Array of Independent Disks." It is a method of storing data on multiple hard disks, but in such a way that your computer sees them all as one very large disk.

The good news is that within this configuration, they operate much more efficiently than a single hard drive.

As a parent, we look for efficiencies in all sectors of our lives. It is why we sometimes raid our children's rooms and computers, looking for things that will make their lives more complicated than necessary —drugs, booze, troubled friends or over-age boyfriends–especially if it results in a school suspension or time in front of a judge.

The great news: within this parental configuration, your children will operate more efficiently without doing a single day of hard time.

"Now that we know Carl is here, we've all got to stay out of sight," I warn Jack and Dominic.

Dominic smiles. "No problem there. Now that we've got

location readings on all the targets' cabins, we're good to go on collecting the rest of the keys."

Jack points to his latex Milton mask. "And I'm hiding in plain sight, remember? Unless we run into a snag, we'll be long gone before they even serve dessert."

"Let's not be so cocky." I don't want to say it out loud, but seeing Carl here has spooked me.

"It works to our favor that there are no security cameras facing the guest quarters," Jack reminds me. "So that we have an extra pair of eyes, the Acme satellite is pointed at Lark Island. Through it Arnie and Abu will track the whereabouts of our targets. He'll know the minute they leave for the cocktail party. With dinner starting around eight, and ending by nine-thirty—maybe a quarter to ten—we should have plenty of time to find the game keys and search Carl's room for the thumb drive containing the full stash of intel, then get the hell out by boat. Abu has it hidden in a cove, about a half mile from here. Take the path to the tennis courts, then veer right when you see the sign for deer crossing. Because everyone is freaked out over ticks, the path is rarely used. When we're all aboard, we set sail for the closest airport—Roche Harbor, on the big island. George is waiting for us there."

"The chickens have scattered," Arnie murmurs in our ear buds.

"I'll take Abdullah and Carl's cabins," Jack says. "Dominic, you take Ivan's. Donna, that leaves you Ji Wong's."

"On it." I grab a couple of towels from Jack's bathroom.

"Where are you going with those?" he asks.

I shrug. "It's my cover. Unlike you two, I'm a mere servant in this joint."

When we reach the door, I caution them, "So that we keep track of each other, and the time, keep your ear buds on at all times."

Before I'm over the threshold, Jack pulls me in for a kiss. It's slow and gentle. It promises so much—mostly his return to me. Apparently, it's also a vow: "This time, Carl goes down for good."

I pray he's right.

I'M STILL IN MY EMPLOYEE GARB——IN OTHER WORDS, INVISIBLE TO those guests heading to the lodge for cocktails, and to the other Gryphon wonks who are scurrying about. The footpaths are clear. Still, it's twilight, and the tall trees cast long shadows.

No one looks twice when I knock on Ji's door with my stash of plush towels.

As Arnie predicted, there is no answer. I enter. The wood panel blinds are closed. The only light in the room illuminates a small Buddha seated on a small altar on the dresser.

I guess Ji won't be leafing through the Gideon Bible in the bed stand drawer.

The closet holds two suitcases. His clothes—mostly slacks and golf shirts—hang in the closet. One suitcase, a hanging bag, and a small valise are on the floor, along with three pairs of shoes: hiking boots, golf shoes, and sneakers.

I search the suitcases first. Nothing is inside of them, or in the pockets. I check for false bottoms, but come up empty-handed.

The same goes for the valise: empty.

The pockets of his clothes are the same: no little gold key.

I search his bed—under the sheets and pillows, the mattress, and the floor beneath it. His bed stand drawers are empty. The toiletries in the bathroom have no false bottoms or sides. He didn't hide it in the toilet tank, or in the showerhead, or the soap dispenser.

I'm getting desperate. Did he take it with him?

"Donna, doll, check Buddha for a false bottom." It's Hal.

"It's okay. Our little buddy has been cleared," Arnie says, as if reading my mind. "He's been scanning our teams' lenses with me, and helping me watch the secure cam feed for trouble."

"Arnie has a new bestie... Arnie has a new bestie..." Emma's sing-song taunt isn't cruel this time, but playful.

"Ah, you're just jealous," Arnie teases her back.

I lift Buddha and shake it. Hal is right—a false bottom.

I take the golden key, and I'm out of there.

"In the clear," I murmur, as I walk toward Jack's cabin.

"My first stop was successful," Jack mutters back. "Now, on to Darth Vader's lair."

"Mr. Fleming, an ETA, please," I ask.

"Finishing...up...now," he gasps.

His breathing is labored. Oh no—did he run into trouble?

I take a detour toward Ivan's cabin, just in case he needs help.

By the time I reach the door, he's coming out of it, hopping into a shoe. His shirt is unbuttoned, too, revealing sculpted abs that are hairless and tanned.

"Jesus, Dominic," I hiss. "What the hell were you doing in there?"

"Whatever it took." He tosses me the golden VIP key.

"With...*Ivan*?" I shake my head in awe. It's true he puts country before anything.

He glares down at me. "Hardly, old girl. I never thought you doubted that I'm into birds! So is he—the big-breasted of the species."

"Next you'll tell me she was guarding the key."

"She was doing nothing of the kind. Naked as a jaybird, in fact."

"What excuse did you give her for being there?"

"I told her one of us was in the wrong cabin. Like me, she thought we could make the best of it." He shrugs. "Alas, I think she's much too exhausted for Ivan."

"You've always gone above and beyond the call of duty," I mutter. "Jack, where do you stand?"

No answer.

"Jack, can you hear me?"

Laughter rings through my ear piece.

Not Jack's.

Carl's.

"Sorry, sweet Donna, but your boyfriend is all tied up." Carl's voice is suddenly vicious. "If you want to see him alive, you'll need to bring those keys with you—*now*."

CARL IS OUT FRONT OF HIS CABIN, ON ONE OF THE ADIRONDACK rockers that grace its wide front porch. He is whittling a short thick stick with a Swiss pocketknife. Already, the point is sharp.

I'd love to stab him in the heart with it.

Instead, I ask, "Where is Jack?"

He nods toward the door. "Inside, waiting for you." As I move toward the threshold, he says, "Nope, not yet."

I stop cold.

"You might as well, wifey. I've got the three that were in Jack's possession, so it's game, set, match." He smiles slyly. "Besides, you want to see him alive, don't you? Timing is of the essence. Or as they say in *Wonderland*, 'tick tock, tick, tock.'"

"You've got him tied to a bomb?"

He shrugs. "Couldn't help it. When you're in the wilderness, you have to improvise. I was saving the big bang surprise for the Lark's closing night nerd fest—you know, a 'last supper' motif, as it were. It was to be blamed on The Clark Kent League and its motley crew of cypherpunks, out to avenge the Mad Hacker's death. Instead, they'll get blamed for blowing me to kingdom come. That's okay. I wasn't cut out to be a desk jockey anyway."

"Good riddance," I mutter as I toss him the game keys and start for the door.

He slips them into his blazer pocket. "Now, the key to the boat."

I hesitate. Finally, I toss it to him too.

"Where will I find it?"

"Follow the footpath on the right to the tennis courts. You'll see another one marked deer crossing, also on the right. It'll be tied to the pier."

He grabs me roughly by the wrist. "Of course, you'll have to play first mate. I can't have witnesses who claim I'm still alive."

I struggle to pull away. My reward is a slap across the face.

"Hey, you've got no one to blame but yourself, little 'Lucy.' That's your name this week, isn't it? You always want to be in the show." His Ricky Ricardo accent leaves a lot to be desired. "Time to blow this joint."

I try to wrench my arm away, but he holds tight, laughing. "Chillax! It's just a figure of speech!" He hands me a cell phone. "He's safe—as long as you're the one holding the detonator, right?" He bows toward the path. "After you, milady."

CARL MAKES ME WALK IN FRONT OF HIM ON THE DARK PATH. THERE

is no moon out tonight. The stars are bright, but their light barely penetrates the canopy of fir branches above us.

When I trip, he snickers.

He never was much of a gentleman.

The boat is dark. Arnie and Abu could see my dilemma via my lenses, so they know the score. No need to be caught in the crossfire. They must stay to fight another day.

Sort of like a video game.

If they haven't gotten to Jack as of yet, perhaps Dominic has, and I'll be out to sea—

With Carl.

They'll never find the body, be it his, or mine.

He shoves me off the pier, onto the boat's deck. I land on all fours.

He whistles appreciatively. "Doggie style. Love it."

He unties the rope at the stern before jumping down himself and tossing it at me. "If you get the urge to hang yourself, I promise I won't talk you out of it."

"Fuck you."

He laughs. "I thought you'd never ask."

The engine purrs as he backs it away from the pier. When he has a wide enough berth, he turns the wheel so that we head in the opposite direction.

We're only a hundred yards or so from shore when we hear the blast—coming from behind us.

My head whips around in time to see the blaze, barely above the treetops.

I charge toward him, fists flying. "You son of a bitch! You said...*you said I was holding the detonator!*"

He slaps me. I stagger backward. "And for once you believed me. Go figure." He shrugs.

Jack is gone.

He was there for me from the start, and had my back until

the end. He was the only man who loved me without question. He was my most passionate lover.

He was a true father to my children.

And if Dominic and Abu and Arnie were with him, I've lost my dear friends and colleagues too.

Right now, I wish that rope were around my neck.

Better yet, Carl's.

My fist will have to do.

I rise too fast for him to react. I aim for his Adam's apple. The punch leaves him gasping. While he's doubled over, I bang his head into the console—a couple of times, in fact, just to make sure he gets the point that I'm more than a little upset with him.

Carl is too groggy to fight me as I take the intel keys—the five game keys, and the master thumb drive— out of his blazer pocket.

His windpipe is bruised enough that his breathing is labored. If I had a plastic bag handy, I could stop it altogether.

At least I have the rope—somewhere topside.

I scurry up the ladder leading to the deck.

I'm on the last rung when I feel Carl's hand grab my ankle.

But before he can yank me backward, I toss the intel keys overboard with all my might.

Like me, he hears six splashes as the keys hit the calm surface of the sea.

His howl of rage echoes over the water.

It is the last thing I hear before my head hits the galley floor, and I black out.

THE ICY WATER SHOCKS ME OUT OF BLISSFUL UNCONSCIOUSNESS AND into my hellish reality.

Carl has hog-tied me. My hands are bound together behind my back, as are my legs, which are folded so that ankles can be tied to my wrists.

His voice is raspy but he still shouts, "I'll make sure that the children remember you fondly." He waves to me as the boat roars away.

I'm still face up, but I know I'll soon be sucked down into the deep, dark abyss below the water's surface, so I try to fill my lungs with as much oxygen as possible.

Easier said than done when the next explosion takes place several moments later. The blast is like a comet, only the fireball flies skyward. The force of it tosses me into the air, too. My flight is only a few seconds, followed by an eternity of dread as I plunge back into sea.

By the time I rise to the surface, my lungs are ready to explode. I'm caught in a an undertow that sucks me down then spits me back out. If I spot stars overhead, I take it as my cue to breathe deeply.

I pray that Carl did not survive the blast, but if so, that the roiling tide is pulling him under, too.

I'd like to think that his final breath comes before mine.

~

"How does it feel to die?" Hal wonders.

"Don't ask," I whisper.

"Must we be maudlin?" Dominic opines.

"Are you here, too?" I struggle to open my eyes, but my lids are weighted with pain.

And with the fear of what I will find when I open them.

No longer tied, my hands shoot out in front of me. I don't know if I should take this as a good sign or not. My children aren't in heaven, so being there without them would be a living hell.

I'm afraid to ask, but I must. "Did Jack…did he make it?"

I am answered with a kiss.

I'd recognize those lips anywhere. They are my heaven.

The kiss has lifted the weights from my eyes. I see stars all around.

We are floating through the air.

When I shift my gaze to the left, I find myself staring into Jack's soft green eyes.

Over the steady chop of blades slicing clouds in the cool night sky, I hear myself ask, "How did you survive the cabin blast?"

"Dominic," he answers as he nuzzles my cheek. "He was smart enough to look in the window and climb through it, as opposed to opening the door, which was attached to a trip wire."

Carl stopped me from going inside.

Carl saved my life.

Still, that doesn't excuse him for being the most awful person in the world.

"Unfortunately, our host, Gaylord, wasn't as lucky," Dominic says. "When he went looking for Carl—a.k.a., Charles Babbage—he took the more civilized entrance."

I shake my head. "The front door."

"Word is already out about his untimely demise, and Gryphon's stock is in free fall," Hal informs us. "Rumor has it that i.Me will acquire—that is, if anyone can get ahold of Milton, so that he can put it in play." Hal sighs. "I guess the sharks will be circling i.Me next."

"Jack, how did Carl ambush you?" I ask.

"He never left his cabin. He opted to eat in his room," Jack explains. "He heard me jiggle the knob and hid behind the door. He hit me with the butt of his gun. When he saw me with Milton's face, I'm sure he panicked at the thought that he'd knocked out one of his bidders. But, at some point he realized I was a fake. In fact, he'd previously met Milton at a Catherine Martin for President fundraiser. When Abu and Arnie heard you were on your way to the boat with Carl, they rigged it to blow when it reached a certain speed. They left the i.Me tablet on the boat. If you had seen it and signed in, Hal would have told you to jump."

I grimace. "I didn't see it. I was too busy fighting Carl." I think for a moment. "If the tablet with Hal blew up with the boat, how can he be here, too?"

"Remember? I sync'd your iOS to my iPad while I vetted it," Arnie explains. He holds it up.

"Miss me?" Hal asks.

"Yes," I answer earnestly. "And you"—I point to Abu —"and you"—I point to Arnie—"but not you." I point to Dominic.

"Bugger off," he mutters. His grin means I'm forgiven.

Jack frowns. "I guess Carl did you a favor by trying to kill you."

"Don't tell him that," I retort.

It dawns on me that neither of us will ever get a chance to tell him anything, ever again.

I should be happy about that. Instead, I feel empty.

Without him, I would never have had Mary, Jeff and Trisha.

And for better or worse, he made me who I am today.

For that I owe him something.

$$\frac{}{}$$

19

PostScript

"PostScript" is a computer language for vector graphics, used in desktop publishing programs. Without PostScript your screens would see gibberish, and your printed manuscripts would look like hell.

"Postscript" (lower-case "s") is a paragraph, or phrase added to a letter that has already been concluded and signed by the writer.

A mother's last thought is always about her children.

Needless to say, she will always have the last word.

Just sayin'.

I CAN NO LONGER LOOK AT STARS IN AN INDIGO NIGHT WITHOUT thinking of death and salvation.

Carl's death was my salvation.

At least, this is what Lee Chiffray is trying to convince me. "Problem solved—for both of us."

We are standing side by side, drinking wine on the terrace of the New York penthouse.

If what Lee says is true, it is our rendezvous spot for the last time.

"The Coast Guard never found his body," I insist.

"The explosion at sea left no shred of evidence. Everything sunk—even the boat's steering wheel. The water is deep, and filled with all sorts of large fish and predators."

I shake my head in disbelief. "Carl is the biggest predator of all. You know that firsthand."

"If he is alive, after what he pulled he has nowhere to go," Lee insists.

"He has friends in Russia and China and North Korea and Dubai," I counter. "Those are big places where it's easy to hide."

"Why would he resurface? Better to be thought dead, than hunted down again." Lee pauses, and adds, "And for political purposes, it allows the U.S. to save face as much as those we trust the least."

"Yes, well, I presume the DOD will want to keep the breach a secret." In other words, business as usual in Spooklandia.

He laughs. "You guessed right." His smile disappears. "Donna, if the decision were yours, would you want it known that Carl Stone sabotaged his country yet again for money and power?"

I wince. "You know very well, that's a trick question. As much as I'd personally love to see him back in jail, now that my children know of his existence I'd hate for them to suffer the shame of being the progeny of a known traitor and terrorist."

"Your children will be affected, either way—even if they were told he was killed serving his country. So, how would you want to see it played out?"

I shrug. "In any event, the decision isn't mine to make."

"It may not be yours, but it's mine," he says.

"Are you saying my wish is your command?" For this I down the rest of the great cabernet in my glass.

He turns to me. "Let's pretend it is. How would you want to play it?"

It breaks my heart, but I have to say it. "The truth. Always."

"Thought so." He shrugs. "As it turns out, you'll get your way without any assistance from me. Just before I came here, I got a call from Ryan. Acme's cryptography team broke the Mad Hacker's Vigenèr cipher. It led to a secure cloud file with a perfect cyber trail and full documentation of all of Carl's actions regarding the stolen intel. And get this—the moment the cloud opened, it automatically released emails to press outlets all over the world, which document the break-in and the intel theft. The article was the work of the Clark Kent League."

"Under whose byline?" I ask.

"Mike Willoughby and N.M. Hacker," he answers.

At least their lives weren't taken in vain.

"So, the decision wasn't either of ours to make."

He nods.

I smile. "Good. I would have hated it if you had disappointed me."

"I pray I never do." Lee isn't laughing. "At least there's the Clark Kent League to keep me on the straight and narrow, along with every other head of state."

"Glad to see you're such a fan. Does this mean you're open to, say, an Edward Snowden pardon?"

He pauses, then says, "My goal is to assure that the Edward Snowdens of the world need not run first, in fear of retaliation for exposing the truth."

"Spoken like a true politician." Suddenly, a thought hits me. "It's you, isn't it?"

He frowns. "I don't know what you mean."

"You're the money behind the Clark Kent League! You protected the Mad Hacker. You told her about the existence of Project Clark Kent."

He says nothing. He merely grins.

But the smiles fade soon enough for both of us at the thought of Nymphette.

I lay my hand in his. "This is good-bye."

He squeezes it. Then he puts it to his lips. "Do you know why Carl took the intel?"

I laugh. "Because he was always a greedy son of a bitch."

Lee shrugs. "Yeah, okay, that's one reason. But there was another one. When Nymphette learned from Susan the role Carl played in the missing intel, she broke into his personal computer to find it."

I nod. "Yes, she told me. Apparently he had a file the size of Kansas, just on me."

"She found my blackmail file too," he admits. "She erased it."

"Without it, it was only a matter of time before Carl was back behind bars," I reason. "Congratulations. You're now a free man."

"If you have a conscience, you're never free from your guilt. Particularly not in this job."

I tip my wine glass toward his. "Long live Nymphette."

We savor her memory over a three-hundred-dollar bottle of Domaine du Pégaü Châteauneuf-du-Pape Cuvée Réservée.

Without her, even the best wine is bittersweet at best.

I HAVE JUST WALKED OFF THE PLANE AND TOWARD PASSENGER PICK-up when the Caller ID on my cell phone shows that Emma is calling. "So, um, what's your ETA?"

I look at my watch. "I'm walking out of the airport now. Why do you ask?"

"Damn it. Not good enough. My water broke, and *it hurts like hell*! We're on our way to the hospital now."

I do the math. "Oh, my God! Emma, aren't you a few weeks early?"

"I know! Aren't first babies usually late?" She's breathing heavily. "It happened the minute Arnie presented me with the wedding rings he designed for us!" Now she's sobbing. "They are so beautiful!"

"Quit crying and keep breathing! The second Jack gets here, we'll head directly to the hospital—I swear."

"Good," Emma sighs with relief. "Listen, I need to put you on speaker. Hal is trying to convince Arnie that home delivery may be better for the baby. In fact, Hal insists the two of them could deliver this kid without a doctor, let alone a doula."

Suddenly, I'm glad I gave Hal a new home. "I think it's time you pull the plug on Hal."

Emma stops heaving long enough to gasp, "I would, but he's just downloaded all these wonderful nursery stories for the baby, and it would be a shame to—"

I'm laughing so hard that the other passengers walking toward pick-up are staring at me. "Okay, but don't say I didn't warn you."

I'm just about to dial Jack when I see him, right outside of the security gate. He is holding a bouquet of yellow roses.

He drops them when I jump into his arms.

When finally we're through making out like teenagers, he murmurs, "Don't ever leave. It's only been twenty-four hours, and my body aches for you."

I tingle at the thought. "Imagine how it will feel when we get home—but first, the hospital. Emma is in labor."

He laughs as he wraps an arm around my waist and leads me out the door.

Just at that moment, my cell buzzes with a text.

"Don't answer it," he warns me.

I laugh. "I have no intention of doing so."

I'm just about to turn it off when I see the caller ID:

MAD HACKER.

I show it to him.

"Heck yes, open it," he insists.

It's a text that reads, simply: *U saved a single soul—mine. Thanks 4 that.*

Jack's eyes reflect my own relief. "How did she escape the drone attack?" he asks.

Great question. I text it to her.

Nymphette's response: *Mirror trick. Decoys R Us*

"So, that's how she got away from the drone's missile," Jack murmurs.

I shake my head. "I don't get it."

"Magicians do it too—create illusions. The drone's operator thought he was firing upon the cabin. Instead, it was a mirrored reflection of the cabin. The illusion was far enough away that she had time to escape through the tunnel."

I swipe to open the attachment included with the text. It's a file labeled DONNA.

Carl's file.

With a click, it's erased.

That a girl…

I think.

When we get home from the hospital, I'll open a very good bottle of wine.

To celebrate a new birth, and a rebirth.

I might even find the words to explain to my children that Carl is our past, and Jack is our future.

—THE END—

Next Up for Donna!

The Housewife Assassin's Hostage Hosting Tips

(Book 9)

It's up to Donna Stone to save a hotel filled with international dignitaries from terrorists whose usual demands are million-dollar ransoms. But this time, the price is much higher, and much more personal, for the housewife assassin.

Other Books by Josie Brown

The True Hollywood Lies Series

Hollywood Hunk

Hollywood Whore

The Totlandia Series

The Onesies - Book 1 (Fall)

The Onesies - Book 2 (Winter)

The Onesies - Book 3 (Spring)

The Onesies - Book 4 (Summer)

The Twosies - Book 5 (Fall)

The Twosies – Book 6 (Winter)

The Twosies - Book 7 (Spring)

The Twosies - Book 8 (Summer)

More Josie Brown Novels

The Candidate

Secret Lives of Husbands and Wives

The Baby Planner

How to Reach Josie

To write Josie, go to:
mailfromjosie@gmail.com

To find out more about Josie, or to get on her eLetter list for book launch announcements, go to her website:
www.JosieBrown.com

You can also find her at:

www.AuthorProvocateur.com

twitter.com/JosieBrownCA

facebook.com/josiebrownauthor

pinterest.com/josiebrownca

instagram.com/josiebrownnovels